Gatekeeper

GATEKEEPER

A NOVEL

Natasha Deen

GREAT PLAINS
TEEN FICTION

Great Plains Teen Fiction
(an imprint of Great Plains Publications)
233 Garfield Street
Winnipeg, MB R3G 2M1
www.greatplains.mb.ca

Great Plains Publications gratefully acknowledges the financial support provided for its publishing program by the Government of Canada through the Canada Book Fund; the Canada Council for the Arts; the Province of Manitoba through the Book Publishing Tax Credit and the Book Publisher Marketing Assistance Program; and the Manitoba Arts Council.

Design & Typography by Relish New Brand Experience

Printed in Canada by Friesens

LIBRARY AND ARCHIVES CANADA CATALOGUING IN PUBLICATION

Deen, Natasha, author
    Gatekeeper / Natasha Deen.

Issued in print and electronic formats.
ISBN 978-1-927855-39-3 (pbk.).--ISBN 978-1-927855-43-0 (epub).--ISBN 978-1-927855-44-7 (mobi)

    I. Title.

PS8607.E444G83 2016   JC813'.6   C2015-908667-1
                                       C2015-908668-X

ENVIRONMENTAL BENEFITS STATEMENT

Great Plains Publications saved the following resources by printing the pages of this book on chlorine free paper made with 100% post-consumer waste.

TREES	WATER	ENERGY	SOLID WASTE	GREENHOUSE GASES
7	3,119	3	209	575
FULLY GROWN	GALLONS	MILLION BTUs	POUNDS	POUNDS

Environmental impact estimates were made using the Environmental Paper Network Paper Calculator3.2. For more information visit www.papercalculator.org.

Canadä

FSC
www.fsc.org
MIX
Paper from responsible sources
FSC® C016245

For Nazra

CHAPTER ONE

Someone was pounding at the front door at 10:30 PM, and common sense said not to answer. Then again, I see the dead, live with a ghost, and was dating a supernatural being who transported souls. Common sense may have been in my neighbourhood, but it wasn't on any street I lived. I opened my bedroom door, looking for Serge, my ghostly roommate and soul brother. He was already in the hallway, the overhead lights highlighting his blond hair and freckles.

"Go see who it is," I told him.

His blue eyes went wide. "You want me to answer the door? You think someone seeing a door seeming to open on its own isn't going to freak them out?"

"No, I want you to go *through* the door and see who's on the other side."

He rubbed his stomach and wrinkled his grey shirt. "What if it's someone bad?"

"Boo-boo, you're a ghost. No one can see you."

"Still scared. You do it."

"How can you possibly—oh." I sighed. "You're messing with me."

He grinned.

I'd been living with Serge for about a month, and his smile still surprised me. In life, I'd hardly seen it. In life, he'd usually treated me to a smirk and an up-close view of his middle finger.

"It's ten-thirty and some nutter is banging down the door. You really think I'm going to let you go near it?"

This was saying something. Serge and I hadn't been friends when he'd been alive. And had he still been breathing, he would've been far more likely to toss me into the path of whoever was on the other side of the door than to help me. His death had changed both of us, and though I mourned the things he'd never get to do—have kids, buy a house—I knew his dying had brought him the one thing he'd never had been able to find in life. Peace.

"It can't be anyone super evil," I said as I headed down the stairs and toward the door. "Buddha's on my bed."

"I saw him run from a mouse during our walk last week. He's probably under your bed right now." Serge pushed past me, took the lead.

"I saw that mouse too, and I think it had Hantavirus. Buddha was just being prudent."

Serge shot me a pitying look from over his shoulder. We hit the bottom of the stairs. The carpet muted the sounds of our footsteps as we crossed the small expanse that would take us to the steps that led to the front door.

The linoleum at the foyer was cold on my feet and I wished I'd worn thicker socks. I pulled my ratty bathrobe closer to block the tendrils of winter air creeping through the cracks of the door.

Serge peered through the peephole. "I can't see who it is." He winced as another round of banging rocked the frame. "I think it might be the hulk, and he's hungry."

"Go through the door." I dropped my voice so whoever was on the other side wouldn't hear me. Though with the noise they were making, I doubted they would hear a sonic boom.

"Okay." Serge hitched his flannel bottoms, pushed back his shoulders, took a breath and went through the door. At least, he tried. His head smacked the wood.

I swallowed my smile.

"Not a word," he said, refusing to look at me. "Not one word." He took another breath, closed his eyes, then lifted his hands into the air. After a moment, he wiggled his fingers.

I rubbed the frown from my forehead. "We don't have time for your holy-roller impression."

Serge kept his eyes closed. "Are you dead?"

"No, but I feel like you're killing me."

"Until you have expertise on how to manipulate solid matter with ectoplasm or whatever goo I'm now made of, shut up. I've been dead for a month, and this is what works for me."

I sighed.

"And stop with the mouth breathing."

The banging continued from the other side as Serge slowly pushed his fingers into the wood. When that worked, he followed with his head. A few seconds later, he pulled himself back into the foyer.

"So? Who is it?"

"It's the lady, y'know…"

"Which lady?"

"The one with the great boobs."

I sighed. Boys. Dead or alive, they were all the same. "Can you give me something else?"

"If you were a guy, I wouldn't need to tell you anything else."

"If you were a girl, I'd—never mind." I pushed him out of the way. "She's safe?"

He nodded.

I flipped on the outside light, unbolted the door, opened it, and ignored the blast of icy air that shot through me. "Mrs.—" Great. Thanks to Serge, I'd totally forgotten her name. Double thanks to Serge, I was also having a hard time *not* staring at her chest…and being mortally jealous. I'm so flat, I'm concave.

"Maggie, thank God! I didn't think you'd answer." She came inside, shoved me sideways, and left the scent of expensive lotion in her wake.

I closed the door and shut out the dark night.

"Is Sheriff Machio around? It's an emergency."

"No, I'm sorry. Nancy and Dad went to the city for dinner and a movie. They won't be back for a while. Maybe midnight"—My brain kicked back into gear—"Mrs. Pierson."

"That will be too late!" Her sharp words and sharper tone made me step back.

"Rori's missing. I went to check on her, but her room's empty and—" Hysteria and panic pitched her voice thin and high. The smell of a mom whose love for her daughter was so strong came through her pores, scented the air with its psychic perfume of cinnamon and vanilla.

For a second, I wondered if my mother had ever smelled like that. I'd never get the answer to that question, and now wasn't the time to brood over the woman who'd abandoned me at birth. I focused on Mrs. Pierson and the fear that bleached the colour from her skin. Holding to calm instead of connecting with her panic, I asked, "Isn't there a deputy at the office?"

"I called, but it's Frank."

Cripes. That guy couldn't find the sky with a compass and a Sherpa. "But you did tell him about Rori, right?"

"Paul—"

Her husband.

"—was talking to him when I left." She turned frightened eyes to me. "I thought if Nancy was here—I know she'd find Rori—." The reality of the situation hit and she started to cry.

I did the only thing I could. I hugged her.

Serge stood to the side, looking as helpless as I felt.

"Oh, God. Nancy's not here." She leaned into me for a minute, then pulled away. Mrs. Pierson pressed the back of her hand to her mouth. "Maggie, my little girl is out there and lost." She squeezed her eyes shut as though that could stop the tears, but they gushed out in a steady, thick stream. "I just want her back so badly," she whispered.

Around her, the air stretched and flickered.

I took a small step back.

The vague outline of a body began to form. Sketchy, grey, no details, but the size and shape definitely made it a kid. The fact that it was appearing beside Mrs. Pierson made it *her* kid.

Serge and I looked at each other.

Her daughter wasn't missing anymore. We'd found her. But then again, we always find the dead.

CHAPTER TWO

I asked Mrs. Pierson to wait, told her I wanted to get dressed, then I would go back and help her look for Rori. While she telephoned her husband to get an update, I ran up the steps, then shut my bedroom door.

"Use my phone," I told Serge. "Text Craig."

"Shouldn't we text Hank and Nancy?"

I shook my head. "I don't want to think of either of them getting that message. Dad will push the minivan to the extreme to get home, and that thing's older than God. It'll disintegrate on the road."

"Just text Craig." If anyone was going to be helpful, it was Craig. After all, he transported the dead. If he didn't know how to lend aid, no one would.

"I'm not an expert at that. Remember what happened the last time I tried to use your electronics?"

"Yeah, you sent an email to your father, and since it was from my email address, I got pulled into the police station and almost charged with slander."

"Libel," he corrected me. "Slander is speech, libel is text."

"Patience is me talking to you." I stayed focused on the conversation with Serge because I didn't want to think about Rori and having to tell her mom she'd never see her daughter grow up.

Problem was, the longer I stayed in the room, the more I wanted to stay in here. Nothing brings out my yellow stripes like a dead kid. But cowardice couldn't win. I reminded myself that Rori deserved a proper funeral and Mrs. Pierson deserved to know where her baby's body was. "It'll save me time if you text him. We need to get this thing with Rori over and done with." I winced at how callous it sounded. "You know what I mean."

He nodded. "I'll try."

I grabbed my jeans and an old football sweater of Dad's, and took a quick sniff. It still smelled of laundry detergent and fabric softener. Good. I raced into the bathroom to change. The hoodie was over my head when I heard, "Oops."

I froze. "Dare I ask?"

"Ignorance is bliss."

"Try again. And try not to get me arrested this time." I pulled on the rest of my clothes, then hopped out of the bathroom as I put on a pair of socks.

"It's all done," he said. "And I texted Nell."

"Why?"

"She'll kill both of us if I don't tell her. I'm not ready to re-die." The cell binged twice. "They're both on their way."

Before I could say anything, Craig materialized in my room.

Serge grinned. "You gotta teach me how to materialize wherever I want."

"No." I put my hand up in a stop gesture. "No one's teaching Serge more peeping Tom tricks. The guy's already an expert. He doesn't need to be a savant."

I had a freaked out mom and a dead kid, and neither of those two things were enough to shut off the rush of hormones and heart when I saw Craig. Brown hair, brown eyes, long legs. But he was more than eye candy. He was like heart fibre. A guy who knew my Big Secret, which meant around him, I could totally be myself.

Craig gave me a tight hug and a quick kiss.

I gave myself a breath to enjoy the warmth and solid strength of him.

"What's going on?" he asked. "The text said something about an emergency situation." His mouth went to the side. "Actually, it said *eked gentry sofia*, but I'm guessing that was an autocorrect fail...unless you're suffering some kind of brain clot and that was your way of calling for help."

"That was Serge."

"Give me a break," said the ghost. "You try not having solid mass and texting during an emergency."

"I'm just messing with you," said Craig. "The text came through perfectly. So what's going on?"

"Some stuff's up with the blond lady with the great boobs," said Serge.

"Loni Pierson?" asked Craig. He caught the expression on my face. "What?"

"Seriously, his only description is 'great boobs' and you know it's Mrs. Pierson?"

Craig grinned. "What can I say? Being ten thousand years old gives a guy a lot of time to learn how to appreciate the female form."

Wow. Boys. Quickly, I gave Craig the rundown. Missing kid. Hysterical mother. Kid's ghostly form appearing beside mommy. "But the weird thing is how she's materializing. She's not all formed."

He stepped back. "Define 'not all formed.'"

"You could see the outline but no details," said Serge, "and it's all … like those old TVs when they can't get reception. Not staticky, but squiggly."

Craig went still. "Is there any colour to her?"

"No, it's like pencil smeared on paper."

"What kind of ghost is she?" I asked. I'd dealt with poltergeists, lost souls, angry ghosts. I figured Rori was too little to be any of those. Then again, she was a six-year-old, which made her an expert at pulling tantrums.

Craig tossed my phone at me. "Start texting as many people as you know. See who's awake and can help."

I caught the phone. "Help with what? The only people who see the dead in this town are standing in this room."

"That's just it," said Craig. "She's not dead. And if we find her in time, she won't have to be."

"Not dead!"

"Not dead," he repeated, his head down, his fingers working the keyboard. "But she's close."

"Can't you ferrier her?"

"Mags," he said, "talk and text. Please."

I tossed the phone on the bed and nodded at Serge. "We already texted Nell," I said. "She knows everyone." I turned back to Craig. "Why can't you use your supernatural abilities?"

"Because it doesn't work that way. I'm just a ferrier."

There was no "just" about his job as a ghost transporter. In their natural state, ferriers were gigantic, with scales, wings, horns, serpentine tails, and hooves. They captured escaped souls—the bad guys were the only ones who attempted escape from the afterlife—and brought them back. But ferriers were also there at death and transported the dead from this plane to the next. Sometimes they were reborn, sometimes they stayed, sometimes...other things happened. I closed my mind to memories of Serge's parents.

"I only get the information on the souls I transport across the bridge... Rori's not my charge; I can't see anything to do with her." He stopped texting and made eye contact. "Although...ferriers are attracted to each other. If one's here to get her, I should be able to see them."

If one was here in Dead Falls, I would be able to see it, too. That gave me hope—all I had to do was look for an enormous creature flying over the town. I'd look like a dork, driving with my head out the window and my gaze on the sky, but if it saved a life, I was okay with that.

He frowned. "It's a slim chance. We usually only come at the point of death."

And there went my hope.

"Still, if I find the ferrier, I'll let you know. And if I find Rori, I'll *definitely* let you know. In the meantime, let's start looking." He shoved his phone into his pocket, gave me a quick kiss, and disappeared.

I turned to Serge. "Wait here for Nell then—" The doorbell rang. "Never mind. Sounds like she's here."

I ran down the stairs and opened the door. Usually, Nell looked like she'd fallen off the cover of a fashion magazine. Tonight, her curly hair stood out like she'd been electrocuted, and she wore no makeup. She'd left her wool jacket unbuttoned and it showed she'd pulled on a sweater over her pajamas. "Serge—" She caught sight of Mrs. Pierson and swallowed her words. "Rori's missing?"

"Nell!" Mrs. Pierson moved forward.

I stepped back so Nell could have room to hug the woman.

"Mrs. P, I'm so sorry," she said. "This isn't like Rori at all."

"I know, I'm just devastated. She's all I have and—"

"It's okay." Nell smiled at her. "We're here and we'll help."

I jumped in. "I'm going to go with Mrs. Pierson. You"—I subtly jerked my head in Serge's direction—"take your car." I pulled Nell into a quick hug. "Thanks. And you have never looked hotter."

She gave me a soft punch to the stomach.

"Let's go." I locked the door behind me and ran down the stone path to Mrs. Pierson's Mercedes.

I climbed into a car that still had its new car smell and leather seats soft enough to compete with churned butter. As I buckled up, Mrs. Pierson climbed in and gunned the engine.

"Mrs. Pierson, shouldn't you put on your seat belt—"

But she was already peeling out of the driveway. The car rocked to a stop as she shoved it from reverse into drive, then rocketed forward as she floored the accelerator.

I glanced behind the driver's seat, where the shadow of Rori lingered. It hadn't changed texture or colour, but I didn't know how long it took for a child to die of hypothermia.

"This is Paul's fault," Mrs. Pierson said as the car gained speed. "Him and his obsessions."

Her tone suggested she was talking more to herself than me. I was happy to stay quiet and keep my attention on the sky for a winged creature, lights, or anything else that would give us a clue where Rori was.

"I'm sorry the boy is dead—"

I jerked my attention from the window to her.

"—and I'm sorry about what happened to the Popov family—"

Okay, she was talking about Serge.

"—but Paul's been obsessed with it. With the kid. Let him rest. What's to be gained by brooding on what wasn't done to help him?"

Probably the chance to make sure no kid ever had to live in the hell on earth that Serge had, but I didn't say that.

"Paul's missing dinners, Rori's parent-teacher interviews, the fall assembly, bath time, bedtime story. He misses so many things, already. I'm not saying he shouldn't be volunteering at the distress lines—" She took a breath, tightened her grip on the steering wheel. "I get it, I do.

We moved from Vancouver so Rori would have a small-town life and we land in the middle of a family scandal that's got the media frothing. But how is that a reason to bail on your family? To forget about your daughter because you're caught up in some privileged middle-class mid-life crisis—" Her breath hissed with frustration and resentment.

So that was the gist of the argument. How much time he was— or wasn't—spending with his family. And Rori, being a kid, blamed herself for her parents' fighting. What I didn't get was Rori running away. Nell babysat her, and from everything I'd heard she was a really good kid. Sweet. Shy. Not the kind to take off from her house in the middle of the night.

I tried to think like Nancy and come up with good cop questions that would help us find Rori. "When did you notice she was missing?"

"She went to bed at eight. I went on the deck, trying to get some air. Paul followed." She took a breath. "God, I'm so tired of fighting with him. We started arguing—"

I figured she was gearing up for another round of husband bashing, but I didn't have time for that. "And Rori. When did you notice she was gone?"

"I went to check on her around nine-forty-five and realized she wasn't in bed." Her voice went tight with fear.

"Mrs. Pierson, where did you look for Rori?"

"Everywhere," she said.

Adults. The most unhelpful group in the world. "Where is everywhere?"

"The house, the yard. Paul started down the block, I phoned Frank." She gulped for breath. "Then I came to you."

The speedometer ticked higher. I stopped talking, started concentrating on staying alive. I've never been the kind to pray, but I found myself wishing, hoping, and praying that no one else was on the road. The streets had a skiff of ice and frost and Mrs. Pierson's driving had us sliding on the road top. I didn't want to add to the body count—and especially, I didn't want to add *my* body to the count.

A few minutes later, we swung onto her street. Mrs. Pierson was a stay-at-home mom. Her husband's practice wasn't gigantic, but he was a doctor with a miraculous talent for investment banking, which explained the gigantic house and the four-car garage in the acreages of Woods Way. The family home bordered an undeveloped tract of forest and field, which equalled a lot of land for a little kid to get lost in.

I stepped out of the car and into the red and blue glow of the flashing police lights. Whatever criticism Mrs. Pierson had about her husband, he'd rallied the town. Calls for Rori sounded down the road and the beams of light from phones and flashlights bobbed in the cold night.

I left Mrs. Pierson to find her husband and headed to the house. As I walked up the driveway, a pair of headlights swung my way and put me in their spotlight. I moved toward the car as Nell cut the engine and got out. The interior lit up, showed Serge unbuckling his seat belt and climbing from the passenger side. I didn't blame him. Dead or not, I'd buckle up if Nell was driving.

"Any luck?" She jogged up to me.

"We just got here. Nell, this doesn't make sense. From everything you've said Rori's not a runaway kind of kid."

"No, but she's not good with noise or fighting, either. Her favourite TV channel is the one where they just show different pictures from around the world."

"In other words, her parents screaming at each other would have her looking for refuge. And all these people roaming around, yelling her name, is more likely to scare her—"

"Than make her realize they're here to help." No one was near us, but Nell came up close. "Serge said she may still be alive?"

"Yes, but who knows for how long that'll last—" I stopped, looked up as I heard the beating of wings. A ferrier flew above us, his speed slow and steady.

"What?" Nell lifted her head to match my gaze.

"Craig, looking for Rori."

She squinted into the dark, but Serge and I were the only ones in town who could see him.

"Help me out. I'm a super-shy six-year-old who wouldn't take off from home, but I've run outside because I can't stand my parents fighting."

"They would've—should've—heard the door beep," said Nell. "The alarm system is set up to make a sound every time a door or window opens."

"Unless the door was already open," I said as Serge joined us. "Mrs. Pierson went on the deck to get some air, Mr. Pierson followed her. If they left the door open, then she snuck out—"

"—and got herself lost. You guys check out the backyard," said Serge, "I'll check the front lawn and the neighbours' lawns, too."

We ran for the backyard and swept the lights from our cells around the space. It was a manicured lawn with skeletons of trees, bushes, and the dead stems of flowers. A playset stood to the left. The night wind pushed the swing with an invisible hand.

High in one of the trees, revealed by the bare branches, was a tree house. It sat to the right of a water wall that flowed into a stagnant pond. Trampled grass said the search party had already come and gone from here. In the distance, I heard their calls for Rori. They grew fainter as the party moved farther away from the property. "I'll check inside the playhouse," I told Nell.

"They would have done that," she said.

"They may have looked inside, but she might be hiding under a blanket or table or something." Even as I said it, I knew it was a weak argument, but it was the best idea I had. I gripped the sides of the ladder. The wood was cold and slick from the frost. It forced me to go slow, which had me cursing under my breath.

Way under.

I may have supernatural abilities, but seeing the dead was nothing compared to Dad's talent of knowing if I was cussing. That was a strict no-no in his books and would get me grounded till the day the sun burned itself out.

Finally, head in the doorway, I pulled out my phone and scanned the interior with my flashlight.

I'd hoped for a bumpy blanket or a chest—something that a kid could hide under, but the tree house held only cushions, small stools, and a table. Ignoring the twist of my heart, I stepped down the rungs. And almost wiped out.

And that's when I knew where Rori was.

CHAPTER THREE

hooked my arm in one of the rungs, then turned the flashlight to the pond. There was a small space between the stone wall and the fence. And I hoped the gap also held Rori. I went down the ladder, then did a slip and slide to the wall. I was right. In between it and the fence, was Rori's motionless body. "Nell! I've got her! Call nine-one-one!" When I didn't get a response, I screamed, "Nell!"

"Doing it, right now!"

Dealing with the dead was one thing. Dealing with a dying child was another, and I wasn't equipped for any of it. The space was too narrow for me to get in and the beam of the flashlight showed blood in her hair. Even if I could get to her, I didn't know if I could touch her.

I did the only thing I could.

"Go in there," I told Serge, my breath fogging the air. "Check and see how she's doing."

"Mags, I don't know about the solid-not-solid thing—"

"You're good at it. You don't fall through the ground, you don't float in the air. You know how to manipulate the space around you. Do it. Get to her, Serge."

He nodded, his Adam's apple bobbing, then moved through the rock and fence to kneel beside her. "There's blood—"

"I think she was trying to get to her tree house and she fell." My breath and the words came out thick as I tried not to cry. "She must have gotten confused, crawled in there."

"—I don't feel a heartbeat," he said. "I don't see any breath."

The tears came despite my best efforts, but I held to the hope that her ferrier hadn't arrived. "Remember the night on the bridge? How you reached into the reverend's chest? Do it again, try to massage her heart."

"Maggie, no! That was totally different! I didn't care about controlling the electricity. This is different! I could kill her!"

"Please, Serge, you have to try."

Hesitant, he did his holy roller impression, and slipped his hand into her chest. The point where his energy met hers glowed white. "I can feel her heart, but I don't know—"

"Hurry." Craig's voice came behind me. "She doesn't have much time left." He put his arm around me and lent me his warmth and calm. Then he did the solid-not-solid thing and moved to crouch beside Serge.

"But—"

"You can do it," said Craig. "You're already connected with her. Remember, you're universal energy, electricity, and her body runs on it. Just breathe, reach in, and imagine her heart restarting."

I felt, rather than saw, Nell come close.

Serge took a breath. "I can do this," he muttered to himself. "I can do this. I'm imagining her heart—"

"Pink, healthy," said Craig.

"Pink, healthy," repeated Serge. The light that connected him and Rori turned green, then pink, then white.

"Beating normally."

"Beating—"

"There. Stop." Craig leaned forward. "I can hear it. That's all you need."

Serge pulled his hand free, crawled out from behind the wall, and cleaned her blood off his hand. "I don't know how doctors do it."

"The paramedics are coming and so is—" Nell stopped as Mr. and Mrs. Pierson's screams for Rori shredded the night. "—I texted Mrs. P. Obviously, she got the message."

We moved to the side as Rori's parents raced our way. I stopped Mrs. Pierson as she tried to grab and pull her daughter by her feet. "She has a head injury. I don't think we should move her."

"Rori, Rori."

The hair on my arms prickled. There was something in the way she called her daughter that was familiar—and creepy—but I didn't know why.

The paramedics came, and I gave them space.

I pushed free of the gathering crowd, Craig, Nell, and Serge behind me. Watching Mrs. Pierson twist herself inside out to save and protect her daughter was a bitter reminder of my absent mother. And being jealous of a six-year-old who'd almost died added a layer of pathetic to my life I didn't need.

I wanted to bail on the whole thing, give the Piersons and myself some privacy, but taking off would've looked weird. Normal kids would've watched, wanted to know what was happening. The paramedics would have to check Rori for concussions, cuts, and bruises. They'd probably take her blood pressure and temperature before taking her to the hospital. Which meant I had to feign interest in the scene for the next fifteen minutes.

I stepped back, pretending to give the adults room. When we were out of grownup earshot but still close enough to look like part of the group, Nell punched Craig softly on the arm. "So, Mr. Destiny, what was with telling Serge to save Rori? Did you break some supernatural protocol in letting her live?"

Craig shook his head. "If they wanted her, I couldn't have stopped it." His breath fogged the air. "I don't like taking kids, no ferrier does."

"But sometimes it's their destiny, isn't it?" I asked.

"Doesn't mean I have to like it. Humans make destiny sound like this great thing," he said, "but the ancient Greeks had it right. Destiny is brutal."

Nell turned her attention from him, looked back at the crowd gathered around Rori. "My dad's on call at the hospital tonight. If she gets him, she's going to be fine. She'll be the old lady you collect in ninety years."

If Craig responded, I didn't hear it. If the conversation continued, I didn't notice. My focus was on the pond behind the crowd and the silver light emanating from it. The water had changed consistency and looked more like liquid mercury. Boiling silver. From its thick depths, something slowly rose.

CHAPTER FOUR

"Is anyone else seeing what I'm seeing?" I nodded at the pond.

"Whoa, I am now," said Serge.

Craig said nothing. He shifted his weight to his heels and loosely folded his arms across his chest. I figured if a boiling lake of mercury didn't stress him out, there probably wasn't much to fear.

"I sense woo-woo." Nell craned her head toward the water. "What supernatural stuff am I not seeing?"

Serge described the scene while I watched The Thing from the Silver Lagoon rise to the surface and step on to the ground. It was still covered with the metallic pond water, so how it managed to walk a straight line was beyond me.

I squinted at the red-orange outline edging The Thing.

"It's coming to us," said Serge.

Nell pulled an elastic off her wrist and wrapped her thick blond hair in a bun. "Just tell me where to kick."

"Thanks Princess of Power, but your ninja skills are no use."

"I'm short but mighty."

"Yeah, and this thing is made up of energy, not solid matter. You'll just be kicking air."

"Oh." Disappointed, she pulled her hair free of the elastic. "Right."

The blob kept coming, and with each step, it burned off the supernatural pond liquid.

Craig stiffened and lifted his gaze to the sky. He cocked his head, listened. "I'm being called."

"What's going on?" I asked.

He stepped backward. "I better see what's going on."

"Now?" I squeaked the question. I'm all about girl power and I live with the dead, so I don't scare easy, but an unidentified thing coming toward us, covered in silvery mercury with a red-orange out-line, equalled me wanting as much help as I could get. "If you're not in trouble for helping Rori, why are they calling you?"

He took a step back, morphed into his ferrier form. Because I had supernatural abilities, and because Serge was a ghost, we were the only one who saw the transformation. Which was a good thing for the non-supernatural-seeing townsfolk. Craig in ferrier form was the stuff of nightmares—horns, pointed tale, scales, wings, red eyes, and sharp, white teeth the length of my hand.

"I'm about to find out." He smiled and took to the sky.

Cursing under my breath, I turned back to watching the blob.

By the time it reached us, it wasn't an it, but a guy, around our age. Blond hair, blue eyes, slim frame.

"Hey," I said. He seemed familiar, seemed like someone I should know, but I couldn't place him.

He responded with a head nod.

"I'm Maggie, this is Nell, Serge."

"I don't see anything," whispered Nell.

I ignored her.

She poked me in the ribs. "Which direction should I wave?"

I cut her a glance from the corner of my eye.

"What?" She gave me a wide gaze. "We're probably the first people he's meant since...you know. We should be polite."

"How do you know it's a he?"

She flipped back her hair. "You have your supernatural abilities, Johnson. I have mine."

I rolled my eyes but pointed to my right.

She waved.

He waved back.

"Is he waving back?" she asked.

"Yes."

"Nell, go stand behind him—across from me. Go stand across from me."

"Why?"

"Because otherwise, to the adults, it'll look like we're having a conversation with the air. And that's going to get us into therapy or tested for drugs. I'll come out of it okay, but they'll never let you see the light of day, again."

"Ha ha. If only your fashion sense was as sharp as your wit." She paused, tapped the side of her mouth with her finger. "Oh. Wait. It is."

I ignored the jab. "If you stand across from me, it'll look like I'm talking to you."

"Oh." She flipped her hair back and took her spot.

The ghost watched as she came to a stop behind him. Then he turned, gave me a confused shrug.

"Do we know him?" she asked.

"Yeah," said Serge. "We do...I just don't know..."

This seemed like a problem that was easily solved. "Who are you?"

He pointed at himself, then looked over his shoulder.

Great. Either he was a smartass or had suffered some kind of head trauma when he died.

"Yes," I said. "You. I'm talking to you."

He opened his mouth, moved his lips. No sound came out. The ghost frowned, tried again to talk, but nothing came out.

"What's he saying?" asked Nell.

"Nothing." I wished Craig were here. "Can you talk?"

Irritation flitted across the ghost's face and he mouthed what looked like, "Yeah." He tried again.

"Did he say anything?" Nell asked.

"Nope."

"Oh, maybe it's a whole Little Mermaid thing," she said. "He needs a kiss from his true love?" She pulled out a tube of lip-gloss. "Tell me where to smack."

"Have you lost what little mind God gave you? Put it away before I smack you," I said. "You're not his true love."

She shoved the tube back in her coat pocket and shrugged. "It's a new millennium, baby. True love is who you make it with. Or who you make out with," she grinned.

"You don't even know if he's cute," I said.

"Nice, Johnson, real nice. The unattractive deserve kisses, too. Besides, I'm all about what's on the inside. Kissing him could be part of my destiny."

"Making out with strange ghosts is not part of your destiny," I said. "But therapy is becoming a definite possibility. This isn't a little mermaid thing."

"What kind of thing is it?" asked Serge.

"I don't know."

"Get him to mouth his name." Nell pulled on my jacket. "Read his lips."

"How is that helpful? I asked. "I can't read lips."

"That's the beauty." She beamed at me. "Because I can."

Serge blinked, like he wasn't sure what she'd said.

Poor schmuck. I, on the other hand, was a pro when it came to Nell logic and one day, that was going to put me in therapy.

"But you can't see him," Serge said.

She glanced down as her cell beeped with his message. "Yeah, but I can see Mags. So, he says what he says, she mimics it, and I translate."

Ye gods. That's just what I needed. Me, playing mime, with Serge directing and Nell translating. "We're not doing this."

"Try it," said Serge. "We're at a loss until we can figure the basics. And that starts with getting his name."

"You're only suggesting this because you want to see me make an idiot of myself."

"Well," he grinned, "that doesn't hurt."

"We don't need his name to cross him over," I said. Since he couldn't talk, there was no asking him if he knew where he was, or what his last memory was. I went for the blunt truth. "You're dead."

The ghost looked at me like I was crazy.

"You're dead," I repeated. "And you need to let go of this life and move on."

Anger wrinkled his face and I didn't need to be a lip reader to know what he said.

"What did he say?" asked Nell.

"Something impolite about my mother. And that he's not dead," I answered then I turned back to him. "What's the last thing you remember?"

The ghost went off but what he said, I didn't know. He finished off with an over-exaggerated mouthing of the words, *I'm not dead!*

"Are they usually this resistant to crossing over?" asked Serge.

Yeah, when they'd died suddenly or painfully. Something about the ghost's reaction said his ending had been both. Which made me feel bad for what I was about to do to him.

A rise of noise and movement from the group of adults caught my attention. I shifted my focus from the ghost and watched as the paramedics buckled Rori into the bed. As they began to wheel the gurney up the lawn, the group moved aside. Some of the adults headed our way. There was no point in talking to the ghost with a bunch of Mrs. Pierson's neighbours closing the distance.

"I should check in with Mrs. P.," said Nell. "I want to know how Rori is."

"Me, too."

"I'll come, too," said Serge.

I turned to the new ghost. "You coming?"

He shrugged and nodded.

I followed Nell. Serge and the spirit fell into step beside me.

"You really are dead," I muttered to him.

He just shook his head.

Mrs. Pierson held her daughter's hand and walked alongside the bed. I scanned the crowd. My gaze flicked over the neighbours, members of the search party, and Deputy Frank. I saw Dr. Pierson—well, the back of him, anyway—as he talked to a couple of people. Tapping Nell on the shoulder with one hand, I pointed out the doctor, who was trying to disengage himself from a couple of hangers-on. "Let's see if we can catch him and get some info before he gets to the ambulance."

"Dr. P., Dr. P." We flanked Rori's dad as Nell touched his shoulder. "What did they say?"

We were close enough to Dr. Pierson that when he took a step back and turned, he walked into ghost. Which had been my big, genius—admittedly lame—plan. Get someone to step through him so he would see he was no longer solid and therefore dead—and it worked.

The action was sudden and unexpected, and the ghost didn't have time to react. He made eye contact with Dr. Pierson, panicked as the older man broke into his personal space. The ghost flickered at the same time the doctor moved into, then out of him.

"They're going to keep her overnight, make sure there's no injury to the brain and no permanent damage with the exposure," said Dr. Pierson.

I kept one eye on the doctor, the other on the ghost. Of the two, the ghost was having the harder time. He grabbed at his stomach, then tried to touch Dr. Pierson. When his hand ran through the older man, he jerked, then stared at his fingers as though he'd never seen them before.

Dr. Pierson ran his hand over his jaw and mouth. "When I think of what could have happened if you hadn't found her. I'm—we're—so grateful."

Slowly, the ghost lifted his gaze from his hands to make eye contact with me. There was a beat of time, an eerie silence as it all came together, and the full realization that he was dead hit.

And that's when he started screaming.

CHAPTER FIVE

The next day, Nell, Serge, and I sat in a line on my bed, facing the ghost who'd found his voice, given us his name—Kent—and now paced from one side of the room to the other. And his name reminded me why I knew him.

Nell. She'd had a huge crush on him a couple years back. And no surprise.

Kent Meagher was Dead Falls' version of a superhero. He'd graduated high school at sixteen, and had been admitted into the medical program at the University of Alberta as a first-year freshman. I wasn't sure exactly what the research was. It had something to do with the genetic testing of tumours and how knowing its DNA could influence which drugs were prescribed. Plus, he'd had that lone wolf, quiet-waters-run-deep shyness that made the girls drool.

Right now, though, he looked less supermodel and more modern art project gone wrong. The lines of his body were blurred and smeared, like someone had painted him then run their hands over the wet paint. His face went dark, as though he'd stepped into shade.

This wasn't surprising. Every soul deals with being dead in a different way. Serge had come into the afterlife sharp and fully formed...till he blew himself up. Rori had never been dead, only close to it, which was why she'd never fully formed.

Until Kent came to grips with being dead and how to exist in the afterlife, his features would blur and sharpen...but you'd think a guy with the kind of brains he had would grasp what "dead" meant.

"I'm dead," he said, not for the first time, not for the fourth time.

Nell's cell binged as Serge transcribed Kent's words to her phone.

I elbowed Nell as she read the text and gave a quiet sigh.

"I don't mind that death has made him a moron," she whispered, "but it would be a lot easier to take if I could feast my eyes on that sweet body."

"Even if you could see him, you know you couldn't do anything on account of him being dead and you being alive."

She grinned. "Challenge accepted."

"Seriously, after I deal with Kent, we're getting your hormone levels checked."

"By someone cute, I hope."

I shook my head and turned my attention to the newest ghost in the room.

"Totally dead." Kent stopped pacing and faced us. He pointed at Serge. "Which is why I can see him, because he's dead, too."

"And she"—He pointed at Nell— "Can't see me."

She looked up from her cell then toward the door.

I cupped her by the chin and turned her to face the window.

"Yep," she said. Her eyes kept a constant scan of the area. "Just like the last seven times you asked, I can't see you." She paused. "But if I could, I'd hold you close and comfort you."

Kent didn't seem to hear that, but the muscle at the base of Serge's jaw pulsed.

"But you hear me because Serge knows how to interact with electronic devices and he's transcribing everything I say," said Kent.

She nodded.

"I'm confused." Kent turned from the frost-lined window. "How can he do that?"

Serge shrugged. "I'm energy. The phone is electricity. It works."

"How?"

"I don't know. It just does."

Kent shook his head. "How is it possible to work something when you don't understand it?"

"People use cars and computers," Nell said. "That doesn't mean they understand the machinery and technology behind it."

Kent tipped his head to the side and considered her argument.

Nell nudged me. "Why did he go silent?"

Kent ran his hand through his hair.

"He's thinking about what you said…" And because I knew it would tweak her, I added, "He's running his hand through his hair. It's catching the light…and his forearms are exposed—he's wearing a zip-up hoodie and grey sweatpants that—"

"You're torturing me with juicy details because I make fun of your clothes, aren't you?"

"I'm just saying a little restraint wouldn't be a bad thing."

"That's what my last boyfriend said."

"That's going to give me nightmares."

"Keep going," she said. "What else is he doing?" Nell wiggled down the bed and laid her head against the pillow. "All the details."

"That's just gross."

"Says the girl giving me the soft porn commentary on a dead guy."

"That's a good point," Kent said. "About using technology and not having a basic understanding of how it works."

Nell's cell binged. She read the text and glowed at the compliment.

Serge saw her reaction and glowered. "This is taking forever." He came over. "How can he not realize he's dead and needs to move on?"

"Don't be a jerk," I told him. "It took you twenty-four hours to realize you were dead."

"I had mitigating circumstances. I'm not a genius. He is."

I stared at him.

"What?"

"Didn't know you knew what the word 'mitigating' meant."

He rolled his eyes.

Kent moved from the window and took a seat on the bed…close to Nell, which had Serge's eyes doing a cowboy at high noon squint.

"There's so much I don't understand. Why don't I sink through this mattress and how come you can see me?"

"You don't think you should sink through the mattress, so you don't," I said. "Your thoughts make reality—more so than when you were alive. But that's all beside the point. You're here instead of being on the other side. The thing to focus on is freeing yourself to move on."

"I'm sorry," he sighed. "Science doesn't have any answer for this. I've never even conceived the possibility of life after death. It's confusing."

"If you cross over," said Serge. "You'll get all the answers you need." He pulled Kent to his feet and pushed him toward the window. "Time's a-wasting. Get on it, genius." He glanced at Nell. "Step on that bridge and move to the other side."

"That's another thing I don't get." Kent pivoted away from Serge. "I should just move on to…whatever's waiting for me, shouldn't I?"

"What about your family?" I asked. "Any unresolved issues?"

His eyes widened and blood rushed from his face. "My mom! Oh my God! With everything I totally forgot about—" A rainbow of colours lit his body up like a strobe light. "My mom, I'm all she has—maybe that's why I'm still here. Maybe I have to say goodbye to her." He looked me. "Do you translate? Is that how it works?"

Only in that old movie Dad once made me watch. It had Patrick Swayze, Demi Moore, and an inventive use of wet clay. "Uh, not really. I'm not a medium. I'm a transitioner."

He kept staring.

"A medium will connect the two of you and let you talk. I just help you let go of life so you can move on." That wasn't exactly true, but Dead Falls was a small town and I wasn't about to become known as the undertaker's crazy daughter who thought she could talk to the dead.

"Oh." Kent's Adam's apple bobbed. "Can I at least go and see her?"

"Sure," I said.

"Do I just zap over or think of her and appear at her side?"

"I have no idea, I'm not dead."

We both turned and looked at Serge, who raised his hands in surrender. "If I knew how to beam myself places with thought, do you think I'd spend most of my time in my room?"

"Naw," said Nell as she finished reading the text. "You'd be at a strip club."

Serge flushed.

"But a really good one like in Vegas."

He smiled, shook his head and rubbed the back of his neck.

"I can drive you to your mom," I told Kent. "Serge will come too. Nell, you up for the ride?"

"Normally, I'd say yes," she said, "but I think I should get to the hospital and check on Rori and her folks. Last night had to be their best-worst night, ever. Dad said when Rori was admitted, she was talking about seeing the boy who saved her." She smiled at Serge. "Of course, I couldn't say anything to Dad, but way to go, Casper. A little girl owes her everything to *the cute blond boy who made everything better.*"

We left my bedroom. I did a quick water bowl check for the animals, then met the group at the front door.

Nell tucked her phone in the pocket then leaned into me for a hug. "If he does anything sexy," she whispered. "For God's sake, let me know."

"There's a word for people like you."

"Yeah, satisfied." She broke the hug then headed out.

Serge, Kent and I piled into my 2014 red Dodge Charger. I used to have a 1952 Ford A Convertible, but that was at the bottom of the lake, thanks to Serge's father. The absence of my automotive true love was the only baggage left between Serge and me. I put the car in gear and started down Rydl Road. Kent's house was in West Ridge, a working-class neighbourhood just off Olive Lane.

Serge—seat-belted in—sat in the front passenger seat. Kent was in the back, his body twisted so he could gaze out the back window. I doubted he was that interested in the diminishing outline of my house. More likely, it gave him a way to keep his face from us, so we didn't see the pain and confusion lining it.

I didn't know much about Kent. He lived with his mom. His dad lived in another town and I don't know how much they saw each other. No siblings. His mom worked long hours at the diner. All I really knew was the legend and his reputation. I stole a glance at Serge and considered the legacy he'd left behind. Reputations were one thing, but they never really told the truth of a person. This had been especially true for Serge and I wondered how accurate Kent's was.

"How long have you been dealing with the dead?" Kent twisted forward to ask me the question.

"I've seen the dead for as long as I can remember."

"I used to pity people who thought they could communicate with the dead. I figured they were delusional," he said.

I didn't say anything.

"Does it run in your family?"

My fingers tightened on the steering wheel. "Not sure. It's not on my dad's side. I don't know my mom—she left when I was a baby."

"Oh. What about the people on her side?"

"Not sure. Don't know them, either." Time for a topic change. "But your mom—she seems like a nice lady."

"Yeah," he said, his voice growing thick, "she was a good mom. Not the best and we didn't always get along but—" He swiped his eyes. "I can't believe after tonight, I'll never see her again. Or my dad. He lives out of town but if I'd known…" He sat up, pivoted and looked out the back window.

I left him to his thoughts and turned my attention back to the blacktop.

"What happens after?"

I glanced at him in the rearview. "Happens after what?"

"I cross over. Do I come back again?" He gripped the back of my chair and Serge's, and wriggled forward. "Is that what you do?" He asked Serge.

"No, I never crossed over."

"Why? How come you're still around?"

"My destiny. I'm bonded to her," said Serge.

"What does that mean?"

"Somewhere in the past, we scripted our lives to become guardians, watchers over the living and the dead. As long as she's alive, I guess I'm here."

"How did you die?"

"Murdered," said Serge.

"Oh." Kent slid back in the chair, then slid forward again. "Did they catch who did it to you?"

His answer was an emotionless, "Yeah."

I reached over and squeezed his hand.

"Did you remember dying?"

He shook his head. "Bits and pieces."

"I can't remember, either." There was silence as he thought it over. "Does that mean someone murdered me?"

"I don't know," I said. "It might just be that death shocked your system. I transitioned a lady one time who'd been hit by a car. It took her a bit to realize she was dead, too."

"Oh." Kent turned back to Serge. "So, being dead and living in this world. Can you do anything cool? Other than texting, I mean."

"Maggie and I have a psychic connection. She can call for me." Serge twisted to get a better view of the ghost. "I can hone in on her and the house, but that's it."

"You saved me," I reminded him, "and Rori."

"Dr. Pierson's kid?" asked Kent. "Is that what all the ambulances were for?"

I gave him the back-story.

"That's decent," said Kent and turned back to Serge. "But you can't go over to the next world then back again?"

"No. I think you have to be a special kind of supernatural to do that. Like Maggie's boyfriend. He transports the dead, so he goes back and forth all the time."

Mention of Craig reminded me that I hadn't heard from him. And reminded me I had been so focused on Kent that I hadn't even thought of him. Was that good or bad?

"But you didn't cross over. Don't you want to?"

"It would be cool to see stuff and know what's on the other side..." He shrugged. "But my afterlife is linked to Mags and I'm okay with that."

"But what about the other stuff? Like knowing you'll never be with a chick, again? How do you handle that?"

Serge's jaw slackened, his eyes lost focus.

Thank God he was already dead. The reminder that Serge would never get to stick his hand up some girl's shirt looked like it was going to kill him. I jumped into the conversation before Kent reminded Serge he couldn't eat or drink either. "I've crossed over souls and it looks like there's a lot of good things on the other side."

The streetlights cast Kent's frown in shadowy light. "I've never considered harps and clouds." He paused. "I've never considered an afterlife. I always thought you live, you die, that's it. You know—the worm goes in, the worm goes out, the worm plays pea knuckle on your snout."

Oh, boy, if he didn't have a concept of life after death, then despite the outwardly calm demeanour, this guy was in for nine kinds of confusion and culture shock. "I'm sorry." Wow, was I Canadian. Had I just apologized to a ghost for him getting his philosophy wrong? "It's not all bad. It's not like your life is over."

"My life *is* over."

"Okay, so it's not like your *existence* is over. There's lots of stuff that can happen to you, now," I said. "You can be reborn, move to a different plane, re-die"—Good one, Maggie—"but not you...it'll be fine for you, I'm sure."

Kent pressed his forehead against the glass. "But this time, this life is gone. I can't go back to my mom or dad. I can't do all the stuff I wanted to—I'll have to start over, all over again." In the rearview mirror, our gazes met. "Do you know how hard I worked? How much I sacrificed to get to where I was? And now it's all trashed and I don't even know why. Was I hit by a car? Or did I die trying to save someone's life?"

"You don't lose everything. Your experiences become part of your subconscious knowledge—"

"Unless you're telling me I can be born again with my high school diploma and acceptance into university already set, then I'm starting over." He groaned. "I hate physics and now I have to do it, again."

Okay, my sales talk for reincarnation wasn't going so well. Time to pitch something else. "It really won't be all bad. When the time comes for you to move on, someone from the other side will claim you. It's a chance to reunite with everyone who's gone before you."

"Someone from the other side?"

I shrugged. "For some people, it's their grandparents or relatives. Other people it's a pet—"

"My grandparents on Dad's side died before I was born. And on my mom's side when I was just little." He rubbed his forehead. "I don't understand. Why didn't they claim me right away?"

The leather seats and springs creaked as he moved closer to my chair. "Did I do something wrong? Is that why they didn't come to pick me up?" There was a beat of silence, then, "Oh, man. Is something else coming for me?" His voice dropped to a whisper. "Something, you know, with horns and who likes fire and brimstone?"

"No. Those guys claim their souls right away. My theory is when people die unexpectedly or if they can't believe they've died or if the death is shocking, there's a gap that's created. I think to transition naturally, either with a previously passed loved one or a ferrier—"

"What's a ferrier?"

Great, Maggie. Go ahead and complicate an already complicated situation. Nice job. "That's Craig but it doesn't matter, sorry. What I mean is because you didn't expect to die, the natural connection that would have occurred, that would have made a bridge between this world and the next, didn't get created. That's why you're still here and I'm involved. We'll get you to your mom and hopefully, it'll go smoothly."

He gave a humourless laugh. "Yeah, smoothly, whatever 'it' is." Kent slid back into his chair.

Serge glanced back then whispered, "How are we going to do this?"

I shrugged. I was really hoping that Kent would see home, be warmed by it, and somehow cross over. What I *didn't* want to do was knock on the door and pass on any messages from the dead.

"I was rude to her," Kent said from the back. "This afternoon, when I saw her, I was mean. And now it's the last thing she'll remember of me."

"See your memory's coming back. That's some good news, right?" I hung a left for Parsons Ave. "You saw her today?"

He nodded. "I came in for the Thanksgiving weekend. We had dinner, then I went for a walk."

Whoa. *What?* I hit the brakes, pulled the car onto the shoulder. "What?"

"This weekend, Thanksgiving weekend. I thought I'd take a couple days from the university. She and I hadn't talked for a while—"

"You came for Thanksgiving."

"Yes."

"Thanksgiving."

He looked at me like I should be checked for a brain injury. "Yeah. Thanksgiving."

"Thanksgiving is the second weekend in October," I said.

"Yeah, I know that."

"It's mid-November."

"No, tonight's the Saturday of the Thanksgiving long weekend—"

"It's Sunday of a regular November weekend." There was no point in preparing him, so I pushed forward. "Kent, you've been dead for weeks."

His outline blurred and his body bowed and went blobby like an amoeba. "If I've been dead for weeks," he asked, his voice faint. "Where's my body? And where's my consciousness been all this time?"

CHAPTER SIX

What an idiot I'd been. I should've been paying more attention. The newly dead always smell like pine trees and evergreens. When I first saw Kent, he didn't put off the smell. That should have tweaked me to the fact he'd been a ghost for a while.

"What does that mean, Maggie?" Contained panic was in his voice. "If I've been dead for weeks—"

"I don't know," I said, "and there's no point in pretending I have answers."

"But you have to have a theory—you've been doing this since you were born."

An exaggeration, but he was right. I had a theory but I didn't think he'd like it. "The only thing I know is we need to transition you. You'll get all your answers on the other side." I spun around and belted myself back in. "Let's get you to your mom."

A few minutes later, I rolled the car to a stop in front of his house.

"Home sweet home," he said. "I wonder if she'll stay in Dead Falls now that I'm gone."

"Does she have friends here?"

"Not really, I mean she knows people, but she doesn't really have friends here...she really doesn't have friends, anywhere. I'm—I was all she had."

"This is where I step in," said Serge. "Thanks for the ride, Mags. Kent, come on. I'll show you how to move through the walls. We'll find your mom and I'll help you cross over."

You're sure you're okay with that? I went for mental communication to talk to Serge.

What choice do we have? You can't go knocking on her door and telling her you have a message from her dead son.

Do you know what to do? You've never crossed anyone over before.

Maybe not, but I have a lot of experience being dead and letting go of the life I lived.

I didn't have an answer for that, only sadness for the way he'd died. *Fair enough.*

Dead Falls didn't have much in the way of cosmopolitan appeal but it had woodland that bordered the town. The city fathers and mothers hadn't developed the land, and most people used the forest for off-leash dog walking, hiking, biking, and running.

Since Kent's house was next to one of the forest entrances, I told Serge I'd park there and he could meet me when it was done—no need for Mrs. Meagher's neighbours to look out their window and see me sitting in front of her place.

He agreed. I told Kent goodbye and good luck, then drove away. I spent the next fifteen minutes worrying about Serge and Kent, and hoping Serge'd be able to do it...and hoping he wouldn't. Not that I wanted to see him fail, but I'd gotten used to having him around—really used to it—and I worried that him seeing the bridge to the afterlife could mean he would cross over, too.

A few minutes later, I looked up to see Serge coming my way. A mixture of relief and pride gave my heart quick twist. The smile on my mouth dipped a few seconds later when I saw Kent jog up beside him.

My phone binged with a text from Craig: **Free to chat?**

Yep, I texted back.

A second later, Craig appeared in my room.

He grinned, then leaned over and gave me a kiss that warmed me to my toes.

"Seriously," I said. "You can never teach Serge how to appear in people's rooms. He'll never leave Nell's bedroom. And while we're at it, let's never tell my dad you can do it, either."

He laughed. "I've taken on a lot of scary things in my life, but taking on Hank is out of my wheelhouse. The secret will die with me." Craig sat on the bed and reached for Ebony.

The cat purred and climbed onto his lap.

He rubbed her head. "How did the transitioning go?"

"Not well."

"Really? I'm surprised Serge isn't here with you, then. I thought he'd be all over solving the mystery."

"They're in Serge's room, trading dead stories." I told him of our abject failure in transitioning Kent then kept going. "Kent's a mess. He's all Type A 'how can I fail at dying? How stupid am I that I can't cross over?' And it's affecting his ability to stay in a coherent form...and Serge isn't happy about it, either. I think that stupid conversation about what he's doing with his afterlife got him all riled up and he wants to prove he's more than an otherworldly text app and defibrillator."

"The answer seems easy enough for Kent," said Craig. "His mom's not the unfinished business that has him lingering."

"That's my guess, too, but...he's dead and he didn't know it at first—"

"That's not unusual—"

"—and he's been in some kind of unconscious state until now because he's been dead for weeks. He still thought it was the Thanksgiving long weekend."

"That's more unusual."

"Have you heard of anything like that?"

Craig nodded. "When the death is so sudden and shocking, the spirit can't process it, and so the soul goes into a limbo state. It falls asleep."

"Like what happened to Serge?"

"Worse—"

Oh, boy. "However Kent died, it's affected his core identity."

"It's more than him not being able to believe he's dead or coming to grips with the fact he knows who killed him," he said. "It's a combination of all of it, and the way he died might factor in, too." He leaned back against the pillows. "What's his view on suicide?"

"That hasn't come up...you think that's how he died?"

"Maybe. Often the limbo state happens with these types of death—but only if the person had thought of suicide as a mortal sin. Priests, pastors, that kind of thing. They sleep until their soul can find peace with the action."

"Kent doesn't believe in an afterlife or divine punishment. At least, he didn't at the point of his death. But even if that's the case, then Kent waking up should mean he's resolved the inner conflict."

"Or it could mean the combined, heightened energies of you, me, and Serge when we were looking for Rori acted like an alarm clock and woke him up. Or maybe he didn't kill himself and it's something else entirely."

"Thanks. You're just so great at clearing these things up."

"Always there for you. Now it's all about you finding out what happened the night he died."

"Any supernatural hints or clues?"

He pulled me into his arms. "Sorry, when it comes to him, I'm clueless."

"Doesn't seem quite right. You have the ability to move through worlds and transport spirits but you're as blind as I am when it comes to Kent."

"Destiny," he smiled. "It sucks but I'll help in any way I can." He grimaced. "When I get back."

"Get back from where?"

"Africa."

I went still. "You're being shipped to Africa? Why? Is it the gang upstairs? Did you get in trouble for helping Rori?"

"No, nothing like that. Like I said, if it had been her time, I wouldn't have been able to stop it. It's the gang down here, actually. Human problems. There's a virus outbreak in western Africa. I'm going to be gone for…" He sighed. "I don't know how long. There's so much death. A lot of ferriers have been called in. I'll be moving souls. It could be a few days, it could be a week. Maybe longer. Depends on how fast the death toll rises."

That sucked on so many levels, I didn't know where to start. We talked for a bit more, did a couple of fun boy-girl things, then he blipped to Africa. I stuffed down the rising sadness and went back to figuring out how to help a ghost with an identity crisis.

CHAPTER SEVEN

"I don't know why we waste our money going to the movies," Nancy said when I came downstairs the next morning. Dad let me skip school when I told them about Kent, the fact that he'd been dead for a while, apparently sleeping in the Piersons' pond, and was now crashing at our house. Now I'd just finished telling them about our failure to transition him. She tossed a smile at my dad. "Hank, your daughter's life is all the drama I need."

She set a cup of coffee in front of me. The wooden legs of the kitchen chair jittered against the linoleum as she pulled it out from under the table and sat. "Let's run through this again. Kent's dead?"

"Yes. Serge is keeping him occupied so we can talk."

"I don't know what's worse." Dad sat beside his girlfriend and put down the plate of chocolate-chip cookies. "Finding out you're dead or finding out you're dead and you've been in some unconscious state for weeks." He reached across the table and put his hand over mine. "I'm sorry this is your problem to solve."

It was a comforting gesture and one I'd come to depend on. My whole life, it's been me and Dad. He and I were teammates against the world and the afterworld, too. Because of my unique skill set, we'd moved a lot. He worried my abilities would come out and set me up for even more bullying or put me in the tabloid spotlight.

Dad never made me feel bad for the moves or my abilities. He'd never complained about having to restart his life. But now that he was with Nancy, I hoped we wouldn't have to move again. Dead Falls was finally a place we could both call home.

"That poor kid," said Dad.

"Something doesn't make sense." I stopped and took two giant bites of Nancy's homemade cookies. "His mother." There was a beat of silence, then I registered the look of confusion on the sheriff's face.

"I appreciate how close we are, kid, but you talking with a mouth full of food is still incomprehensible to me."

I swallowed my mouthful and tried again. "His mother. Kent's been dead for weeks. How did his mom not know?"

Nancy made a sound and I didn't need a translator to know the meaning: Kent's mom was a pain in the sheriff's neck. "That woman."

I helped myself to another cookie and waited.

"She has problems."

"Kent said she was a good mom."

"That's because Kent's a saint. He put up with a lot from her." Her gaze drifted to the stairs. "Actually, when you think about it, his relationship with his mother was a lot like Serge's relationship with his mom. Fragile women who make their sons the parent in the relationship."

Great. Another whack-job mother for me to deal with. "You said Kent put up with a lot. What kind of problems did she give him?"

"The kind that comes from an ugly divorce and an even uglier custody fight. She and Kent's dad, Doug, split when the kid was five or six, and she never stopped being out for blood where Doug was involved. If Kent was two minutes late coming home from school, she was phoning me a missing person's report." Nancy leaned back, flipped her thick, blond braid over her shoulder. "There's a difference between a legitimate call and a nuisance. There wasn't a dedicated police station in Dead Falls at the time." She paused for a breath. "That woman wouldn't even call to say he was home and we could disregard. She'd make us drive the forty-five minutes to Dead Falls so we could verify he was really okay. Her anxieties over her son and her grudge with her ex-husband got so bad that Doug ended up leaving the town when Kent was in junior high. He just couldn't stand it anymore."

"You were never worried for him? Kent, I mean."

"At first, when Kent wouldn't tell me where he'd been." She shrugged. "But when I went to check up on Doug, I realized what was going on. When Kent was little, he'd sneak off to see his dad. Doug was a long-haul truck driver and when he was in town, that's where

I'd find Kent. Then the kid got older. If he wasn't with his dad, he was jogging or at the library or volunteering. Trust me, there was nothing to worry about with him. He was too focused on becoming a doctor and too much a creature of habit to get himself in trouble. Saving the world through medicine and running the same path through town, that was Kent in a nutshell." She pushed her mug around in a circle. "But I felt for him." She sighed. "Much as I wanted to take my Taser to Marlo, I felt for her, too, but her overprotectiveness frustrated me, I could only imagine what it was like for Kent to be on the receiving end of her fears."

"Not that anyone's asking my opinion," said Dad. "But I think the reason he did so well in school was because he wanted out of this town. The family was poor, getting that university scholarship was the only way he was going to fund his escape."

"But if she was such an anxious mother, how did Kent die and no one know? You'd think if he missed checking in with her once he arrived back at school, she'd have called in the army."

"Which begs the question, did he make it back to the university after Thanksgiving," Dad said. "Or is his body somewhere between us and Edmonton?"

"That's probably a question best asked by a member of law enforcement," I said and gave Nancy my best begging face. "If only there was someone who could step in and help."

"Oh boy, stop before you pull a muscle. I'll put in a phone call." She checked her watch. "It'll have to wait until the offices open." She frowned. "Don't you have a supernatural, superhero boyfriend? Can't Craig answer this?"

I made a face, then made another one when I realized I hadn't thought of him. Again. Craig was my first boyfriend. Was it bad girl-friend karma to forget about him because of everything going on with Kent? Or was that the healthy relationship thing of each of us having separate lives? I dug my cell out of my pocket and checked to see if he'd texted. "Battery's dead."

"Don't we have an agreement about that cell always being charged?" asked Dad.

"Give me a break," I said. "It was probably because of Craig. Between the psychic energy he puts off and the electricity Serge puts out when we're doing our supernatural thing, I'm lucky the phone doesn't explode."

His expression smoothed out, then shifted as his mouth pulled down. "I thought you guys figured out how to avoid the shorting out of the cell?"

"We did, but the other night with Rori and Kent...all of our energies were spiking. That's probably why the phone shorted out."

Dad pulled off his glasses, rubbed the bridge of his nose, and sighed. "There should be some kind of support group for parents like me. At least he was with you, if anything had happened." Setting his glasses back on his nose, he asked, "Any updates on Rori?"

"Nell said she's doing better."

"Everyone living is good, which brings me back to Craig," said Nancy. "Can't he help?"

"I don't think so." I talked around a mouthful of chocolate chips. "He only gets info on souls that he's charged with transitioning, and Kent's not his charge."

She sighed. "Too bad. It would've made things...less complicated for me when I put in the call to Margo and the school tomorrow."

"Thanks for coming up with a reason to talk to the university." I lifted what was left of the cookie. "And baking. Thanks for that, too."

They stood, shoved their chairs under the table.

"Hopefully, you'll be able to transition Kent to the afterlife by the end of the week," said Nancy. "Maybe even in a couple of days." She stopped as her phone buzzed, then let out a string of Italian.

"Bad news?"

"Some idiot's vandalized the Pierson home."

"Are you kidding?"

"I wish." Another string of Italian. "I got to go and check this out."

"Will you be gone for the rest of the day?" I asked.

"Nah. For sure I'll be back in time to tell you goodnight."

If I ever had delusions about being cool, Nancy's words obliterated the fantasy. Maybe normal seventeen-year-old girls detest their parents hugging them goodnight. Not me. There was something about having Dad and Nancy around me that made me feel like things—no matter how crazy they could get—would always work out. Let's face it, with my life, I needed all the confirmation I could get.

"I'll check out Kent's stuff ASAP, and who knows? We may have it all figured out by noon tomorrow."

I smiled, nodded. I didn't have the heart to obliterate her fantasy, but the facts didn't support her dream. Kent was dead, had been missing for weeks. The university didn't know anything. If they had, there would have been a report or questions, and for sure, Kent's mom would have been notified. Which meant Nancy would have been notified. Instinct said whatever had caused Kent's death was going to be complicated, ugly, and that by the time we were through, I'd wish Kent had just stayed in the pond.

I found Serge coming out of his room. "Everything okay?"

"Need a break," he said. "His story is a lot like my story, and it's putting me in a bad place. Thought I'd do a lap around the house and come back."

"So, not going well?"

He shrugged. "As good as can be. His relationship with his mother is almost as complicated as mine." He gave me a small smile. "Almost. She's more independent than my mother was, but he's just as protective...and resentful."

Dysfunctional parental relationships. No wonder Serge was having a rough time.

I left him and knocked on the door. "Kent," I said, "Can we talk?"

Kent turned from the window and nodded. "Sure, it's your house, your rules, right?"

"Yeah, but for the time being it's kind of your room."

"I want to leave," he said.

"I'm trying to help with that—"

"No, I mean your place. I don't want to be here anymore."

Well, gee, I'd have been a better hostess but since you don't eat or drink or breathe—

"I'm worried about my mom. I think I should go back home and look out for her."

Oh. That stopped my inner rant. "Sure, I can drive you in a bit, if you like."

He smiled and I understood why Nell had crushed out on him. There was a genuineness in the way Kent looked at you, like he *saw* the you that you wanted to be, and wanted to you to know he was present, listening, and happy to be around you. "You would have made a really good doctor."

His eyes turned glassy. "Thanks."

"Did you always want to do that?"

"Actually, I wanted to be a vet, but I wasn't smart enough."

"That's hard to believe."

"No, really. Doctors have to know the human body but a vet has to know dogs, cats, birds—plus..." He laughed sheepishly. "Besides, I have a better shot at objectivity with people." I crossed the room to where he stood. There was no easy way to broach the topic, so I dived in. "I wondered how you felt about suicide?"

"Huh?"

"Do you believe in it?"

He laughed. "Suicide isn't an intangible thing like Santa Claus or faith, Maggie. You don't believe or not believe in it. It's an act, a choice."

"Okay...how do you feel about suicide as a choice?"

"I saw a lot when I volunteered at the hospital and some of it..." He leaned his shoulder against the window jamb and looked out into the grey morning. "There were some patients that were in all kinds of pain and the only way to help them was to dope them with so much morphine, they weren't even conscious anymore. And I'd think, if this person was a dog or a cat, I could euthanize them and people would congratulate me on my act of mercy. But they're human and I can't do anything but watch." He turned his gaze from the window back to me.

His eyes were clear, blue, the sincerity in them, unencumbered.

"The majority of the time I see people speaking out against doctor-assisted suicide, they're healthy people. Think on that."

I had asked about suicide and he'd answered with euthanasia and terminally ill patients. "So...you're not against it?"

He watched me for a second, then, "Holy crap! You think that's what I did? That I killed myself?"

"I'm trying to figure out why you would have gone into limbo and I was wondering..."

"Geez! No, I didn't off myself. I know that, for sure!"

"But how—"

"Because I'm a med student and I've learned all the possible ways to kill yourself. Trust me, the sure-fire methods involve a lot of pain and blood." A flush of red touched his cheeks. "I'm kind of a wuss when it comes to *my* pain and *my* blood."

"But there are other ways—"

"And those aren't a 100%. Believe me, whenever I do anything it's at 100% but suicide isn't one of those things."

"Okay. Fair enough."

He exhaled a long, slow breath, slid to the floor.

I joined him.

"Any other theories?"

I shrugged. "I've never really had anyone with your circumstances before. I mean, I've transitioned souls who've wandered for days, even hundreds of years, before deciding to move on...but I never had a conversation with them about why they wandered or if they'd been asleep..."

"Trust me to be the outlier in your experiences," he said.

I put my hand on his shoulder. "It's not so bad."

"It kind of is. I used to hear about ghosts that could move furniture or make objects spin—"

"Hey." Serge came into the room. "Is this a private conversation or can any ghoul join in?"

"We're talking poltergeists," I said.

"You'd think if all I am now is energy," said Kent. "I'd be able to do amazing things."

"Serge blew up a house last month," I said.

Kent's eyes went wide. "You did? Why?"

"It was part of my anger management training." He sat down with us.

I checked him out. "Wait a second, Serge, there's something else you can do."

"What's that?"

"You text and fix hearts and blow up houses—" I pointed at him. "But you change clothes, too."

He looked down at his jeans and long-sleeve crewneck. "Yeah, I guess I do...so?"

"I don't know. It just seems like another talent," I said.

Kent pulled on his sweater. "This is the last thing I remember wearing when I was alive."

"It's also the same thing you've been wearing since we found you," I said.

Kent looked at his jogging pants and hoodie. "I wonder what the practical applications of that talent would be?"

Serge was staring at his outfit. "Actually, that's kind of weird and random. It's not like anyone sees me except you and Craig—and Kent, now." He looked up at me. "Why would it matter, anyway?"

"It's part of your self-identity," I said.

"So what does that mean?" asked Kent.

"I think it means whatever happened to you, you are *really* stuck in it," I said to Kent.

"Great," he muttered, "just great. I'm going to be here, forever."

CHAPTER EIGHT

Early the next morning, bleary-eyed and barely aware of what clothes I'd tossed on, I sat in the passenger seat of Nell's car, waiting in the drive-thru of the Tim Hortons'.

"What do you think Nancy will find out when she calls the university?" Nell asked.

"Nothing. The university probably doesn't even know Kent's gone."

"That's what I figure, too." She glanced in the rearview mirror. "How's Casper doing with his new brother?"

"They were both sleeping when I left." I checked out the overturned garbage cans along the street. Of the things I'll never understand, vandalism has to be in my top twenty. "I'm assuming they're fine. Kent said he's going to go home today. He can't do much, but he wants to be around his mom."

"It must be nice for him—Serge, I mean. Having someone who understands his situation."

"I understand his situation!"

Nell gave me a soft smile. "You *know* his situation, but Serge gets it. Serge's living it." Her eyes squeezed shut. "No pun intended." She put the car in gear and pulled up to the menu board.

"My treat," I said when she'd finished ordering two large double-doubles and a pack of ten Timbits.

She shook her head. "Save your money." She glanced at my sweater. "Use it to pay for a nice funeral for that outfit."

"Hey!"

Nell pulled up to the next window, paid, and got our breakfast. "I suggest cremation. That sweater should be burned."

"I would, but considering your top looks like it's painted on, the fumes might present a fire hazard."

Nell grinned at me from the top of her cup. "Baby, *I* am a fire hazard." She took a pull of her drink. "Since we're talking hot topics, did you hear from Craig?"

"Radio silence." I pulled the tab off my cup and let the vapours of dark roast coffee scent the air. "Should I be worried?"

"I don't think his silence is regular boyfriend silence, and I don't think you should worry."

Her mention of worry reminded me of Rori. "Does your dad have any updates on Rori?"

She nodded. "He said Dr. Pierson's been hovering and so's Mrs. Pierson. They're a couple of basket cases. I guess one of the nurses had to ask them to leave because they were fighting in her room."

Whoa. "A nurse kicking out worried parents—one of whom is a doctor at the hospital? That's big."

"Major big, but it was upsetting the kid. Other than that, Rori's doing great. They're waiting on the test results, but so far she has a mild concussion and they're going to keep her for a couple of days—mostly to give her a break from her folks, but she should be fine. Her mom says she's asking about us. You up for a visit when she gets home?"

I nodded, pulled a Timbit from the box, and bit into the bite-sized frosted pastry. Man, nothing like sugar, caffeine, a warm car and a good friend to help me feel like I was going to figure out Kent and his death. I scarfed down the Timbit, reached for another, and let the town pass me by in a blur of grey sky and barren trees.

The buzz of my cell caught my attention. I pulled it out and checked the screen. "It's a text from Craig." I opened the app and read, **In the middle of all of it, there is still beauty.** I smiled and turned the phone so Nell could see the picture he'd included: zebras silhouetted against the red sky of a setting sun.

"Don't you think it's weird, that kid going missing?" Bruce asked when Nell and I found him and Tammy in the school cafeteria.

The faint smell of bacon and hash browns wafted from the kitchen but I was happy with the cup of coffee in my hand. "Weird?"

"Come on." He leaned forward. "First Serge, then you, some doctor's kid."

"Rori," said Nell. "Her name is Rori."

He leaned back, made the blue plastic chair squeak. "Don't you see the connection?"

I figured he was missing a connection—or three. Judging from the earnest look on his face, saying so would have been hurtful, so I went with, "No, sorry, I'm missing it."

"Serge died, then you almost died, then Rori almost died."

"Serge was murdered, I was caught in the crosshairs of a murder investigation, and Rori slipped on a ladder."

Bruce shook his head. "It's Serge."

Disbelief worked like a psychic homing beacon and brought Serge to me.

He flashed into the seat beside me. "What's going on? I was just teaching Kent about using text apps—"

"Serge?" I said as Nell's phone beeped his text.

She glanced at it and I continued, "You think Serge was behind what happened to Rori Pierson."

Serge's eyes went wide, then narrowed into slits. "Are you kidding me? Even dead, I'm being blamed for the bad stuff that happens in this town?"

Bruce nodded. "Until Serge, how many people had been murdered in town?"

I shrugged. So did the rest of the group.

"There have been two murders in the last twenty-seven years," said Bruce. "Then Serge dies. That's one death—well, plus the stuff with his folks. But then you almost die, so does that little kid. All within the last month." He folded his arms across his chest. "Trust me, Serge is behind this."

"I suppose I shouldn't be surprised—" Serge said, shaking his head.

Nell looked up from her phone. "Why are you blaming him? He's dead."

Bruce straightened. "I'm not blaming—the opposite. I think Serge is trapped in between our world and the next. He's calling for help—"

"—and almost killing kids in the process?" I asked.

Bruce shrugged. "It's Serge. It's not like he's going to write a polite note asking for help."

Serge laughed, the sound partly hollow and mostly sad. "He's got a point."

Confusion made wrinkles in Nell's face. "How do you figure kids dying and Serge—"

Oh, no. No way. I wasn't going get into Bruce logic. I had enough to deal with when it came to Nell logic. "Uh, that can wait. You want to talk to Serge—"

"To see if he's okay," said Tammy.

Serge went still, then laughed. "What do they think I'm going to say? Like...HHHEELLLPP?"

I went for mental communication with the ghost. *Seriously. No more Scooby Doo.*

"We think Serge is trapped in this plane," said Tammy, "and we want to free him."

He stopped laughing. "Actually, that's kind of sweet." He blinked, then blinked again. "And more than I deserve."

"Exactly. We'll cross him over." Bruce's fingers twitched. "Maybe get a chance to say sorry for being such a jerk to him."

"I think he knows," said Nell.

Under the table, I kicked her foot.

"—he would know and forgive you." Nell gave me a bland smile made sarcastic because she knew the truth.

Tammy's shake of her head made strands of her hair stick in her lip-gloss. "Not if he's trapped. Then he may not know anything. He might be in pain."

"How are you going to do it?" I asked.

"An Ouija board," she said. "You in?"

That was going to be problematic. Me plus anything that acted as a magnet for spirits was going to equal every ghost showing up at my door.

Can I come?

Serge's question sounded in my head.

Rattle some chains?

I'll rattle your chains if you do.

"You need to be there," said Bruce. "I think you have a special connection with him."

Serge laughed. *Boy, they don't know the half of it, do they, Mags?*

"Nell's coming—" Bruce continued.

Of course she was. Had Nell been at the burning of Rome, she'd have brought marshmallows.

"—if you come that's four of us. Five if we can get a hold of Craig." Bruce's face scrunched together. "I tried texting but he hasn't responded." His gaze found me. "You're his girlfriend. Do you know what's going on?"

"Uh, he had to visit family. They live in a remote area. Not sure if they get cell reception where they're at."

Nell had a sudden coughing fit.

"Anyway, you on board?" He grinned. "For the board?"

"Um, I'm not sure..."

"You gotta come."

Dang. He looked so sincere. "Let me think on it, okay?"

Bruce's disappointment was almost palatable. He stood. "This isn't just about him, it's about you too."

Oh, boy. He didn't know the half of it.

CHAPTER NINE

"What do you mean I dropped out of school?" A few days after Nancy put in the query, Kent stood at the kitchen table, his arms folded and a look of disbelief on his face. Well, what was left of his face. Half of it had gone black. I guess he was still wrestling with the reality of being dead. His outline remained sharp, which seemed like a positive step.

Nancy glanced at the screen of her cell. "Is that Kent or is Serge transcribing?"

"Serge taught me how to tap into the phones."

Her phone beeped the text. "Oh, okay." Nancy slid close to me and whispered, "Should I congratulate him or is that just weird?"

"I'd hold off on the kudos, for now," said Serge.

Kent raised his hands in the air, then let them drop with a *slap* against his thighs. "I'd never drop out of university. I gave up having a life just to get into med school!"

Nancy's phone beeped.

"The university's registration system recorded someone logging in with Kent's ID and passcode, then dropping all of his classes. They also received an email from his address to the dean, saying he couldn't handle the pressure and was withdrawing."

"Couldn't handle the pressure? After pulling off perfect marks and perfect attendance, being on almost every sports team, volunteering at the hospital, and getting to university on a scholarship that *still* doesn't pay for everything, and they think I caved under pressure?"

"Maybe Kent needs some time to consider this," I said.

"I don't need time, I need answers! Don't you get it? My body's missing, plus all this stuff at school. People are going to think I flaked out on my life—or that I really *did* kill myself! I didn't do either!" He put his head between his legs and took a few deep breaths.

Nancy held up her phone. "I got nothing, what's he saying?"

"He's hyperventilating," I said. "Give him a minute."

She set down her phone. "This is a weird life you live, kid. And all this time, when I dealt with murder victims, I always thought, if I could just talk to them, I'd solve this case in a heartbeat."

"Yeah, well, violent deaths have a way of erasing memories," I said. "I'm getting that."

"Did you get anything from his mom?"

Nancy shook her head. "She's on sick leave from work. I tried calling, then going to the house when she didn't pick up, but she didn't come to the door."

"Let's hope it's because she's actually sick and she didn't have anything to do with her son's death," I said.

"Kent." Nancy's gaze washed the room.

"He's standing across from you."

"If it wasn't you, then who? Who knows you well enough to know your passwords and code, and could access your student records?"

He stood up, shook his head, miserable. His body rippled, like he was a piece of laundry left on the line during a storm. "That's just it. No one. I don't have any close friends—"

Serge and I glanced at each other, but the sadness of the statement seemed to bypass Kent because he didn't miss a breath or a word.

"—and sending a letter to the dean, having me drop out because of stress? That's someone who hated me. Wanted people to think I was some kind of flake." His misery turned to confusion. "But to hate me that much they'd rip my reputation? I don't know anyone like that."

Great. Now, I was chasing two ghosts. Kent and the shadowy phantom who'd ruined his life.

I found Kent in Serge's room a couple hours later. "Hey."

"Hey."

"I'd ask how you're doing but it's pretty obvious." I gestured to his face. "But you look like you're doing better...I can see all of you, now."

He blinked and wiped his eyes. "I'd say this is a nightmare come true, but in my wildest nightmares, I never imagined this." He reached his hand out to me. "Sorry about the freak out earlier."

"Understandable, no worries." I sat beside him on the duvet-covered bed and went silent. A lifetime of transitioning the dead had taught me lesson number one: let the dead talk. They needed to tell someone their story to free themselves from this plane and move on.

"My whole life has revolved around being a doctor. I volunteered at the hospital on weeknights, got temp jobs there during the summer. Made sure my application to med school was well rounded: volunteered at the animal shelter and the distress line, joined track teams, did extra homework. I didn't have time for friends or a girlfriend. I've never been on a sleepover, never had a birthday party. I spent my entire life making hard choices and sacrificing for my future." He broke off. "All of it, for what? To end up dead before I was twenty-one."

I took his hand and squeezed. "I'm so sorry."

"I was going to help kids with ADHD. Fight for better health-care options for the poor and elderly." He laughed through his tears. "I was trying to do it all and I probably wasn't going to get any of it done, but all I've ever wanted was to leave the world a better place than I found it. And now I'm dead and the world hasn't been made better. The world doesn't even know I'm gone."

I put my arms around his shoulders, rested my chin against the top of his head, let him cry.

Craig's text woke me up the next morning. **Wish you were here** it said, along with a photo of a waterfall.

Wish you were here, I texted back, **'cause then you'd know there's an eight hour time difference and it's three in the morning over here.**

ROFL.

I blinked fast. I really did wish he was here so I could hear his laugh in person. **I heart you.**

Heart you back.

I set the phone back on the night table, squirmed back into a comfortable spot between Ebony and Buddha, and closed my eyes.

Tammy and Bruce were waiting at my locker on Monday morning, and I managed to get around another request for a séance by claiming

I was so upset by what happened to Rori that I needed a couple days to recover.

After school, I grabbed Nell, went to my house to get Kent and Serge. Then we headed to Kent's house.

"What's the plan?" Nell asked as we drove. Snowflakes fell from a dark grey sky and a sharp wind heralded the coming of a bitter storm.

"We need to get a missing person report filed—" I glanced over my shoulder at Serge. "You know you're dead, right? And don't need the seat belt?"

"Have you seen her driving?" He buckled himself into the seat.

Kent shrugged and did the same.

"I see you grinning, Johnson," said Nell, "but since I'm not one to text and drive, I don't know what's going on."

"Do you ever know what's going on?"

"I know if you keep sassing me, I'm pulling over and you can walk to Mrs. Meagher's house in the snowstorm."

"I take it back. You're a visionary, Nell."

"That's better. Why are we doing this?"

"Mrs. Meagher's not answering her door, but I bet if she thought it was about her kid, she'd answer. His mom is the only one who should file a report." I looked at Nell. "You're going to tell her you wanted to talk to Kent about med school, but you can't get a response from him and you're worried."

The streetlights illuminated her frown. "My dad's a doctor. Why would I talk to Kent?"

"Because it's been light years since your dad was at med school and you want an opinion from someone who's not a geriatric."

She snorted. "Don't let Dad hear you say that. Okay, that works… wait, you think that will work?"

"If what Nancy says about Kent's mom is true, one whiff of her kid going missing and she'll call in the marines."

"She'll call the marines," said Kent. "Mom's super protective."

Then why hasn't she called yet?

I glanced at Serge and gave a subtle shrug as my answer.

"And when they can't find him, she'll call Nancy and the sheriff will get it done."

I laughed.

"Is that true?" asked Kent. "The sheriff—she's really good? She'll find my body and figure out what happened to me?"

"Yeah," I said. "She's the best."

"When she does…find my body, how will she tell my mom? She'll be nice, right?" Kent pulled on the seat belt like the shoulder strap was too tight and he couldn't breathe. "She doesn't have anyone. God! How could I be so stupid that I died?"

"I don't think stupidity has anything to do with it," I said.

"I still can't figure out how I died—car accident doesn't seem likely. I don't have any genetic problems, so it can't be a heart problem—"

It was murder.

I took a breath, thankful for the telepathy that kept my conversation with Serge private. *We don't know that.*

I got a feeling.

Maybe, but I think his death is pushing your buttons.

No, it's murder. Trust me, I can see him in ways you can't. He looks like a puzzle someone put together, but the pieces don't all match. There are gaps in his body—that's not suicide or an accident.

"All I know is I'm dead, Mom's stuck here, stuck in a dead end job, and she'll have to live with that."

"Let's take it one thing at a time," I said. "Let's get the report filed and then we'll figure out the next step." Serge's conviction about murder aside, there still was the possibility of an accident. And though Kent denied it, suicide. He didn't need to believe in it like Santa Claus to do it, maybe that explained his amnesia about his death.

I was hoping for an accident. Suicide was going to re-kill Kent. I'd already lived through one murder, I didn't want to go through it again.

From the backseat, Kent gave me a miserable nod and went back to pulling on the seat belt.

Maggie.

Yes.

It's me, Serge.

Is this a Judy Blume joke? Like, are you there, God, it's me, Margaret? Huh? No. I'm just telling you it's me calling you.

I gave myself a minute. *I know. You know how come I know?*

Because you can hear my voice?

Because, Boo-Boo, yours is the only voice in my head. Oh, right, and we just had a telepathic conversation. *But thanks for identifying yourself.*

Nell watched me from the corner of her eye.

I put my finger to my lips, then gave a quick nod to Kent.

A thumbs up from her and she went back to watching the road. *What's going on?* I asked.

That maybe we shouldn't let Kent be part of this conversation with his mom.

Why?

Because he thinks he's gotten the ultimate F for getting murdered and he's been freaking out over his mom.

Now wasn't the time to point out—again—we didn't have any evidence that Kent had been murdered. My memory flashed back to me, Serge, and our sometimes unpleasant conversations about his mom. And the even more unpleasant results of those conversations. *How much is he freaking out? Like he's going-to-blow-something-up freak out?*

In the rearview mirror, Serge gave a quick, helpless shrug. *Kent was really protective and looked out for her. He feels like he's failed her, not just by dying, but that because of his death, she'll never get out of the financial hole she's trapped in.*

When you say protective…like you and your mom?

He shook his head. *No, more like you and your dad…maybe like my mom. He pays the bills, makes appointments for plumbers or furnace guys. I get the feeling she's going to be lost without him.*

Oh. Oh, man.

Yeah. I don't know how he's going to deal with seeing his mom again—especially when we're telling her that he's missing.

I had seen what one ghost exploding could do. I wasn't in the mood to see the sequel. The tires crunched the gravel shoulder as I asked Nell to pull the car over and put it in park.

"Kent," I said. "We should talk."

Nell took out her phone to follow along.

"Okay."

"We're driving to your house to tell your mom you're missing. And we want her to file a police report."

He nodded.

"There's nothing on my phone," said Nell. "What's he doing?"

"He's nodding."

"Oh, okay." She glanced up. "Casper, can you be a good little ghosty and give me the action stuff?" Her cell binged and she beamed in Serge's direction. "Great, thanks."

"Uh, yeah, sure."

Good thing the lights were off because I was sure Serge was blushing. "Kent," I said. "Have you thought about how you're going to react to your mom reacting to us telling her you're missing?"

"Yeah," he answered. "She'll file a report and—"

"No. To her *reacting to hearing you're missing*. That all the silence between you isn't because you're busy at school, it's because of something else. And her mind is going to start thinking about you being lost or kidnapped or—"

"Dead in a gutter somewhere," he finished. "Oh, God. Then she's going to freak—" He put his head between his knees. "She's going to cry so hard—"

I put myself in Kent's shoes, imagined standing by my dad's side as someone told him I'd gone missing. There would be disbelief in his eyes, then denial. He'd track back in time, to the last moment we'd spoken, run through every word of the conversation. Then it would hit. I was missing. Gone. Maybe dead. Probably dead.

And I would be a ghost, unable to tell him I was still by his side, unable to hug him or let him know I hadn't gone anywhere—not really. It would be the tears I couldn't stand.

I thought about what Kent had said, that the last time he and his mom had talked, they'd had a fight. The guilt would weigh on both of them. Kent would move on, but Mrs. Meagher would be trapped in this life, with no friends or family to comfort her. What would she do? Soldier on? Survive but waste away a little every day? Or would she make the ultimate solution to her pain?

I met Kent's eyes and saw the same questions I had mirrored there. "You don't have to come," I said. "It's going to be hard enough for you—"

"No, I have to be there." His body flashed transparent. "I need to make sure she's...I'll know if she's in trouble and I can tell you."

"Are you sure?"

He rubbed the back of his hand across his mouth. "Yeah, I am."

"Okay." I looked at Nell. "Drive on."

"On the way here," she said, "I was thinking of the adventure. Figuring out the mystery. But now...now it's hitting me. We're setting the stage for her to find out her kid's dead. We're about to destroy her, aren't we?"

I squeezed her hand. "Let's go."

CHAPTER TEN

She sighed and put the car in gear.

We drove the rest of the way in silence and when we arrived, Nell cut the engine. A couple seconds to unbuckle the seat belt, zip up my jacket, then I was ignoring the sting of the wind against my skin as I headed up the walk, Nell and Serge behind me, Kent beside me. I knocked on the door.

Nell pressed her ear against the scarred wood. "I can hear someone moving around."

"Mrs. Meagher! Mrs. Meagher! It's about your son!" I banged on the door, then almost fell into the threshold when it was suddenly wrenched open.

Marlo Meagher swayed in front of me, one hand on the doorframe, the other around an etched glass filled with gold-coloured liquid.

That tweaked me. She was anxious and flighty, but I'd never heard anything about her being a drinker.

It tweaked Kent, too, because his eyes went panic-wide. "She's doesn't drink. She hates it. What's going on—why does she have alcohol?"

Liquor was a great anesthetic, but I just couldn't see her killing her son then drowning the guilt in alcohol. Then again, I didn't know her and was basing my premise on her being like my dad.

"I'm going to sneak inside," said Serge. "Take a look around the house, Maybe I'll find something that can help."

Nell read his text and nodded.

"What do you want?" Mrs. Meagher squinted in Nell's direction then peered at me. "If you're fund-raising for school or band, I don't have money."

Kent stepped close to her. "Unsteady footing, slurred words, pupils dilated…"

"No, ma'am," I said. "It's not—"

"The diner pays nothing and the customers tip like crap. You see that car in the driveway? Don't let the fact it's a newer model fool you. It's held together by duct tape and cardboard."

"Yes, ma'am—"

"Or prom. I don't have money to help you with limousines or dresses. Frankly, you kids should be—"

"That's not why we're here. We were...my name is Maggie. I—we know your son, Kent," I said. "And we're worried about him."

That snapped her out of her stupor.

Kent jerked back then leaned forward and scanned her face.

Her eyes suddenly bright, she said, "You're friends with Kent?"

"Sort of." I stamped the snow off my boots and onto the rubber mat. Nell did the same.

"My friend, Nell, she wants to be a doctor, like Kent. They've been emailing back and forth but Kent suddenly went quiet."

"At first I thought he was buried under school stuff." Nell tightened the scarf around her neck. "But it's been over a month and I haven't heard anything. That's not like him. Kent's very...conscientious about keeping in touch."

Mrs. Meagher's mouth pulled down. She glanced at our feet. "Take off your boots and come inside."

I shucked my shoes and followed her into a living room full of mismatched furniture. I scanned the room for a hint of the truth behind the family. Everything was old and worn—faded fabric on the couch, the dull sheen of the wood tables. But everything was also in order. Tidy. The coffee table may have been scratched, but the smell of lemon wax polish scented the air.

Mrs. Meagher sat. She was a sturdy woman, the kind you expected—and liked—to be the one handing you greasy bacon, eggs, and hash browns at the diner.

"Mrs. Meagher, are you okay?" I asked. I stepped forward, put my hand on her shoulder, and caught a whiff of the drink in her hand. Apple juice. So she hadn't suddenly started drinking. I took it from her. "Can I get you some more apple juice?"

Kent's shoulders dropped, his breath left in a *whoosh.*

She nodded. "It's the medication, gives me a dry mouth—"

I set the glass down.

"Medication?" Kent frowned. "For what? She doesn't have any medical issues."

Okay, her son didn't know anything about her being on meds.

"—they're fixing my dosage." Mrs. Meagher squinted at the glass on the coffee table. "I think they said something about side effects."

Kent frowned. "Unless they've given her a too-high dosage, her symptoms are more in line with mixed medications—listen to her. Her speech is slurred."

Another question answered about why she was unsteady on her feet. I was super curious about what medications she was on, but figured that would get me a glare if I got too nosy. Still... "Are you sick? What medication are you on?"

"You said you haven't heard from Kent in over a month."

Okay, I could take the hint.

"I'm going to check her room," said Kent. "Find those pills." He took a couple of steps, froze, then turned back to me. "Maggie, I'm dead, and we don't know why. It could be a lot of things, but no one's found my body, and it's been weeks. And now my mom is suddenly on medication with a dosage high enough to make her look drunk. Do you think there's a link?"

I shrugged, then made a mental note to talk to him about what he'd said. It was weird he'd even think there was a connection, unless he was remembering things from the night he died...things that would make his death more deliberate than accidental.

"Okay, maybe I'm being paranoid and letting my imagination run wild. But meds? I just saw her—" He stopped. "I guess a lot can happen in a month," he muttered and headed down the hallway.

I squinted at the trail of green fog that hung off his heels. I blinked and it was gone.

Turning my attention back to his mom, I asked, "Yes, ma'am. It's not like him..."

"I thought maybe you might know what's going on?" Nell perched on the edge of the couch.

Shadows darkened her face. "No, Kent's..." A smile flitted across her face. "He's very busy. His class load plus he works at the hospital. He's probably just caught up with work and school."

"It's possible," I said. "But since it's been a while since he's talked to anyone—"

"I'm sure he's just busy and will email you as soon as he can."

Crap. Nell and I glanced at each other. I was hoping for more hysteria and less calm.

Serge came into the room. "Any luck? There's a laptop in his room that might have stuff." He moved closer to me. "I thought about zapping it but I was scared I might short-circuit the computer." He did a three-sixty of the living room. "Where's Kent?"

Looking for her medication bottle.

"Holy smokes, is she not taking her meds? That's no good—"

No, she's not on any meds—not that he remembers. And this stuff is pretty strong going by her lack of balance.

Nell glanced at her phone and started typing.

"Mrs. Meagher," I said, "I'm worried. I didn't know Kent well, but he wasn't the kind of guy to bail on someone who needed help. Besides, Nell's dad is a doctor, too. For sure, Kent would've wanted to be nice to her. You know, as a way to get in good with her dad and maybe get a residency here at the hospital."

Mrs. Meagher frowned. "I suppose, but he was close with a lot of the doctors—"

"I emailed him a few times and we were supposed to meet on the Thanksgiving weekend." Nell cut me a quick look, then continued. "He didn't show and I figured maybe he just got caught up with family stuff. I gave him a few days, then I emailed him. But when he didn't email me back, I started getting worried."

"We're a couple years younger than him," I said, "so we don't really know any of his friends."

"Kent had a lot of friends, here." Pride straightened her shoulders. "Smart, good looking, all the girls love him. But of course, university is his first love and he lost touch—"

As Mrs. Meagher continued to count the ways her son was amazing, I tuned out. This really wasn't going well. What happened to the hysterical mother who would phone the cops if her kid was five minutes late?

"Isn't there anyone we can talk to about him? Find out where he might be?"

She shook her head. "I'm afraid when Kent left for school, I lost touch with most of his friends. I think he did, too. It's not often he gets to come home. The holidays, that's it."

"Did he have a Facebook page or—"

"No, I didn't." Kent came back into the living room. "That stuff's never really been my style."

"Maybe we should call Nancy?" I suggested.

Mrs. Meagher's eyes went wide. "Oh, no! Kent will be so angry if I—" She stopped, took a breath.

"Mrs. Meagher, I really don't think Kent would be angry if you told Nancy—"

"No, I promised him after the last time, I wouldn't do it, again." She gave me an embarrassed smile. "I'm afraid I've been a little overprotective where he's been concerned and I'd been good the last couple of years. Did my best to give him space to be a normal high school kid. Didn't ask him about doing drugs or girls…I didn't mean to be a nag or smother him—"

"I know you didn't, Mom," said Kent.

"But at Thanksgiving he went out for a jog and he was late. Really, really late. And it started to rain. I thought he might have rolled his ankle or was having a hard time of the run, so I went looking for him."

The outline of Kent's body got a fuzzy, low-res, pixilated look to it. "I remember that, now. I was at the forest, running, just trying to clear my head—"

"I found him coming out of the forest on the highway. Beeped the horn at him. I thought he'd be happy to get a ride home. It was so cold that night and raining—"

Kent's body went blurry and shiny, like oil mixed with water.

"Instead, he was so mad—"

"And I started yelling at her," he said. He body returned to a normal state and he spoke through his tears. "She'd driven around town, looking for me, wanting to give me a ride home so I didn't get cold and wet in the rain, and all I could see was—"

"I didn't realize how smothered he'd felt," she whispered. "All those years, I thought I was being a good mom and instead, I was building up his resentment—"

"—the times she'd called the cops to look for me, how she and Dad would fight over visitation and custody—" He used the sleeve of his shirt to wipe his face. "—I was so stupid and arrogant, told her—"

"—he was a grown man, he didn't need me coddling him. He was right—"

"—I was so wrong. I yelled at her. Told her the next time we talked, it was going to be because I phoned her. She wasn't to call or text, or email." His body started losing cohesion, the edges of him went fuzzy and wavy. "It was the last time I ever talked to her. Those were the last words I ever said to my mother."

"I tried phoning him but he refused to talk to me for the rest of the night," said Mrs. Meagher. "And the next day, he was gone before I woke up." She gave me a trembling smile. "I can't help you with Kent. He hasn't talked to me since that day."

"But Mrs. Meagher, he hasn't talked to *anyone* since that day. Don't you think that's odd?" I wanted to point out that he'd left his laptop at her house, but since there was no way for me to explain how I knew that, I kept quiet.

"Not really. When he got involved in a science project, I could lose him for weeks." She gave me a wobbly smile. "When he comes back, he's going to be real proud of me. He'll see the changes I made—therapy and medication to deal with this overprotectiveness."

Kent moaned. "She doesn't need to be on medication." He directed his comments to his knees. "She's drugging herself because I was a jerk. And now I'm dead and she's drugging herself for nothing."

She was earnest, sincere, and the way she clutched my hand transmitted her vulnerability. Knowing I was further upsetting her but also knowing it had to be done, I said, "But he's missing."

"No, no he's not! Look!" She sprang to her feet.

There was a heart-stopping minute when I wasn't sure she was going to stay on her feet, but she stayed upright then disappeared into the kitchen. She returned with a stack of papers in her hand. "See? All our bills are paid. On time, as usual. If he was missing, how could that be?"

It was a good question. But there had to be an answer. After all, Kent was dead. But how was he paying the bills from beyond the grave?

CHAPTER ELEVEN

"**P**re-arranged payment," Dad said when I told him about the conversation with Mrs. Meagher. "With online banking. You can set it up to pay a set amount to your utilities and services every month. That's how he's doing it."

"Okay, thanks."

He pushed a cup of tea my way. "This thing with Kent's wearing on you."

"There are some creepy similarities between his life and Serge's—"

Dad's laser gaze honed in on me. "How are you doing with that? The run off with Serge and his family, I mean."

I shrugged. "Okay. Having Serge around helps."

He sighed. "I wish I could do something, get you professional therapy, but—"

"What are you going to say? My daughter needs help because she sees the dead and transitions souls? We'll both end up in therapy. Or a nut house."

"I guess..."

"Honest, between you, Nancy, Serge, Craig, and Nell, I have all the therapists and emotional support I need. Still, this situation with Kent and his mother..."

"It's destroying both of them."

"He's drowning in guilt and she's oblivious...and when she realizes why he's been quiet...." I took a sip of tea, then leaned back in the kitchen chair. "Kent still can't remember anything and his mom won't file a report so we can start getting information. How am I supposed to transition him when I can't get a straight answer from anyone?"

"You didn't have help from Serge's parents."

"Yeah, but I had Serge. Kent's a mess. Not only can he not remember what happened to him, but he's all screwed up about not being able to help his mom. When we left, he was just sitting beside her, looking miserable."

"Maybe it's time to stop trying to get the answers and time to start finding them."

"Thanks, Zen Master. Your words of wisdom are as empty as the calories from Nancy's coffee cake."

"Maybe." Dad helped himself to a slice of the frosted dessert. "But my words and this cake both give you something to chew on."

I rolled my eyes. "I'm going to find Serge. You see how you've upset me? I'd rather spend time with a ghost than you."

Dad shrugged. "He's got good taste in TV. I like spending time with him, too."

"But now you're all alone. Even Nancy's deserted you on account of your poor puns."

"No desertion involved." He sighed. "She's back at the Piersons'. More vandalism. And it looks like it's spreading around town."

I made a face. "What kind of jerk goes after a family whose daughter almost died?"

"A big one," Dad said. "I heard some people talking about it at the Tin Shack—town council's going to have a meeting if it doesn't get resolved soon."

Grabbing my drink with one hand and a slice of cake with the other, I headed upstairs. Serge was on the bed with Ebony and Buddha.

"Did you hear anything from Kent?" he asked.

"Not yet, but I don't think he can hone in on me like you can." I flopped down beside him. "It's good he's with his mom. We need some alone time. You and I haven't really had a chance to talk about stuff."

"If this is going to be a conversation about feelings, you need to put on a tighter shirt." He smirked. "And try to take some deep breaths."

I punched him on the shoulder. "Be serious. How are you doing with all this?"

"If he doesn't transition, I think he'll make a good roommate. It's hard to wake him in the mornings, though. I hear he sleeps like the dead."

That made me laugh. "Come on, I'm trying to be a good soul sister. You and Kent have a lot in common."

"Well, we are both dead."

"You both had difficult home lives, can't remember how you died..."

"What you're really asking is if he's bringing up any bad memories, giving me the ghostly version of PTSD."

"Yeah, but aren't you glad I'm not asking about your feelings?"

"You started this. We're going to talk about my feelings." He punched the pillow and laid back on it. "Just to be clear, sometimes, the only thing that comforts me is a strong hug." He wriggled his eyebrows. "Make sure you press those mosquito bites close to my chest."

"Deflection. The last resort of the desperate. You must really not want to talk."

His mouth pulled down. "It's making me feel weird but not for myself. There's lots of people with screwy mothers and absent fathers. And ever since that night I exploded"—He shrugged—"I don't feel tied to my life. Not anymore. I feel bad for Kent, though. I know how much it sucks to wake up dead and not know why. And then to find out you've been murdered, sucks."

"We don't know it's murder—"

"Finding out that people don't believe you when you tell them other people have been murdered, sucks."

I rolled my eyes. "Why are you so sure?"

"I can't explain it—it's just a feeling. Someone off'd him, I know it. I feel it. Maybe it takes a murder victim to sense a murder victim."

I hoped not. I'd already seen what one murderer could do, I wasn't anxious to see what another one would do.

"But that's not the worst of it for Kent. It's going to be him finding out how much people didn't like him or know him...that sucks most." After a second, he added, "That's one thing we have in common: our funerals will be small."

A month ago, I would have felt gleeful that he didn't have enough friends to carry his casket. Now it made me sad.

Serge took my hand. "I don't mind. At least I have an afterlife to make up for my mistakes. Plus, I have you." He smiled. "We're on a strange destiny, Mags. Transitioning souls, dealing with weird creatures and things that crawl out of hell. On this path, you're all the friend I need. As long as you're beside me, I'm cool."

"That's really sweet—"

He loosened his grip and closed his eyes. "I figure if anything really freaky comes at us, all I need to do is toss you in between me and it. That should give me enough time to disappear."

"Seriously?"

"Totally. First sign of trouble, I'm punting you like a football and running the other way."

"You know what you are?"

"Dead funny?"

I looked away so he wouldn't get the satisfaction of seeing me laugh.

He opened his eyes and watched me. "How are you doing? You know, with everything that happened with me…"

"Boo-Boo, I wish I could say I was completely traumatized, but that stuff's kind of what I've done my whole life. Your case took it to a whole new level, but it's nothing I ain't seen before."

"Okay, Xena."

"Gross, you're imagining me in that outfit, aren't you?"

"Already there." He grinned. Then the watchful look was back on his face, again. "You sure you're okay?"

"Sadly, my biggest problem is this dating thing."

"You and Craig? You guys are great together—"

"Yeah, but we're not exactly normal. I mean, shouldn't I be trying harder to stay in touch and shouldn't he be doing the same?"

Serge gave me an incredulous look. "You're both busy saving the world and when you're not doing that, he's transporting souls, you're transitioning souls. I think you need to take a deep breath and calm down."

"Yeah?"

"A really big, deep breath. Get those lungs to inflate. Come on, I'll watch and make sure you're doing it right."

I shoved him sideways and he laughed.

"I just thought of something. Didn't Kent say he volunteered at the distress line?"

Serge nodded.

The number for the phone line I knew off by heart—their posters were plastered on the back of every bathroom stall at school. I dialled the number then perked up as Harriet's distinctive voice growled hello.

"Hey Harriet, it's—"

"No names, kid." Her smoked-since-the-womb-voice rumbled over the line. "This is an anonymous service."

"Oh, uh, I was calling about Kent Meagher."

"Watch the names," she said. "We're here to help, not to—"

"Oh! No! This isn't a distress call. Not the regular kind, anyway. I've been trying to get a hold of Kent Meagher but I can't reach him."

"This isn't a messenger service, honey, and you're tying up the line for someone who really needs to talk."

"Yes, ma'am, I understand what you're saying. But Kent worked with you at the distress line and I'm worried about him. I was hoping maybe he's talked to you...?" I trailed off and waited in silence.

After a minute, Harriet said, "I'm sorry, kid, but this Kent guy never volunteered with us. And I don't know him. Try his folks, maybe."

"Yeah, sure, thanks Harriet." I shut down the call. "That was weird." I told Serge what happened.

"You're sure he said he volunteered at the distress line?"

I nodded. "Why would he lie about something like that?"

"I don't know. It doesn't sound right. Maybe you misheard?"

"Maybe. I'll have to ask him when I—" The phone binged with a text from Nell. I read the message and frowned. "Nell says she's coming over. Something about the Piersons acting like babies."

Downstairs, the doorbell rang.

Serge sat up. "Wow, that was fast."

As we headed for the living room, Dad emerged from the kitchen. "I got this," he said, opened the door, and frowned. "Someone pranking us?"

He stepped into the pool of porch light, intending to investigate, but I stopped him. "It's Kent," I said. Then I looked over the ghost's shoulder. "Craig!" I wanted to run down the stairs and throw myself into his arms, but Dad was there. PDA in front of the parent wasn't big on my list, so I opted for a casual, "Hey!"

"Come on in, guys." Dad stepped back. He glanced up at me. "You probably have lots of catching up to do." He raised his eyebrows and tilted his head at me.

Message received. Catch up with Craig but not *too much*.

Dad started to close the door.

"Hey! Mr. Johnson, tiny blond girl headed your way!"

"Oops, sorry, Nell, I didn't see you," said Dad.

"If that's a dig at my height, I'll let you know I'm short but mighty."

"Don't I know it," Dad said, smiling. "You guys go on up. I'll put on some tea and you can get it later, okay?"

"Thanks, Dad."

He closed the door and headed into the kitchen while Craig and Nell took off their shoes and coats.

Serge pushed past me and headed to the ghost. "You rang the bell?" The question held a combination of disbelief, respect, and envy.

"I was working on the theory of everything being electrical. Figured it was worth a shot. It's a lot harder than just sending a text, though." He leaned against the doorjamb. "It takes a lot of energy. I'm bagged."

Craig and Nell followed as Kent headed up the steps.

"But how did you do that? I'm still figuring out computers and phones," asked Serge as the four of us headed to the bedroom.

"The theory of passing through solid matter is the same as connecting with electronic devices," said Kent. "I just modified it for practical application. I can show you, if you like."

"Geez," muttered Serge. "Captain Canuck's been dead two minutes and he's already a better ghost than me." He glanced over his shoulder at Craig then said to me, "I'll take Kent for a couple of minutes so you can do whatever with Craig, but then we should regroup."

"I'll hang with Casper and company," whispered Nell.

Craig and I went to my room. "How bad was Africa?" I asked.

"I stop counting after three hundred souls." He lay on my bed and closed his eyes. "You lose track when you're ferrying the dead—especially since time in this plane and the others don't match up." He opened his eyes and. Exhaustion turned his brown eyes the colour of mud.

I crawled beside him and snuggled into the cradle of his arms. "I'm sorry."

He kissed the top of my forehead. "It's life. Death's just a part of it."

"I liked the pictures."

There was a smile in his voice as he said, "I thought you might. I'm sorry I was too busy to send you more."

He didn't seem to want to talk, and there was nothing I had to say, so we just lay there until Kent, Nell, and Serge came in.

"We have to talk about my mom," said Kent. He glanced at Craig. "He's the guy from the other night, right?"

Craig nodded and held out his hand. "Craig. Maggie's boyfriend—"

Kent jerked back then stepped forward. "You can see me? Right, you're a supernatural something-or-other."

The side of Craig's mouth lifted. "I've been called worse. Yeah, I'm a ferrier. I transport souls."

"To where?"

"To wherever they need to go. It depends on their religion, the kind of life they've led, their destiny—"

"Are you saying it was my destiny to have my life end before I was twenty-one? To never become a doctor?"

"I don't know," said Craig. "I'm not your ferrier, so I can't see the threads of your lives." ·

"Lives." Kent blinked. Then blinked again. "What's on the other side? What's waiting for me?"

"I can't give you any answers," said Craig. "Everyone crosses over to an individual path and unless you're my charge, I don't get information on you."

"That's not right! You're supernatural, you should be able to see—everything—all the ways I was and am and will be—"

"Trust me," said Craig. "You don't want me and my kind having that type of power."

"But if you knew—"

"I could make some terrible mistakes." Craig swung his legs off the bed and rested his elbows on his knees. "Pretend I could see everything about the living and the dead. See all the ways they are and will be. And I'm walking down the street and I see a guy and everything—his aura, his energies, smell—all of it says he's a bad guy about to do an even badder thing. So I take him out. Prevent whatever tragedy he was going to inflict."

"Are you arguing for not having power?" I asked. "Cause your scenario sounds pretty good."

"Except what if, on his way to do the bad thing, he was supposed to run into someone, someone who would change the trajectory of his life's path? I've robbed him of the possibility for change and redemption. And more than that, I've taken a soul at its lowest state, shackled him to an afterlife and karma he may not deserve."

"Oh." Kent went quiet. "I guess you have a point."

I gave him a minute, then said, "We should talk about your last moments alive and—"

His eyes squeezed shut. "I can't get over watching my mom stumble around like she's drunk."

Nell looked up from her phone. "I can't believe it's any doctor here in Dead Falls who's prescribing the meds. I know all of them, thanks to my dad. If she's stumbling around, then her dosages are too high. Or they've prescribed her more than one med and they're having interactions." Her mouth twisted to the side. "That still wouldn't be one of our doctors. This town is too small to get away with doing something like that."

"She doesn't need to be on medication." Kent took a sharp breath. "I couldn't find the pill bottle, but maybe that's why I'm still here. If she's gone out of town to get help and they're misdiagnosing and messing with her meds, it can be dangerous. Fatal, even. Maybe I'm supposed to help her get proper help and then I can transition...you know, like make up for being so mean to her that night."

"Maybe, but we still need her to file a report. If I'd known you better when you were alive, I could have done it. But since that's not the case, it's just going to look weird. A report gives Nancy the chance to search your room, to access your computers, find out what happened to you the day you died," I said, "unless you remember something?"

He shook his head. "I still got nothing."

"I wondered because you thought maybe your mom being on meds and your death were connected—"

He waved away my words. "Yeah, till she said she was in therapy and taking pills. I keep thinking if I walk, it'll clear my mind and bring back my memory. But all I'm getting is foot calluses. I thought being dead meant no body effects."

"It's your background in long distance running, I bet," said Serge. "You think you should show signs of repetitive movements, so you are."

"I'm sorry my mom won't help," he said. He snapped his fingers. "Hey, but I can send texts, right? Maybe I can text something to her, like a message I'm in trouble?"

"You're dead. You start texting, it'll create way more questions—especially once your body's found." I took a quick breath. "And we need to talk about something else. You said you volunteered at the distress line?"

He nodded. "Yeah."

"When I called Harriet, she said she never worked with you." I held my hand up in case he started yelling, then dropped it when he smiled sheepishly.

"Sorry. I meant the distress line at university. Being dead is leaving my brains scrambled."

"It's okay," said Serge. "Time and stuff can get a little confusing in the first while after you're dead."

"Which sounds like the faster we get me over to the other side, the better. So, how are we going to do this?"

After a couple of minutes, I reached for my socks. "I think I have an idea on the police report. You guys coming?"

CHAPTER TWELVE

Craig opted to go home and catch up on sleep. Nell went back to check up on Rori. Kent, Serge, and I headed to the police station where we found Nancy at her desk, cup of coffee in hand.

"You alone?" she asked when she saw me.

"Brought a couple of friends."

She pulled out her cell so she could read any texts Serge and Kent sent her way.

"Here." I handed an extra-large cup of the Tin Shack's house blend. "I've tasted station coffee. It's a great negotiation tool. It's bad enough to make me confess to the murder of JFK if I thought you'd make me drink it."

She leaned back, threaded her fingers behind her head. "Bringing me drinks?"

"And a slice of your cake." I slid the paper plate to her.

"Oh boy." She sat up. "Tell me whatever you need isn't illegal."

"No, just questions."

"Sit. Have some cake." Nancy took a sip of coffee. "I could use the break. The city police are driving me crazy."

"Did they call you about Kent—maybe they found his body in the city?"

"Nah, the usual stuff about drugs."

I gave her a blank look. "There's usual stuff about drugs?"

"Small towns are great for drug manufacturing and distribution. So are the national parks. Less law enforcement. We usually stay in touch with the bigger centers, get updated on drugs or suspects. Lately, both Calgary and Edmonton have had a rash of drug-related deaths." Nancy pushed the files to the side. "That's a problem for another time. Along with their updated list of their most wanted. Small towns are great for criminals to hide in, too. Sit."

I did.

Serge leaned against the desk.

Kent remained standing.

"What's going on?"

"Kent's dad. What do you know about him?"

"Normal. Average. Nice guy." She made a face. "According to me, not Marlo Meagher."

Kent snorted. "Mom drove him crazy, even after the divorce—it's why he moved away when I was in junior high."

"One of the worst things about being a cop is the family disputes. Doug never tried to take his son, but he did struggle with his custodial rights. Marlo was a nut when they were getting divorced…and after, too. She found ways to deny the dad visitation. It all got really ugly." Nancy took a breath and reached for the cake.

"They bankrupted themselves," clarified Kent. "Then, when they had no money, they found some sense. At least, Dad did."

Nancy read the text. "It's true about Doug. He ended giving Marlo primary custody and agreed to the least amount of weekends and visits with Kent."

"This makes no sense," I said. "Kent's dad had a right to see his son. She couldn't deny him—"

"Oh, kid, you have no idea. When love turns to hate and bitterness, it gets ugly."

"But I don't understand. Why would Mr. Meagher just give up his rights to Kent like that?"

"Because he thought it was best for Kent," said Nancy.

Emotion flashed across Kent's face. It happened so fast, I couldn't tell if he was sad or mad, agreeing or disagreeing with Nancy. "And because of the money," he said. "They spent so much money fighting each other, they had to declare bankruptcy. That freaked out Dad, but Mom was still willing to spend money she didn't have to fight him. In the end, Dad gave in. He said he didn't want any more money being wasted on them instead of being spent on me."

"Wait a second. Are you saying your folks are still married?" I asked.

He nodded. "They didn't have enough money to get divorced. Dad eventually left town, and I guess they just let it go."

"How did you feel about it?"

Typical guy, he went with a shrug over sharing his feelings. "Dad said any money not spent on a lawyer was money spent on me. So, I went with it. Anyway, we found workarounds." He stood. "I'm—" He ran his hand through his hair. "You care if I just jet for a bit? This is kind of hard to talk about."

"No problem," I said. "I'll see you later."

He left.

"I'll go with him," said Serge. "Even if we don't talk, maybe he'll appreciate the company."

I nodded, reached for the file and flipped through it. "Okay, when Kent was small, the times he was late coming home, he was with his dad. But starting"—I did the math—"in grade nine, he wasn't at home but he wasn't with his dad, either."

"I'd find him at the library or the park. It was right about then he started going hard-core for his marks. I think he realized how expensive med school was and that neither parent was going to be able to pay for him. If he was going to go to university, it was going to have to be through bursaries and scholarships. There wasn't a job in town that kid wouldn't take if it paid for college. I'd see him around, shovelling walks, mowing lawns, flipping burgers. He worked with the parks cleaning port-a-potties one summer." She took her seat. "Amazing kid. How did you talk with his mom go? I'd like to find his body, bring him home. Any luck with Marlo?"

I shook my head. "She's convinced he's just busy. When we were there, Serge searched the house for any clues. He said Kent left a laptop in his room. I bet it has answers."

"I need a reason to take the laptop. That woman can be stubborn. She won't just let me take it. Of all the times for her to take a measured approach with her kid, this is where she plants her flag."

"In her defense, she said Kent was really pissed with her the last time, and she'd promised she would never call the cops again."

Nancy sighed. "Of all the luck." Then her eyes lit up. "You know who could help—?"

"His dad." I smiled. "That's why I'm here."

"Smart girl. I've got his number in the file." She found it and handed it to me.

I checked my watch. 9:30. Not too late for a call. I dialled the number. There was a ton of static on the line, but I was finally able to explain why I was calling, then laid it on thick with Kent's lack of communication.

I gave Nancy the thumbs up when worry crept into his voice. "Yes, sir," I said. "It's been over a month. I haven't heard from him. Have you?"

"No." It was hard to hear him over the static. "But we didn't really talk a lot in the last few months. I figured it was just school."

"Yes, sir, but now I'm worried. It's just not like him."

There was a long silence. "No, it's not. Let me look into this. Is there a number I can reach you?"

I gave him my cell number, then thanked him and hung up.

A few seconds later, Nancy's line rang.

She picked up. "Sheriff's office. Nancy Machio speaking." She listened. "Doug, how are you?" A pause. "Kent? Yes, it's been a while. What's going on?"

I had a moment of elation, of glee that we were finally getting some traction on Kent. The feeling was fleeting because I immediately realized I was the only one who'd see the full circle. I'd see Kent get closure. But for his mom and dad, there would only be questions, sorrow, and loss. Thanks to me, a family was about to come apart at the seams.

The next day after school, I went with Nell to visit Rori Pierson.

"Bruce and Tammy were asking about you and the séance, again," said Nell as we drove to the house. "I told them to go ahead without you. That it might be hard for both you and Serge to have any kind of an Ouija conversation with company."

"You're genius. How will I ever find a way to thank you?"

"We'll start by throwing out that coat and work from there."

"I said you were genius. I didn't say you were divine."

"Yeah, well, that coat looks like it's already halfway to the pearly gates."

I rolled my eyes and changed the conversation.

We got to the house and I saw what Nancy had meant about the vandalism. Someone had hacked their bushes, broken the windows in the garage. The world was a crazy place full of crazy people, and someone deciding to add to the trauma of a missing child by tormenting the family wasn't unheard of. But it put that person lower than pond scum and I hoped karma would nail their butts.

Nell and I headed to the front entrance. I rang the bell. A few seconds later, Mrs. Pierson, dressed in yoga gear, opened the door and ushered us into the kitchen.

"Sorry it took so long," she said. "The housekeeper's off and I'm trying to do her job and mine. Rori's been asking about you," she said as she walked us inside and seated us around the glass dining table. "She wants to thank you both for saving her."

"Oh, it was nothing, really," I said.

"You girls help yourselves to some juice and squares, I'll go get her."

When she was out of earshot I asked Nell, "How can you babysit in here? The whole place looks like it's been prepped for a photo shoot." I leaned to the side, closed one eye and ran my gaze along the glass table. "There are no fingerprints on this table. They have a small child. Shouldn't there be jam smears or toys?" I sat up. "Perfectly arranged flowers, white marble floors, glass tables—"

"They have money and a live-in housekeeper."

"Baby, I think they've got a team of them of housekeeping elves." The place made me nervous. It wasn't the cleanliness. It was the antiseptic quality of it. For all the luxury, there was ...I didn't know. Not like the house was unloved, but more like the people who lived in it were hyper aware of appearances. That projecting an air of perfection wasn't just something they wanted but something they *needed* to do.

"Here she is." Mrs. Pierson sang the words as she walked hand-in-hand with Rori.

Nell got up, went to the girl and swept her into a hug.

I didn't know Rori, so I hung back, gave her a little wave when she looked my way. She smiled, wiggled her fingers at me.

"How are you feeling?" I asked.

"Good," she said. She squirmed out of Nell's arms and looked around. "Where are the boys? I made them a picture." She waved the piece of paper she held in her hand.

"The boys?" Nell put her hand on Rori's shoulder. "What boys?"

"The boys from the night."

I went still and did my best not to look at Nell.

"Oh, this again." Mrs. Pierson gave a dismissive wave of her hand. "The doctors said it was the head injury, but she's convinced there were boys with her that night."

Rori nodded. "They were! One of them had wings." She frowned. "The blond one didn't have wings, but he made me feel better."

"And scales." Her mom gave me a good-natured roll of her eyes. "Don't forget the angel with scales."

"He had them! They were there!"

"Of course he did." Mrs. Pierson set out a plate for her daughter. "Sit with your friends." To us, she said, "The doctors think her imaginary friends—"

"They're not imaginary!"

"—are part of her dealing with the trauma of the injury. They told us to go along with it, that she'll outgrow it eventually." Mrs. Pierson turned toward the hallway. "It's funny. She was never into imaginary play until now."

I cut a glance to Rori, whose red face said everything. "I believe you."

She gave me a wary look. "You do?"

I nodded. "Yep, I have those kinds of friends, too."

Mrs. Pierson smiled at me from over her shoulder. "That's very sweet of you, Maggie." She directed her attention to her daughter, started giving her the usual parent spiel, don't eat too many treats, don't spill the juice.

While she was talking, Nell came up to me. "I meant to ask you about that. How come she can see Serge and Craig and I can't?"

I shrugged. "She was on the border between life and death. I guess it makes sense."

"You think she can still see them?"

"There's only one way to find out." I called Serge to me.

"Thank God," he said as he appeared. "I decided to hang out with Kent. Any more walking and I was going to start feeling like Moses in the desert. A bored Moses."

Rori says she saw you the night of her accident. Head over, see if she can still see you.

"No problem, I'll take any friends I can find, right now. Even tiny ones." He turned her way. *Maggie, what does she look like to you?*

A little girl. Why? What does she look like to you?

A little, normal girl? Chubby cheeks and rosy complexion?

Rori wasn't exactly a chubby-cheeked kind of girl. *She's too skinny for the cheek thing. She looks about the same as she did when we found her that night. Why? What does she look like to you?*

You know those commercials with starving kids with flies on their eyes? Like that?

Like that, but no flies. He gave Mrs. Pierson a once over. *She doesn't look any better. Like a skeleton with a skin covering.*

What do you think it means?

Rori's starved for love and Mrs. Pierson's anorexic. What do you think?

I think you're right.

Geez. With a house like this and all that money, you'd think they'd be happy.

Why can you see all that?

He shrugged. *I had my hand in her heart. Maybe that formed a special connection.* He headed over to Rori, tapped her on the shoulder. "Hey."

"The boy is here, but he's all fuzzy," said Rori. "Can you see him?"

"No, sweetie." Her mom had the distracted tone of an adult whose focus was on something else. "Only you can."

I went over to the little girl. "I see him, too."

"What's his name?"

Oh, boy.

"Shaggy," said Serge, then lifted his eyebrows at me. "What? It's better than The Boy, and besides, it works. I got a gang and one of my best friends is a dog who'll eat anything."

Nell read the text and grinned.

"Did you hear that?" I asked Rori.

She shook her head.

"His name is Shaggy," I said.

"Thanks for making me feel better," said Rori.

"Yeah, no problem, kid." Serge sat in the chair next to her.

"While you kids visit, I'm going to go downstairs to the gym. I have to do my therapy for my torn rotator—"

"It's still giving you trouble, huh, Mrs. P?" asked Nell.

"My own fault. I shouldn't have dived for the tennis ball. The exercises shouldn't be more than a half-hour," said Mrs. Pierson. "It's Mrs. Humphrey's day off and I'm not comfortable leaving Rori unsupervised—"

"No problem," said Nell. "We're happy to hang out."

As soon as Rori's mom left, I asked, "Rori, do you see the boys all the time?"

She shook her head. "Only that night and right now."

"Before then, did you ever see people that no one else did?"

She shook her head, again. "It's kind of hard to see Shaggy, now. He's all fuzzy."

Nell elbowed me. "What does that mean?"

"I don't know. I've never met anyone else who could see what I did." Maybe it was a brain injury thing. If Serge was fuzzy, maybe that meant eventually Rori would lose the ability to see ghosts. Part of me hoped she wouldn't. It was nice knowing there was someone else like me. Most of me hoped she would. Nice or not, it was a crap life she was chained to.

"How are you feeling?" Serge asked her.

Nell translated.

"Good. I'm getting lots of cards." She nodded at a circular table where a stack of get-well cards lay amid a pile of mail. "People are really nice."

"Bet you're happy to be home," I said.

Rori kicked at the chair legs. "It's loud here."

"Loud?" I asked.

She glanced at the hallway.

Oh. *Loud.*

She looked up at Nell. "Can I come live with you?"

"Oh, honey, "said Nell. "Your mom and dad are just worried for you. They don't mean to be loud."

"They yell all the time. Please, can I stay with you?"

"How about this? Let me talk to your mom and maybe you can spend a weekend with me." Nell glanced my way. "Maybe Maggie and Shaggy will come—"

"Absolutely."

"—and we can have a whole slumber party."

"Can you talk to Mom and Dad? Ask them to not be so loud?"

"Uh, well, honey, when it comes to grown-ups—"

I stood, went over to the table. "You said people were sending you cards. Any favourites?" I picked up a pile. The mail caught my eye. I set down the cards and picked up the envelopes.

"Should you really be reading other people's mail?"

I jumped at Nell's voice, then looked over her shoulder. Serge and Rori were talking.

Nell tracked my gaze. "He distracted her from parent talk by letting her play on my cell. They're talking about the picture she made about the submarine she had in her brain."

"The submarine in her brain?"

Nell shrugged.

Okay, that was a new one. "Are we talking the sandwich or the military equipment?"

"Her drawing's a little on the abstract side and I didn't want to showcase my artistic illiteracy by asking her to clarify. Anyway, it's probably part of how she's dealing with the trauma."

"Probably." I held up the envelopes. "Doesn't this seem strange to you?"

She rifled through them. "Bills, offers for credit cards, medicine dispensaries promotions, flyers for furniture stores, and charities asking for money. Seems normal to me."

"Yeah, but look at the charities."

Nell did. "Homeless, animal shelters...so?"

"Mrs. Pierson was angry the night Rori disappeared. She said her husband was ignoring his family because he was busy doing volunteer stuff on account of Serge's death."

"So?"

"So what's with the animal and homeless charities? Think about it. You see some news report about a murdered kid, dysfunctional family. Wouldn't you start donating to charities connected with that, like domestic violence shelters or organizations for runaways?"

Nell shrugged. "Maybe he's been moved to donate to all causes."

I shook my head. "No, it's like this house. Everything's about appearances. Besides, if he was really volunteering for a phone line like Mrs. Pierson said, then where's the mail to prove it? Charities are always asking for money—look at what we do for the blood drive. Plus, the mail here is a few weeks old. If he was really volunteering with a support line, there would be something here." I took the envelopes from Nell and put them back. "He's lying to his wife. Something's going on here."

"One mystery at a time, Johnson. Maybe one charity sold his name to the other, and the mailings are only now coming in."

"I just think—"

"Yeah, well I know you should stop thinking about this. You're frustrated with Kent and your inability to cross him over. I think you're freaked out because stuff's happening and Craig can't help, and I think you're compensating by looking for mysteries where none exist." Nell lowered her voice. "This is an unhappy family, okay? Fact is, they're unhappy people. The doc"—She exhaled sharply—"he makes good money as a doctor, which already ticks off people. But he's also got a

Midas touch with investment. Only he won't share his knowledge or invest for other people."

I glanced behind me to make sure Rori couldn't hear us talking about her parents.

"People think he's greedy and wants to be the richest guy in town but it's actually about integrity. He doesn't want to be responsible for losing someone else's money. Imagine how it feels to be him—saving lives and protecting other people from potential financial ruin and having them hate you for it. And for Mrs. P. She married for wealth, security, and status, but she never thought they'd end up in some tiny town. There's nothing for her here—no charity balls, no big volunteer circuit to join—and she's got an absent husband, too. He's always travelling to conferences without her, taking boys-only vacations. The only thing they have in common is Rori. And even then,…they barely do stuff as a family. Mrs. P and the doc live separate, unhappy lives. He's probably not volunteering for anything, okay? He's probably having an affair and so is she."

I lifted my hands in surrender.

"It's a mystery, but it can wait. Let's deal with Kent, then we'll worry about the Piersons, okay?" She left me and went over to Rori and Serge.

I sighed. She had a point. I was probably overthinking everything, but I couldn't shake the feeling we weren't doing enough and I was missing something really obvious.

CHAPTER THIRTEEN

joined the group and we hung out for a little longer. It was easy to see why Nell liked babysitting Rori. She was a fun kid, sweet, smart. And sad. Whatever was going on between her mom and dad, it was bringing her way down. I did my best to make her laugh, joined in her ninja hero party games. A half-hour later, Mrs. Pierson came upstairs.

"Thanks for visiting girls, I appreciate it." She smiled and hugged her daughter. "Mommy just heard about a great new ride for us. What do you think? Would you like to have a trip with Mommy tomorrow and we'll go look at convertibles? We can have a spa day—it'll be so much fun! We'll get our nails done and everything!"

Rori nodded, then whispered to Nell. "What's a convertible?"

After we left, I dropped Nell at her house, then phoned Nancy.

"If you're calling to tell me about more vandalism in town, I'm not in," she said.

"Wow. Still? The Piersons?"

"Thankfully, not today. But someone tossed stones at the windows of the grocery store, wrecked havoc in the hospital storage. The mayor is up one side of me and down the other, but I don't have enough deputies or patience to deal with this. If the town wants to put a stop to this, they'll have to do more than just complain to me."

"I suppose asking if you had any leads on Kent might put me in line for no dessert tonight?" I put her on speaker so Serge could hear.

"Nah, you're fine. I got some leads but a lot more questions. Kent was living in campus housing. His roommate said he got an email from Kent a couple days after Thanksgiving. In it, Kent says he's dropping out and someone was coming to pick up his stuff. A day or so later, a moving guy came and packed up all Kent's things."

"Did he save the email?"

"You're kidding, right?"

"Moving guy? Did he get the name of the company?"

"No. Just some average-looking guy of average build and dark-ish hair, dressed in khakis and carrying boxes. The roommate didn't think anything of it—"

"Because he had the email from Kent."

"Right. The only thing he remembers is the moving guy asking about the laptop. Seemed real upset it wasn't around. Unfortunately for us, that's as much as the kid can remember. The university's sending the paperwork they have but I don't think it'll be much help. I visited Mrs. Meagher, did a walkthrough of his room and collected his laptop."

"How's she taking Kent being a missing person?"

"She's still convinced Kent's taking time off and we're all over-reacting."

"I bet that's because of the fight she had with Kent." I thought about Mrs. Meagher and the medication, and made a mental note to talk to Nell about it. In the meantime, I said, "Serge is convinced Kent was murdered. A mysterious email and an even more mysterious figure emptying out Kent's room seem to support that. Especially when if the mystery man wanted the computer and didn't realize Kent had brought it home."

"Maybe," said Nancy. "Has Kent been of any help?"

"The poor guy's in shock. He's doing his best but it's hard going. He's spending most of his time doing his Heathcliff impression of walking the moors. In this case, it's the forest."

Laughter was in her voice as she said, "And people think public education's a waste."

"Can you bring the laptop home?"

"No, but if"—Her voice went quiet —"someone were to stop by and read over my shoulder..."

"Serge is with me; I'll drive him to you. See you in a bit."

Of course, after I left Serge at the police station and texted Nancy he was there, I realized I had no way to track Kent and let him know about my conversation with Nancy. I headed home and did a walk-through of the house but didn't see the ghost. After I changed the water for Buddha and Ebony and gave them some treats and cuddles, I headed out.

I'd heard of something called psychic magnetism—the ability to attract and bring an object or person to you. I didn't know if it worked with anyone other than Serge, and based on my inability to find lost keys, I suspected I didn't have it. Still, ghosts found me. Theoretically, it should work in the reverse. Since I had nothing else to go on, I climbed back in the car and drove around town. After a half-hour of doing nothing but wasting gas, I got smart and called Serge to me.

"Thank God," he said as he appeared in the passenger seat. "There's nothing worthwhile on his laptop. Just a bunch of nature photos and school stuff."

"That it?"

Serge nodded. "The guy didn't even have porn on the computer."

"Man, it was like he was dead already."

"Tell me about it."

Sarcasm was lost on him. "I need your help to find—"

"Nell?" He closed his eyes and raised his left hand. "I bet I can hone in on her."

"I know exactly what you want to hone in on with her." I slapped down his hand. "Help me find Kent."

"Give me someone fun."

"Seriously, I'm trying to find him but I'm not having any luck."

"You don't need luck. All you need is his route. Trust me, drive it and you'll find him."

"I've been driving all over town—"

"Yeah, but did you do his route?"

"I don't know what that is."

With his directions, I did a loop of the town. Nancy hadn't been kidding about the vandalism. Broken windows, busted lamps. Serge and I did two laps.

"No Kent."

"Did you try the lot by the mill?" he asked.

I frowned, slowed the car, then took a left toward the park he'd mentioned. "You think he's there? No one goes there."

"If he's not on the streets, then yeah, he's there. I walked with him a few times, trying to help him understand being dead but..." He shrugged. "Death is a journey you make by yourself."

"Are you going to be okay going there?"

He laughed. "I've already been there a few times with Kent, remember? Don't worry, it doesn't bother me to revisit the spot of my death."

I drove us to the mill, parked the car in the lot and stepped out. "We'll cover more ground if we split up," I said. "If you find him, text me."

Serge nodded and headed to the left.

I turned on my flashlight app, went right. The night was cold and the wind left me wishing I'd brought my toque. I walked the trail as fast as I could but halfway through the path, I still hadn't seen him. The phone rang and I pulled it out, figuring it was Dad. Or Nancy.

I checked the caller id: unknown. The only unknown caller I knew was Serge, but what was he doing phoning instead of texting? I answered the call. "Going old school?" The words were out before my brain twigged into the sound on the other line.

Static. The creepy, otherworldly static that heralded The Voice.

My legs did a weird combination of getting cement heavy at the same time they went weightless and did a wobbly jellyfish impression.

"*Maggie—*"

The hair on the back of my neck stood to attention. Usually, The Voice came through the radio. It would take over the airwaves to warn—or threaten me—the jury was still out on whether it was my protector or tormentor. The last time it had made an appearance, it had proven it could do more than talk. It could reach through time and space, crush my heart and bend me to its will.

"*Oh, Maggie—*"

I unstuck my tongue from the roof of my mouth. My eyes darted for escape even as my brain laughed at the stupidity of it all. The Voice could and would always find me. That it was able to get control over my phone said it had upped its game. Which could only mean big, bad things for me.

"*He's coming for you*," The Voice wept. "*Maggie. Ohh, Maggie.*"

Footsteps, quick and hard, came up behind me. I felt a sharp crack on the back of my head, then a rough push as someone shoved me over the trail's path and down the hill.

CHAPTER FOURTEEN

I woke to beeping, rough sheets, and the taste of plastic in my mouth.

"Maggie, thank God!" Dad grabbed my hand.

My vision cleared to a private hospital room, with Dad, Nancy, Nell, Craig Kent, and Serge standing around my bed. "What happened?" I croaked.

"I was hoping you could tell me that," said Nancy.

"I texted you." Serge came over and sitting, took my hand. "To tell you I couldn't find Kent"—He glared at the ghost—"when you didn't answer, I figured something bad had happened, so I texted everyone—"

"I used the Find My Phone app," said Dad, "and tracked you to the bottom of a gully."

I told them about The Voice and the unknown assailant who bonked me on the head. Judging from their faces, they were more upset about The Voice than they were about the mystery man. Me, too. Flesh and blood I sort of stood a chance with—round one went to the creep who crept up on me—but there was no fighting a non-corporeal form.

"You didn't hear or see anything?"

I shook my head at Nancy's question. Then immediately regretted the action—it felt like someone was taking a hammer to my skull. "Other than The Voice, no."

"Is it weird she's warning you when a month ago she tried to kill you?" asked Serge.

"How do we know she was trying to warn her?" Dad asked irritably. "She could've been trying to kill Maggie. Maybe she's the one who shoved my kid down a hill."

"If she had the ability to kill me," I said, "you think she would've done it a long time ago. Besides, she said he's coming. It was a warning."

Dad opened his mouth to argue.

"We'll figure out the other-worldly motives later. Right now, I want the bastard that decided to use your head like a baseball," said Nancy. "What about smell? Was there any unusual odours?"

Another shake of my head. Another painful moment of regret. "The mill always stinks, but I didn't smell anything extra weird."

"No woo-woo, either?" Nell's voice had a hopeful lift.

"No." My lips quirked at her description of my abilities. "No woo-woo."

"It's not all bad," said Nell, which got a simultaneous eyebrow raise from both Dad and Nancy. "There was some good news."

"And what was that?"

"You may not have found Kent the ghost tonight—" she said.

The overhead lights caught the brilliance of excitement in Nell's eyes. Or mania. With her, it was a 50/50 shot.

"—but you found my body," finished Kent.

"I *what!*"

"The point where you fell," he said. "You landed by my body."

The body that had been dead for weeks. I tried not to focus on the imagery.

Nancy looked up from her phone, where she'd been tracking the ghostly contribution to the conversation. "Based on the scene, I think you were in the wrong place at the wrong time."

"Tell me something I don't know," I muttered.

"No, what I mean is I think you interrupted someone as they were trying to move the body."

"You think it was murder?" I asked.

"I can't say for sure, not until we get an autopsy," she sighed. "The first glance shows head trauma. Either he was hit over the head or he fell and hit his head. But there are fresh drag marks by his body, which means someone knew he was there and they were trying to move him. Maybe it's murder, or maybe Kent died by accident but the person is somehow involved." She grimaced. "Maybe Kent fell, this person happened by the body tonight, and...had plans for it."

"There's something I'll never be able to unhear," murmured Kent.

"What is weird," said Nancy, "is the mysterious guy tossing you down the hill. I don't know why he didn't run when he heard you coming."

"Unless your last idea is the right one," said Kent, "and the guy was looking for a matching pair."

"Let's change the subject," said Dad.

I tried to wrap my brain around what everyone was saying. Unfortunately, I was full of some kind of medication that was strong enough to leave me loopy but not strong enough to dull the increasing volume of the aches from the fall. "Huh?" was all I could come up with.

"There were drag marks in the dirt," said Nancy. "One set of shoe prints, from whoever attacked you and—" She glanced around the room.

"It's okay to say it," said Kent. "Murdered me."

Serge leaned in to me. "Told you."

I raised my hands in surrender. "I give. He was murdered. Whether by accident or on purpose, someone killed Kent. And it's probably on purpose, because that person hacked his student account, dropped him out of school, and took all his stuff."

"You can call it murder, but as law enforcement, all I can say at this point is Kent died under suspicious circumstances," Nancy said, "but the person there tonight must have heard Maggie coming, panicked—"

"—and tried to kill you, too." Dad's mouth fell into a grim line and his shoulders tightened with all he wanted to say but didn't.

Nancy gave him a quick once-over then continued, "—and panicked. The only thing I can figure is with Serge texting you, the messages must have shown up on the screen and told the murderer folks were coming for you—"

"—and he didn't have time to finish the job," said Dad.

Everyone—ghosts included—took a step away from Dad.

"But I'm not dead," I told him. "So maybe it's time to stop scaring everyone in the room with your Scarface impression."

"If I find this guy," said Dad, "I'll do more than tell him to 'say hello to my little friend.'" He moved toward the door. "You and I will talk, but later, when it's just the two of us."

"Bet that's going to be scarier than being bonked on the head," said Nell after Dad left.

"Given the choice between a ticked-off Dad and a murderer—"

"They call them unsubs on TV," Nell offered.

"—doesn't matter what you call them, I'd still rather take on one of them than Dad."

Nancy snorted. "Don't let him hear you say that. Listen, kid, I got to get back and see how the team's doing with the evidence. You gonna be okay on your own?"

I nodded then opened my mouth to tell her to check in on Dad. Before I could get out a word, she said, "I'll check on your dad, first. Make sure he's okay."

Two seconds later, it was just me, Nell, Serge, Craig and Kent.

"Your dad kept asking Craig if he couldn't detect or sense anything that would give us a clue to the murderer," said Nell.

"When your dad calms down"—My boyfriend took a spot beside me on the bed—"we'll have a talk about the difference between a ferrier and a bloodhound."

"That's going to take awhile. His aura was red and black," said Serge. "And it wasn't just an outline. It had edges, like it was on fire."

I winced and decided to worry about Dad later. "Was there no evidence?" I asked. "No clues?"

Craig shrugged. "Nothing definitive. It's a guy, that's for sure. You can tell by the shoe prints in the dirt, the gait—"

"And the drag marks," finished Nell. "Whoever was toting Kent's body—"

Kent closed his eyes.

"—wasn't struggling to do so."

So we were looking for a big guy.

"My mom," said Kent. "Someone's put my mom on drugs when there's no need for it."

"If it's an anti-anxiety," said Nell, "you can't argue it's wasted on your mother."

"The dose is too high," he said.

"That you can argue. I've been asking my dad without asking my dad—if you know what I mean—about Mrs. Meagher and the pills," said Nell. "But he's got nothing."

"It's no one from around here," said Kent. "I got into her car and checked the GPS history. The only places she's been are work, the grocery store, and the Tin Shack. No doctor visits."

"Why would someone drug your mom?" asked Serge. "It's not like she witnessed your death or anything."

"But if she's too stoned to think," said Kent. "She's too stoned to wonder about me and start asking questions, like why am I not calling her. I know what she said about waiting for me to call, but trust me, that's not her style. If it wasn't for the drugs, she'd be phoning. I bet we find that guy, we'll see it's the same guy behind my death."

"If Nell gives me a ride to Mrs. Meagher's house," said Serge, "then I can go inside and find the bottle. The doctor's name has to be on it, right?"

"Right," said Nell, "Then we can do a search for him."

"I can do that." Kent waved them down.

"You should spend time with your mom," said Craig. "Let them handle this side of it."

He nodded.

"Hey, guys," I said, "can Kent and I have a minute?"

I got a round of hugs. Then they left. I took a second to choose my words.

"How are you feeling?"

He shrugged. "I'm dead."

No duh, I wanted to say. "Yeah, but you seem more upset about it, now. Is because they've found your body? Or because it really is looking like murder?"

There was silence.

"It makes it feel…real." Kent scratched his head and did an awkward shuffle. "That probably sounds stupid."

"No, it doesn't." Part of me hoped the conversation would be enough for him to cross over—that he'd only been hanging on until his body was found. The fact he was still here meant he was probably hanging on until his killer was caught, but whoever murdered him had landed me in the hospital. I didn't want to think about where else that person could land me if I kept investigating.

He moved to the window, watched the night. "I thought...Serge was talking about manipulating electricity and I'd figured out how to turn solid enough to knock on the front door...and I—I thought if I could find my body—I've been walking around, practising like an idiot, trying to hone the ability—"

"Wait. You've been practising around town?"

"Yeah."

"On your regular route?"

He nodded. "Do you know how amazing it would be to be able to harness that kind of power? To be able to turn yourself solid or move things with your mind?"

I followed his train of thought along the overachiever trail. "You could pull a Frankenstein. Enter your body and somehow manipulate universal energies to reanimate yourself?"

He laughed, the sound hollow and echoing in the stark room. "Imagine what I could bring to science and medicine. Death isn't death. It's just another state of being."

"You would have revolutionized everything."

"It would have been *amazing*." In a softer voice, he said, "*I* would've been amazing." He took a ragged breath, covered his face with his hands.

Now wasn't the time to do the whole kick a guy while he's down, but there's never a perfect time to deal with some things, so I said, "When I was looking for you earlier tonight, I did the same route you took when you'd run."

"It's a good one," he said. "Hills and level ground, different types of ground..."

"I noticed there was a lot of vandalism along the route."

"I didn't think of it," he said. "Give me a second—I'm trying to remember if I saw anything suspicious..."

Not the path I was aiming for. "That wasn't what I meant."

"Do you want my help in finding out who did it? Might not be a bad idea. It'd take my mind off of all this...stuff. At least it'll distract me until Serge and Nell figure out what's going on with my mom."

"Uh—not"—I took a breath—"I think you're the one doing it."

He shot to his feet. "You think I'd destroy property? Thanks a lot Maggie. I may not be thrilled about being dead but it's not like I've gone off my rocker!"

Man, I have to work on my bedside manner. "I didn't mean it like that."

He stepped in towards me, then retreated a step. "Then what did you mean?"

"You're trying to turn solid, right?"

"Not anymore."

Boys and their adherence to details just to win a fight. "You *were* trying to turn solid, though, right?"

"Fine."

"Okay, that takes energy."

"Yeah, I was totally bagged from doing it. But thanks for thinking I had strength left to vandalize the town."

I took a breath and exhaled my impatience. "You were trying to become solid and stay that way, you were trying to find your body so you could enter it. You're the scientist. Energy can't be destroyed, right?"

"Yeah, the law of conservation of energy."

"So all that energy you used in your experiments, where did it go?"

"Sometimes I could turn solid for a bit or move through different kinds of matter." He waved his hands in disgust. "I don't know where you're going but if you're trying to rub in that I failed—"

Man, he was Type A, all the way. "When Serge first became a ghost, he caused all kinds of havoc trying to figure out how he could do stuff without having a body. I'm not saying *all* the broken windows and stuff is all you. I'm saying is it possible that some of it *might* be you? That the energy waves caused when you were trying to turn solid could've have spread out and damaged windows and property?"

He opened his mouth, his denial in the tight lines of his face. Then he slumped into the chair by my bed. "Maybe."

"Okay. Can we connect with Nancy and find out about the places where the vandalism occurred and see if any of it matches up to you?"

He nodded.

I patted the spot by my bed. "I'll share. It's way more comfortable than the chair."

He gave me a small, quick smile. "Thanks."

I shifted over—careful not to move too fast and hurt myself—and he took the empty space.

Kent didn't bother to hide the tears in his eyes. "It's really all over, isn't it? I'm never going to any of the things I wanted."

I reached out.

He took my hand.

That night, after Kent had left and Dad had stopped by for a hug—and another threat of a *long* talk—I lay alone in the hospital bed, wide awake but quieted by the chocolate milkshake Nell had snuck in. I tried to piece together what I knew about Kent and who could've killed him. Nothing was coming.

"Knock, knock."

"Dr. Pierson?" I sat up in bed as he flipped on the light. "What are you doing here…and why are you wearing a clown nose?"

"Oh! Sorry!" He pulled the red nose off and stuck it in his lab coat. "I was in the kids' wing. The clown thing is a favourite. I go in, pretend I'm Dr. Bob and I can't do anything right." He smiled. "You get them laughing and they relax, and it's much easier to take blood samples or do a check up. Mind if I come in?"

"No"—I did a quick check to make sure the hospital gown was still covering everything—"not at all. I'm sorry about your house. Nancy told me about the vandalism."

"Some people are jerks. But it's nothing a little paint and sparkle can't fix. It's terrible, I heard they're taking the vandalism to the hospital and Main Street." Dr. Pierson stepped in, let the door swing shut, and walked to my bed. "I wanted to tell you thank you for saving Rori. I don't know what I would've done if something had happened to my little girl." He came to a stop by my pillow. "She's my everything."

"I had a chance to meet her—"

"Yes, I know.

"She's a very sweet little girl."

His smile couldn't hide the worry or the weariness in his eyes. "Neither her mom nor I are getting much sleep these days. We're constantly checking on her. I just don't know what possessed her to run away."

"She wasn't running away. She went to her playhouse and slipped on the ladder."

"It doesn't matter where she was going," he said. "She's a six-year-old girl who walked out of her home in the middle of the night."

Because you and your wife were screaming at each other, I wanted to say. Instead, I went with, "She's home now and safe."

"Thanks to you." He gave a half-chuckle. "And a medical miracle, though I'm not a man who normally believes in such things."

"Sir?"

"Her X-rays. It's the damnedest thing. It looks like she'd suffered a subdural—sorry, doctor speak—a brain injury, but somehow it was fixed. And the cold. Considering her age, the injury, her heart should've stopped before we ever found her."

"I'm glad everything worked out."

"It's thanks to you that she remains in our sight."

Thanks to me and a ghost.

He reached out and squeezed my shoulder. "I should let you rest. I only wanted to express my gratitude."

"My pleasure."

He turned to walk away but when he was at the door, I stopped him by calling his name.

He turned around.

"Did you know Kent Meagher?"

"Sure, the whole town knows about that wunder-kid."

"No, I meant personally."

He laughed. "I've been told I have boyish good looks, but I don't think I'm cool enough to hang with a university kid."

I blushed. "Sorry, I meant when he volunteered at the hospital."

"Oh, of course. Forgive my vanity in assuming you meant he and I were friends. Kent was a good kid, did a lot of great work for the hospital. You could always count on him to take initiative and pitch in." He strode back to my bed. "We crossed paths a few times when I was doing patient rounds, and of course like the rest of the doctors, I made myself available to him if he needed someone to talk to about becoming a doctor."

"But you didn't really know him, on more than a superficial level?"

"Do we ever know anyone on more than a superficial level?" he asked with a smile. "I apologize. I shouldn't tease you after your accident and the horrible shock of finding his body—" He gave me a quick, sad smile. "The Dead Falls gossip network. Uploads rumour and speculation faster than Google." He sighed. "I hope the sheriff got to his mother before the rumours did. And you, you found the body. That must have been terrible."

"I'm doing okay...for now"

"Sure?" he asked. "No emotional trauma or memory coming back? Not that I'm pushing—"

"Nothing, sadly," I said. "Whoever knocked me out did a great job of hiding themselves. I don't know if it's a boy or girl who did it. And as for my 'find,' I didn't see anything."

"I suppose, on some levels, that's a good thing."

"Yeah, I think I'll sleep better not knowing what his corpse looked like."

"That poor kid. I'm sorry I didn't know him better. I feel like if I had, if I'd extended myself maybe I could've..." He sighed. "I don't know what I could've done, but it's a terrible thing to find out someone you worked with was murdered. Makes you wonder if you weren't paying attention. That maybe he was in trouble and we were all too busy with our lives to notice." He tucked his pen into his lab pocket. "Was he a friend of yours?"

"Sort of. Lately, I hadn't been able to get him on email or text, and I know he'd been going through a rough time with school—"

"Huh. You know he stopped by the hospital around Thanksgiving but he never mentioned anything about problems with grades. In fact, he said he was doing great. Funny, isn't it? The things we'll tell one person but not the other. I suppose he didn't want any of us—the doctors and nurses—to think he was struggling in case it affected his chance of getting a residency here."

"I imagine it was hard for him to get into the school and get that scholarship. Did he ever say anything to you about any of the other kids getting mad when he won and they didn't?"

Dr. Pierson cocked his head. "Isn't that more likely something he'd share with you?"

I shrugged. "It's what you said about the things we share and the things we keep. I'm a girl. I think it was okay for him to tell me he was having trouble with school, but I don't think he wanted me to think he was weak or worried about other people's opinions of him."

"Well, he certainly didn't tell me anything. Besides, I can't imagine anyone not liking Kent. He was the nicest guy and he'd worked through some difficult circumstances to get to where he was. Who would be mad at him for that?"

That was the same question I kept asking myself.

CHAPTER FIFTEEN

By the time I was released a few days later, word had officially spread all over town and social media. Kent was dead, his demise classified as suspicious by the police, and I had found him. The tablet clicked off as I flipped the cover closed. "Don't make me go to school today," I said as Dad walked into the kitchen, "and I promise I'll never put you in a home. I'll keep you in my house and take care of you until you die."

His eyebrows went up. "You're taking care of me in my old age?"

I nodded.

"Cooking and everything?"

I nodded again.

"You're definitely going to school. I've tasted your cooking. And I'm terrified of the 'everything.'"

"What if I found you the best old folks' home in the city?"

"What city?"

"Any one you want."

"All this, as long as you get to stay home."

"It's a low, low price."

He poured himself a cup of coffee and took a long, slow sip from the cracked mug. "Deal."

"Sweet."

"In fact, take the week off."

"Oh, you're kidding."

"Dead serious." He winced. "No pun intended. This is a small town and you've found two bodies in just over a month. People will either support or vilify you. Until we know which one they're choosing, you stay home."

"What about walking Buddha?"

"Nancy or I will do it."

"Junk food run?"

"Time you ate healthy." He gulped the rest of his coffee and stuffed some toast in his mouth.

I groaned. "Come on, I want to stay away from the gossipy kids, not crawl into a hole—"

"Don't even joke about something like that." He shuddered. "No mention of you or anything that could be construed as a grave."

"Deal, if you let me occasionally go to the grocery store, have burgers with Nell, and walk my dog."

"*Our* dog. Yes to all, as long as Nell's with you." He ate the rest of his toast. "That girl would send Attila the Hun running for his mommy." Dad gave me a quick kiss on the forehead and headed out.

I grabbed another cup of the good stuff and headed back upstairs, where I tapped softly on Serge's door.

Serge opened. "Hey," he whispered. "Kent came by last night. He's still here."

"Hey," I kept my voice down. "How's he doing?"

He stepped back and let the door swing open.

A solitary lamp through the room into dark relief. Kent was in a corner where the light couldn't reach, curled into a shadowy ball.

"He's been like that ever since he came by last night," whispered Serge. "Won't talk. Won't move."

"I had thought he'd transition once we found his body."

"He's not ready to let go."

"I imagine it's not easy," I kept my voice low.

"At first, I lingered because I was angry but Kent's not mad…"

"He's heartbroken."

Serge nodded. "I'll take mad over sad, any day."

"Should I say something?"

"Leave him." Serge closed the door. "I have my issues with Captain Canuck, but I can't imagine a worst punishment for him. I keep thinking of what Craig said about why Kent was in limbo…"

"And you're thinking maybe it would have been best if he'd never woken up?"

Serge nodded. "Dead is one thing. But dead like him…it really is a fate worse than death."

We stepped away from the door and left Kent to a silence he wanted but one I wasn't sure he needed.

"I've got to find a way to get into Kent's room." Two days of being stuck at home and it was enough. I'd done my chores, watched as much reality TV as I could stomach. Five minutes into watching two rich women fight like toddlers, and I'd climbed in the car, and was now at the police station.

Nancy spun from the computer to face me. "Why?"

"Because he's a total basket case and I need to transition him before he gets stuck here, permanently." I unzipped my coat and brushed the snow from my hair.

"He's not co-operating with you?"

"He's in shock." I sat down across from her beat up desk and flipped my braid over my shoulder. "Finding his body finally made his death a reality. He left to see his mom. If I don't transition him, he's going to shadow her and linger forever."

"How did *finding* his body make his death real? Didn't he realize—?"

I waved away the question. "It's a long story about his delusion that he could re-enter his body and—"

"Pull some kind of Lazarus? Oh, boy. No wonder he's messed up."

There was a plate of lavender cookies with rosewater icing on her desk. I helped myself to two of them. "He still doesn't remember anything—"

She watched me scarf down the pastries and pushed her cup of coffee my way. "You're sure he's not just playing you? Lying to you."

I took a sip of the hot coffee, gave myself a second to enjoy the combination of coffee and sugar, then sat back. "That's a lovely thought."

"Oh kid, don't be naive," said Nancy. "Of course he's lying to you. They all lie."

"Optimistic. You kiss my father with that mouth?"

Her grin was quick. "It's realistic, and if you're going to survive this world and the next, you'd better learn it, quick. Everyone has something to hide."

"I don't think that's the case with Kent."

Nancy shrugged. "He may not know that's what he was doing. People try to cover up the things they're ashamed of, meanwhile, that lie they're telling is helping a criminal go free."

"The only thing Kent probably has to hide is a B- on a test." I sat down. "When Serge died, he had all kinds of things to say about the people around him and the life he'd led. But Kent didn't really know anyone here anymore. Plus, the poor guy's a train wreck over being murdered and unable to use those brains of his to solve the problem. It's like he can't remember anything about this life. Oh and his mom's on medication and it's freaking him out."

"That all sounded like English but you lost me on the last part."

"Kent said his mom wasn't taking anything. But she was. And she told us they were still tweaking her meds. Which means she's only been on them for a short time."

"Still sounding like English. Still beyond my comprehension. Why does this matter?"

"I'm wondering if maybe he's here to help with that. Make sure she's on the right meds and dosage. But I can't shake the feeling that it's weirdly coincidental that she started on the meds just around the time he was murdered."

Her lips quirked. "You think his mom going on some kind of medication—"

"It's making her loopy and confused. She's like Kent. Can't really remember anything specific about the night he died. She might have clues she can't give us."

"You think she's got the key to figuring out his murder."

"It's not totally out of the realm—"

"And based on the 'weird coincidence' you suspect the murderer's drugging his mom?"

She was full on laughing at me, now, but I didn't care. I figured if Sherlock Holmes could have a motto of "once you eliminate the impossible, whatever remains, no matter how improbable, must be the truth," then I could have a moment or two of considering the fantastic. "Maybe."

"And they're dosing his mom because...?"

"They killed him, right? Maybe his mom knows something or saw something?"

"And what?" Her lips quirked. "They're injecting her—"

"She's on pills, not needles—"

"—pilling her—"

"Now you're just being sarcastic."

"—so she can't rat them out? How do you think 'they' are getting the meds in her. Crushing it in her coffee?" She gave me a smart-aleck grin. "Maybe they're hiding it in the strained peas. And when they make the airplane noise to get her to open her mouth that's when they slip in the meds."

"You're spending too much time with Nell."

"You're not spending enough time with common sense, kid. She's a grown woman. How is it even possible to force her to take medication? Your motive is out of the realm of reason."

"Go ahead and laugh. But tell me again who was behind Serge's death and what was the motive?"

There was a beat of silence. She lifted her arms in surrender. "Well-played. Promise you'll tread lightly. I'll call and set up a time with Marlo. I doubt think she had anything to do with Kent's death, even as a witness, but we have to be careful and do this right. Capisce?"

"But—"

"No buts, ands, or any other conjunctions—coordinating, subordinating, or correlative. I'll keep her busy while you poke around. But no finding out something important to the investigation and keeping it from me. You got me?"

I sighed. "Yeah, I got you."

"Good." She glanced out the window, watched as a guy on a Spider motorcycle drove by. "Man, that's either really manly or really stupid. It's got to be minus five out there and he's riding a motorcycle."

"I haven't seen that one before."

"It's probably his first time driving through, heading to the Territories."

"You know, it could be a woman. And local. Maybe someone just bought it."

"No way." Nancy shook her head. "Only a man would be dumb enough to ride a motorcycle this late in the year. Alberta weather changes at the drop of the hat, and no one local is crazy enough to take on the roads to the Territories on a bike."

I flashed back to the conversation with Nell and Serge. "Holy crap! The murderer. He's local, isn't he? That night, when I went looking for Kent, I was the only car in the lot. This town's so small you sneeze and you could miss us. Any non-local in town would catch people's attention—"

"Because they wouldn't recognize the vehicle the guy was driving. That's what I thought, too. High-five, kid. If this dead thing doesn't work out, you may have a career in law enforcement. I've been quietly asking around."

"Any luck?"

"Not yet. No one saw anything unusual."

"They're probably lying."

"See? You're already learning."

"Yeah, yeah. So funny." I stood. This was the worst case, ever. No leads. No clues. Only one thing could make me feel better. "I want to do a junk food run. You gonna narc me out if I go to the store unsupervised?"

"Nah," she said. "I'll keep it on the down-low from the man—if you empty the dishwasher for the next two days."

"I always empty the dishwasher."

"Then we're good."

"You want anything while I'm there?"

"Since you asked, I need a couple of things—"

After Nancy gave me her list, I gave her the rundown on Kent and his accidental vandalism. Twenty minutes later, I walked into the Golden Chicken Market. I didn't bother with hiding behind sunglasses. This town was too small for Superman-esque disguises.

Luckily, it was the perfect time. Too late for the stay-at-home-crew, too early for the people coming off work. I resisted the urge to follow my nose to the origin of the amazing roasted chicken with rosemary scent and headed straight for the junk food aisle. Chips, chocolate, gummies, and fruit chews vied for my attention.

After I'd put enough empty calories in the cart to get me a personal warning from the surgeon general, I headed to the cash register. There was one guy in front of me, buying toothpaste, deodorant, and a toothbrush.

My phone binged with a text and I reached for it.

The cashier, Jason, looked up from the items he was ringing through and gave me a sympathetic smile. "You doing okay, Maggie?"

"Oh—" I shoved my phone back in my pocket. "I'm—"

The guy in front of me jerked upright and spun around. "Maggie?"

I gave the guy a wary once-over. Average height, greying hair mixed with brown, belly going to paunch. "Yeah. Do I know you?"

His face crumpled and he began to cry.

If I'd known him, I would've hugged him or at least put my hand on his shoulder. But he was a stranger and his tears made me go stupid. I proved the point by standing there like a moron while the guy heaved and sobbed in front of me.

"I'm—I'm—" on the fifth try, he got out, "I'm Kent's dad. You and I talked a few days ago…"

The basket slipped from my suddenly weak grip and I awkwardly grabbed for the metal handles as it went to ground. "Mr. Meagher. I'm so sorry." I hoped he would nod and go on his way.

Jason was in eavesdropping range, which meant I had to watch my words because he was a huge gossip.

"I'm real sorry about your boy," said Jason. "It's shook up the town. Serge Popov, then Kent. It's like there's a target on the backs of the boys in Dead Falls." He glanced at me. "And of course, you almost died, too."

Mr. Meagher managed a wet snuffle.

"Folks are scared," Jason continued. "There hasn't been a murder in years and now two—almost three—in a month?" His gaze keyed in. "Serge, I guess he was just a matter of time, but Kent, he was a real good kid."

He remained silent on the topic of my almost demise and I wasn't sure how to take it.

Mr. Meagher bent over as the sobs wracked his body.

I shot Jason a look that screamed, "shut up!"

Of course he didn't catch the hint. "And you, Maggie, finding the boys each time."

If he hinted at my being an angel of death, I was going to grab him by whatever hair was left on his head. "I've never really been known for my good luck," I said. "Maybe you should finish ringing in Mr. Meagher so he can go."

Jason nodded. "We're all real sorry for you too, Maggie."

Yeah, thanks. Totally believed the insincere tone.

"It's kinda weird, isn't it? With your dad being an undertaker and all. Those bodies get funnelled his way."

Did he just imply I was offing the guys in Dead Falls to bring my dad work?

"I'm so sorry," Mr. Meagher wheezed, "I hadn't seen my son in mon—months and now I'll never—" He gripped the edges of the counter, holding on to it as though it was the only thing between him and collapsing on the floor.

Considering he was about to bury his son, the counter probably was the only thing between him and an up-close meeting of the ground.

I awkwardly patted him on the shoulder. What could I say? Even if Mr. Meagher believed in life after death, Kent wasn't exactly in a great space emotionally, and I wasn't in a great space—location-wise—to let him in on my secret abilities.

"Marlo will want to talk to you." He wrenched off his glasses and wiped his eyes. "We owe you thanks for—we both thought Kent was just busy—"

"Oh, um…"

"You can follow me to the house."

From the corner of my eye, Jason perked up. I could almost see him mentally transcribing what was happening for future posting on his social network feeds.

"Thanks, Mr. Meagher, but I wouldn't want to intrude, and—"

"Please." He lifted his hand toward me. "It would mean so much to Marlo and me. You were one of the last people to talk to Kent."

Oh boy, he didn't know the half of it.

"You and that other girl, Belle, she talked to Marlo."

"Nell."

"We just want to know if—" Mr. Meagher's hands dropped back to the counter.

"Sir, I don't think that's a good idea."

Jason vibed his displeasure at my turning down a grieving father's request.

Nancy had commanded me to *not* go to the house without her. Trying to explain the wrath I would face from both Dad and her would be longwinded. There was a faster way to end this conversation. "Let me phone my dad, okay? Get his approval."

On the other end of my cell phone, Dad's voicemail kicked in. Great. I tried for Nancy but got her voicemail, too. "I should probably take my groceries home, first."

"None of that is perishable," said Jason.

Maybe not but I wished *he* was.

"My wife and I just lost our son," said Mr. Meagher. "We just want to talk to the girl who saw him last. Is that too much to ask?"

Now what? Either disobey Dad and Nancy, and get dark looks and grounded for a week, or tell Mr. Meagher no and have Jason spread all kinds of stories about what a heartless kid I was and how my dad had done a crap job raising me.

I didn't care about the bad-mouthing of me, but no one gets to say anything negative about my dad. Shoving my phone in my pocket, I said, "Just let me pay for my stuff and I'll follow you out."

CHAPTER SIXTEEN

In the car, I texted Dad and Nancy...and hoped it wouldn't be the last text I ever sent as a living person. Then I put the vehicle in gear, called Serge to me, and headed to the Meagher house.

"What's up?"

"I ran into Kent's dad at the grocery store and now I'm heading to have a coffee with him and Marlo."

Serge checked the backseat. "Is Nell following?"

"No. Why would Nell be here?"

"Because your dad said you were only allowed out of the house if she was with you."

"I was caught off guard, okay? Nell's not in on this."

He did a double take. "How do you get caught off guard going into the store? That seems like a conscious decision—"

"Nancy okayed the store. Mr. Meagher blindsided me."

"You should've said no."

"Yeah, I should've done a lot of things in my life. Can you stop grinding me on this?"

"You know your dad's going to kill you, right?"

I groaned. "This is you letting up on me?"

"I'm just saying we should text Nell—"

"Yeah, cause her suddenly showing up at the Meaghers' house will look super casual."

"Why didn't you just say no?"

"Thanks, Nancy Reagan."

He beamed at me. "And you thought the oldies TV wasn't doing anything for you. See how it's teaching you accurate pop history. But back to this thing you're doing that's going to have Hank and Nancy doing their impression of the exorcist—"

"I ran into Mr. Meagher at the cash and Jason was at the till."

"Oh, boy. No further explanation needed. That guy's got a mouth like the Grand Canyon."

"Exactly. I tried calling Dad and Nancy because for sure, they'd have said no—"

"Mags, I sympathize and empathize, heck, I'll even prioritize, but your dad is still going to have a fit."

"Tell me about it," I groaned.

"I hope we get something out of this talk with the Meaghers," he said. "Maybe it'll help ease your dad's screaming or mitigate any lifetime groundings." He sighed. "And maybe it'll help Kent, too. I felt bad for him when he was with us. Just sitting there, staring into a corner."

"Maybe he's just processing?"

"He thinks he's lingering to save his mom from an accidental overdose or medication mix-up." Serge shrugged. "But you get the feeling he's not moving on until we find his murderer?"

I nodded. "I just hope the murderer doesn't find us first—if it was a murderer and—"

"Not some guy finding a dead body he wanted to keep, then panicking when he heard you on the path?

"Thanks for that image."

The last few minutes of the ride we did in silence. I pulled behind Mr. Meagher's truck and shut off the car. "You wander the house," I told Serge. "Look for anything—especially the meds."

He nodded.

Mr. Meagher waited for me by the front door. "Marlo's...fragile."

Talk about a conflict of interest. I could use Mrs. Meagher's emotional state as a way to bail on the visit—and save myself from punitive groundings. But this was a chance to be nosy and find out stuff, and transition Kent. But...this was an even bigger opportunity *not* to get hearing loss by Dad yelling at me for breaking our agreement. Then yelling louder for disobeying Nancy.

"I can come back later," I said. I'm all for sleuthing, but Dad had this vein that would pulse when he got super mad. I'd only seen in a couple times in my life and I'd die happy if I never saw it again. Besides, Serge was here and could do all the nosing around we needed.

"No, you're here, now." He opened the door and stepped inside, leaving me no choice but to follow.

The house was sweltering. I closed the door behind me and immediately started to melt.

"I'm going to look around again," said Serge. "See if I can't find something useful." He pointed to a box with the University of Alberta logo on it. "That must be Kent's stuff—homework or papers. Think you can find a way to get into it?"

I gave him a small nod.

He gave Mr. Meagher a once-over. "He looks horrible—can you see it?"

He just lost his son. Of course he looks horrible.

"No, I mean…there's a halo of colour around his body. Like mud."

His energies are off because of Kent.

"But you can't see the colour or how his outline looks kind of shaky?"

Boo-Boo, if I could read the living, I'd be a lot more popular.

"Good point." He jerked his thumb at the hallway. "I'll head down there and see what I can find." Serge moved away as Mr. Meagher came toward me.

"Let me take your coat," he said.

I handed it to him and resisted the urge to peel off my sweater and stand there in my tank top. After he'd put my coat in the closet, we headed for the living room.

Mrs. Meagher emerged from one of the bedrooms. "Hold on," she said. "It's so cold in here. Let me turn up the heat."

Great. I was going to be Dead Falls' first victim of spontaneous combustion. As soon as I had the thought, I felt guilty. I was here because I needed knowledge, needed information to transition Kent. But knowledge for Mrs. Meagher hadn't been a lantern to her life path. It was a winter's storm and it had frozen all the life and vitality from her and taken that which she most loved from her. The fragments of her previous life were held together by a combination of shock and grief, and the torment she was in showed itself in her painful shuffle to the thermostat.

She squinted at the case. "It's as high as it can go. It must be broken. I'm sorry, I'll have it fixed later." She pulled her sweater close, wrapped her arms around herself. "You were kind to come. I should have listened to you—"

"No, ma'am, it was—"

Her lips trembled. "Should've filed that report. Maybe they could've done something—"

"He was long dead," Doug said softly. "There was nothing you could have done."

"They could have found him sooner if I'd filed that report! Could've brought my boy home." She pressed her hands to her face. The sobs came, primal and raw, and wracked her body. "I think of him lying there. Cold and alone—"

I swiped the wetness from my eyes with the back of my hand. This was the worst part of being me. Knowing I could tell her how he was doing.

Knowing I could *never* tell her.

"Sit, Marlo." Mr. Meagher moved to her, put his hand on her shoulder.

She threw it off, wrenched herself from him. "This is your fault!" She spat the words. "If you had been a decent man—"

"What, he'd be alive now? You're blaming me for his death? What about you? You smothered him. The kid couldn't breathe around you—"

Poor choice of words and it took him a breath to realize it.

"God, Marlo, I didn't mean—"

"I hate you. I hate you for deserting this family. I hate you for being an absentee father and forcing Kent to look to strangers for his role models. I hate every breath you breathe," she hissed. Mrs. Meagher lurched for the couch, collapsed into it, then reached into the right pocket of her cardigan. From its depths, she pulled out the bottle of meds. Her fingers closed over the top and she struggled to open it.

Mr. Meagher rose to help, but odds were great if he touched his wife, there would be a blood bath.

"Let me," I said. I took the bottle. "How many do you take?" I asked.

"Two."

I handed them to her and palmed a third pill.

"I'll get you some water," said Mr. Meagher.

"Don't need it." She dry-swallowed the pill then turned to me. "You talked to Kent. Maybe you were the last one to ever talk to him. How was he?"

Oh, crap. This was the problem with lying. I couldn't remember exactly what I'd said to get in the door that night. Something about Nell and wanting to be a doctor. But what had I said to Mr. Meagher on the phone?

I swallowed, folded my hands, and looked down. Hoped they would buy my delay tactic as an attempt to compose myself. "Well, Nell and I had talked about a career in medicine. It was really her idea to talk to Kent." I peeked at them, checked to see if my ambiguous start had satisfied both their memories.

Each of them had the expression of people who were zoned out—unfocused gazes, mouths in straight lines, no light in their eyes—waiting for the cue word so they could zone back in. They were too locked in their grief to even remember what I'd said that night. Terrible for them. Great for me and my crappy ability to lie.

"Mostly, he talked about his family," I said. Which was true.

That set the light glowing in their eyes again.

Mrs. Meagher leaned forward. "He did?"

I nodded and went for a general overview. "Just about growing up here, how..." Okay, Maggie, *do not* mention anything about him having issues with his parents over the divorce. "...much he was looking forward to being a doctor."

"Thank God for that scholarship," said Mr. Meagher. "He could never have gone through school without it."

Cue my opportunity to wedge myself into their lives and start some digging. "What happens to it, now?" I asked. Not that I cared, but asking easy questions—and ones not directly related to Kent's death—seemed a good way to segue into the stuff I really needed to know. "Will they do a special bursary in his name or anything?"

He frowned. "I don't know. I hadn't even thought—" He turned to his ex-wife. "We'll have to notify them."

She gave him a half-nod.

"Maybe that's something I can help with?" I asked. "You'll have enough to do with the funeral arrangements. I'd like to help. I mean, I wouldn't be on this path in my life if it wasn't for Kent. We should probably tidy up all his affairs. Let his friends know about the funeral, talk to the school about any paperwork…"

"What else did he say about his family?" asked Mrs. Meagher.

I glanced at Mr. Meagher.

"Marlo," he said gently. "The scholarship, school, his friends. Maggie's right. They'll need to be notified—"

"Who cares! My boy is dead!"

"We have to care." Mr. Meagher kept his patience. "Because someone else's Kent may need the money—"

"There is no one else's Kent." Her voice was thin and high. "There was only one and now he's gone!"

Mr. Meagher took a soft breath. "It's what Kent would have wanted."

"What he would've wanted was a father who was present! Who didn't skip town and bankrupt the family!" She shoved herself from the chair and stumbled to her bedroom, and slammed the door closed.

"I'm so sorry, Maggie—"

"It's okay, Mr. Meagher. It's just her way of grieving."

"Maybe." He sounded doubtful. "The scholarship." His head swivelled left then right. "I'm not sure where he would've kept the papers."

"It's probably in his room." I stood. "Shall we go and check?" I started for the hallway.

Mr. Meagher followed.

"Had it really been months since you'd last talked?"

"He was just always so busy. We'd text. Email. But a phone conversation? Six weeks, at least. And seeing him in person…"

"I'm sorry."

He gave me a small smile, then gave a confused glance at the closed doors. "I'm not sure which one is his. This isn't my house—we had to sell to pay for the lawyers we'd hired…" He trailed off and gave me an embarrassed smile.

"Only one way to find out." I opened one door that turned out to be the washroom. The second door was his. I expected to see Kent, but the room was empty, except for the bed, desk, dresser. Posters of sports celebrities, scientists, and the occasional model hung on the walls.

Serge wasn't there and I wondered if he was in with Mrs. Meagher. "Sir, do you want to check his desk?"

Mr. Meagher didn't answer.

"Mr.—?" I looked over my shoulder. Kent's dad stood at the threshold of the room.

"I c-c-can't—" He took a rattling breath. "I just—"

"It's okay. Just stand—sit—sit there and I'll look for it, okay?"

He nodded, sank to his knees. "You never think this will happen. The doctor tells you that you're having a kid and all you want—all you pray for—is for the baby to be healthy. Every day, you pray and hope. And when he's born with ten fingers, ten toes, and healthy heart—" Words failed as the tears took over.

I turned my back to him—partly out of cowardice because I didn't know how to comfort him, mostly to give him some privacy—and started digging through Kent's desk.

Hey, Mags.

Did you see Kent?

No. I figure he's probably out. No matter how much he may love his mom, he'd need a break from sitting Shiva with her. Serge looked over at Mr. Meagher. *Parent-kid issues or not, it must still be nice to have someone who'll cry at your passing.*

I'd cry if you left.

Aw, really?

The joy would be unbearable.

Ha ha. Deadhead.

Where were you?

I was doing looking between the walls to see if he had any hidden compartments.

And?

And yeah. There are papers in it. I sent you an image to your phone.

Really? I thought you only did text.

I figure if Kent could turn solid enough to ring a bell, I should be able to send pictures.

Okay, I'll forward it to Nancy.

He flopped down next to me. *What are you doing?*

Looking for information on his scholarship. Can you look in on Mrs. Meagher? She's carrying the bottle in her coat pocket. I stole a pill but I didn't get a chance to read the label.

Yeah, no problem. He left the room.

I sighed and sat back. "Mr. Meagher, I'm sorry. The only things in his desk are articles on ADHD medication, and some stuff for bio class, maybe." I gestured to the papers on plant growth.

"It's okay, I can look for the paperwork later."

He sounded like looking for his next breath would be a struggle. "Do you remember the name of the scholarship? I can Google it and contact them on your behalf."

"Oh. Give me a minute..."

"Take your time," I said. "Maybe he kept the files in his dresser." I went to the piece of furniture and opened the top drawer. Man, this guy was meticulous. The socks were arranged according to shade—the whites at the top left, the darks at the bottom right—and they had been folded into precise squares.

I took out half of the pairs, checked to see if there was anything underneath and did a quick tug on the bottom of the drawer. No false bottom. I did the same to the remaining drawers.

I saw the bottle on her night table. Serge came back. *It says it's for strep throat and the expiry date is from two years ago.*

Great. Another set of questions. Look at this drawer. Do you think this is weird?

No, I think he's got some kind of anal-retentive disorder.

Not his tidiness—the clothes. Look at these labels. This is high end, designer stuff.

Serge's eyebrows went up.

Don't look so surprised. Hanging out with Nell is a master class in fashion. Just because I don't wear labels doesn't mean I don't know what they are.

What do his clothes have to do with anything?

So how does a kid who's on scholarship for school afford this kind of stuff?

Maybe he had a part-time job.

Maybe. Definitely, we'll be talking to him about this.

Serge laughed. *I can't wait. Kent, I can't help but notice your boxers are high-end silk and those wife-beaters run about $70 a pop. Please tell us about your buying habits.*

Ha ha. This doesn't make sense. Maybe getting him to talk about this will jog his memory about the night he died and who might have done it.

No argument there. I want to know what's in the secret box.

I did some more searching of his room, but found nothing except more questions. Finally, I stood. "Mr. Meagher, I can't find the papers. Maybe I can come back later and try again?"

He nodded and slowly got to his feet. "Thanks, Maggie. I should go and check on Marlo."

"And I should go. My dad will be wondering where I am."

He walked me to the door. Serge followed.

My nose twitched at the smell of burnt electronics and when Mr. Meagher took my coat from the closet, I knew why.

"What happened?" He spun the coat to where a dark spot stained the front pocket.

"Oh, man," groaned Serge. "I bet I overheated the phone and burned it when I was trying to text the picture. Captain Canuck can turn himself solid enough to knock on a door. I trash your phone."

I took the cell out. Oh, man. If Dad wasn't going to kill me before, for sure I was going to get it when he saw what I'd done to my phone.

CHAPTER SEVENTEEN

"What's the damage?" asked Nell as she came into my room the next evening.

I waved my hand toward the plate on the night table. "See any of Nancy's treats?"

"No."

"That's my punishment. For a month."

"Ouch, your dad plays hardball."

"You're not kidding. I had to beg for him not to take Nancy off cooking duties and install himself."

"Whoa." She flopped down beside me on the bed. "He must have been really ticked."

"He's not the only one." I told her about Kent, the hidden box of files, the clothes.

"Don't wig out just yet. He may have shopped consignment or online for the clothes."

"Okay but what about the hidden stash of papers?"

"Have you seen what they are?"

"No."

"So it could be porn."

"A cut-out hole in a wall is pretty far to go for dirty pictures."

She shrugged. "With his mom, maybe it was the only step to take." Nell sat up. "Where is he, anyway?"

"Serge went looking for him. He thought he should talk to Kent first. Thinks it's better than me going in and asking about Kent's underwear."

"I could always ask about them."

"Your questions would be inappropriate." I dug in my pocket and pulled out the green and black capsule. "Abriule." I told her about the old bottle and the strep throat. "That bottle said the doctor was Dr. Auger. Does the name ring any bells?"

"Just because my dad's a doctor with doctorly connections doesn't mean I can Rain Man the information—"

"What's a rain man?"

She sighed and snatched the pill from my hand. "We really got to up your knowledge of 80s movies."

"You know all the doctors."

"Yeah, I do, but I don't like you taking my knowledge for granted."

"*Nell*...I'd never do that. I firmly believe you not only rain man information, you can thunderstorm girl it, too."

She rolled her eyes but grinned. "Dr. Auger retired a couple years ago."

"Scratch him as a lead. What about the pill? Doesn't your dad have that giant textbook with every medication listed? Pictures and descriptions?"

"What you, living in the stone age? We have technology, now." Nell took out her phone and plugged the drug's name into the search engine. "It's used to treat anxiety. And alcohol withdrawal, but my money's on anxiety with Mrs. Meagher." Nell pressed the capsule back into my hand. "Sometimes doctors give it to patients before surgery, but that wouldn't be the case with her."

The door opened. Serge and Kent came in.

I shoved the pill back into my jeans.

"I'm sorry I missed you when you came over," Kent said. "And I'm sorry you think I was keeping stuff and not being more helpful. I was—part of me is so used to going things alone—and everything's so confusing right now..." He took a breath and then took another one. "Serge asked me about the clothes. When I volunteered at the hospital, I got friendly with a nurse..."

"Or five," said Serge.

Kent's face went red. "It was flattering to get the attention of older women. And some of them bought me stuff—"

"Good enough for me," I said. Nancy had been right in her belief he hadn't been covering up anything illegal, just something embarrassing. "Were any of them married?"

"God no!"

Okay, so no death at the hands of a jealous spouse. "What about the papers?"

"In the wall hole? That's just me being overprotective about my research and intellectual property. You can go ahead and look—it's just a project I was working on for ADHD. Refining the drug so it's more effective, with fewer side effects for patients."

Nell followed all of this on her cell. "I thought you were into healthcare reform."

"I wanted to do more than one thing."

"Are you talking about the research or the nurses?" she asked.

His cheeks flared red. "I'm ready to help now," he mumbled. "No more hiding stuff from you."

"Speaking of which, your scholarship. Your folks have to contact them. Where's all the information?"

He frowned. "It's not in the desk?"

"No."

"What about the emails on the computer?"

"Didn't check."

"The information should be there. I'm not sure why the paper files are gone, but I'd scanned and made back-ups on the laptop. It was the Le Lorche Scholarship, through the university." He paused. "That's really nice of you to help my parents."

Not really. As long as I was "helping," I was in a position to poke around the house and their lives. But since I couldn't trust that Kent could or would remember vital information, no way was I going to tell him any of this. "It's a hard time for them," I said. "And anything I can do to help with the paperwork gives them a chance to grieve."

"On it!" Nell looked up from his text, then returned her focus to the phone. "I'm texting my dad to call her in for an appointment." She told Kent about the medication his mom was taking.

"I get her taking something for anxiety," he said, "but that stuff's hard core."

"I'm going to get my dad to bring in your mom, talk to her and make sure she's not on any medications that might have a bad interaction—"

"She takes Aspirin sometimes."

"Geez," said Nell. "No wonder she was listing like a drunken sailor. The web page said those two meds would definitely interact—" She paused as her phone binged and read the text. "Dad says he'll get on it right away."

"What does that mean?" asked Kent.

"Let's find out." Nell typed, then waited. Another bing. She read then rolled her eyes. "It's amazing how he conveys sarcasm over the phone. He's going to stop by and visit with Mrs. Meagher."

Kent stood, rubbed his palms against his jeans. "I should go and...I don't know but I should be with my mom. You guys mind?"

"No, go ahead—"

"For sure, totally understand."

Kent walked into the door. He bounced off the wood and grabbed for his head. "What happened?"

"When you're really emotional, it can affect your ability to manipulate objects," said Serge.

"I'll get the door." Nell stood. "I should go, anyway. I want to make sure Rori's okay." She gave me a quick hug. "Kent, why don't you come with me? I'll drive by and you can do a drop and roll out the car."

Serge's face darkened as he watched them walk out the door. "Maybe I should go—"

I grabbed his arm and held him back while the other two left. "Rein it in. We need to work."

"On what?"

"I got in the door with the Meaghers, but if I'm going to stay in and find out stuff, I need to do my part."

"Which is...?"

"That scholarship. If we can get some basics, then I have a reason to visit Mr. and Mrs. Meagher and start asking questions." I pulled out my laptop and opened a search page. I entered the Le Lorche scholarship. Nothing came up. "That's weird."

"What?"

"No results."

"Is that even possible?" He came over. "Maybe you spelled it wrong."

I tried a few variations. "Nothing."

"Try searching out medical scholarships, University of Alberta."

I did, then scrolled through the hits. "Still nothing."

"What about the doctor? Maybe you can find it via his foundation."

I tried that. "No."

Serge put his head next to mine. "You've got to be spelling it wrong."

I shrugged and went with a few variations of the spelling. Could I have heard wrong? I tried again, using different words that sort of sounded like Lorche. "Still nothing."

"Keep trying." He stepped away from me and headed back to the bed.

"You're not going to help?"

"I'm moral support." He un-muted the TV, tucked his arm behind his head and went back to watching the cop show.

"Thanks." I went for using another search engine to see if that helped.

"Hold on a second." Serge turned down the volume. "What did you say the name of the scholarship was?"

"Le Lorche."

He stared at me for a minute.

"What? You're creeping me out."

"I'm thinking."

"Could you blink or something? You're looking like a shark and I feel like chum."

"Hold the metaphor—"

"I think that's more like a simile." I waited.

"You realize if you rearrange those letters it spells Rori's name."

"It doesn't spell—oh, man, it spells Rochelle. Crap. I'm such an idiot.."

"Maybe it's a coincidence."

"What kind of coincidence could possibly explain this?"

He shrugged. "I've got nothing. What does that mean?"

"It means it's time to go and see Kent. Wait. Check that. I think it's better to go and see Dr. Pierson. Then we'll go talk to Kent." I texted Dad to let him know what was going on, then we headed to the hospital.

I climbed out of the car, crinkled my nose against the smell of burned trees and brush, and surveyed the damage to the park. "I don't understand what happened here."

"When an incendiary device and dry wood mix," said Serge, "a chemical reaction known as fire occurs when oxygen from the air—"

"Thanks smart guy. I meant how could a fire happen? The ground's covered in snow."

Serge sniffed the air. "Smells like chemicals on the wind."

I pulled out my cell and phoned in the sheriff's office. "Hey, Frank," I said when the deputy picked up. "I'm out on Garden Road, south of Running Creek and I think there's been a fire. I can smell smoke in the air and I there's a chemical tinge to it." I stopped, listened to him. "Yeah, I know it's weird that there's a fire when there's snow on the ground but"—I swallowed my sigh, rolled my eyes at Serge—"yeah, could be that someone's camping but..." I listened some more and practised not letting my breathing give away my impatience. "I was just taking a drive..." No need to tell him I was aimlessly loping the streets and trying to figure out how to confront Dr. Pierson "...because it helps me think and I'm pretty sure we can agree, I've got a lot to think about." More listening. "I just thought, since you were dealing with the vandalism, you'd want the head's up. Yeah...yeah, you too. Have a good night."

"Frank the Intrepid strikes again?" asked Serge as I disconnected the call.

"I'm going to have to move out of this town sooner rather than later. Between you, Kent, and now the fire, Frank thinks I'm more suspect than victim."

"Think he'll look into this?"

I shrugged. "Who knows? Maybe Frank's right and this is just some camper with too much fire-starter—"

"But it doesn't smell like it and given the stuff's that's been going on in town with the vandalism..."

I filled Serge in on my theory of Kent's involvement in the property destruction and finished with, "Nancy was able to take a bunch of buildings off the list, but that still leaves a bunch of unexplained property damage and graffiti. This area isn't on Kent's loop, and he's a total creature of habit. I can't see him going out of his way to burn a park. I bet the same guy who did this, did the other stuff."

"Might be a girl," he said.

"Maybe, but arsonists are usually male."

Serge sighed and scrubbed his forehead. "None of it makes sense. Why would there suddenly be a fire in the middle of snow-packed ground and why someone would destroy a park?"

Good questions. I wish I had the answers. I headed back to the car. Time to confront Dr. Pierson and try to solve one mystery.

CHAPTER EIGHTEEN

Ten minutes later, the car was parked, and Serge and I were walking into the hospital. "Hi," I said to the nurse at the reception desk. "I'm wondering if I could see Dr. Pierson."

Her dark eyes gave me the once over. "Are you his patient? You have an appointment?" She said it like she was challenging me to prove Dr. Pierson saw patients at night.

"No, ma'am."

"Then I'm sorry. Unless you have an appointment, I can't help you. Dr. Pierson's on rounds and—"

"Oh, of course. I'm Maggie." I paused, waited to see if there was a flicker of recognition. All I got was a flare of irritation. "I'm one of the kids who found Rori Pierson." I gave her a split-second to process. "I'm one of the girls who saved his daughter's life—"

"Oh! Honey!"

"—and I just wanted to see him during one of his breaks, maybe get an update on how his family is doing."

She went from ice queen to melted milk chocolate. "Sure thing, honey. Let me just check his schedule." Turning from me, she flipped through some sheets. "It looks like he'll be free in an hour. Did you want to wait? There's a staff lounge I can take you to—"

"Sure, thank you."

She pushed back from her rolling chair, then came out from behind the glass partition. "That was a great thing you did."

"Right place, right time."

"Well, thank the Lord you were there."

I smiled.

She led me down the hallway, the air sharp with the smell of disinfectant, then turned down the second corridor.

"Ma'am, did you know Kent Meagher?"

She chuckled. "That kid was a shadow in this hospital. You'd have thought he was one of the doctors."

"It must have hit hard, then, finding out about him."

The nurse slammed to a stop. "Little Kenny. *Dead*."

Serge snorted. "Little Kenny. Nice. You think that's what his other nurse girlfriends nicknamed him?"

Down boy. To the nurse, I nodded.

"I was in Calgary visiting my sister when I got the text... Oh my Lord, what is going on in this town?" She put her hand to her chest and leaned against the wall. "Sergei Popov, Rochelle Pierson, Kent Meagher. What is going on with this town and its children?" The recitation in names must have triggered her memory because she was suddenly looking at me like she *knew* me. "Maggie. Lord, honey, you too. I'm sorry. When you said your name, I didn't put it together with—"

"It's okay."

"You found Serge."

"It's keeping me awake at night."

"Is that a dig at all those late night movies I make you watch?" asked Serge.

"And Kent." She stared at me for a long—too long—moment. "Are you okay?" she asked.

I hate it when adults ask me that. I never know how to answer. "Oh, uh...good as can be, I guess."

"What was it like? Finding both boys?"

"Horrifying." Realizing she was in control of the conversation and I was in danger of becoming the hot topic around the water cooler, I said, "Especially with Kent. Coming so soon after Serge." I shivered. "You said you knew Kent?"

"He was such a good kid. A real favourite with everyone—"

"Especially the nurses," muttered Serge. His eyes went wide as I shot him an exasperated side-glance. "What? You think being dead means I'm not going to have petty moments."

You know he's dead, right? That you're both dead. You'd think the pettiness would have died with you.

"I know," he sighed. "But as far as the cool dead guy goes, the do-gooder model about to be doctor has way more fantasy appeal than some jerk."

C'mon. You're the bad boy.

"Yeah?"

Yeah.

His shoulders went back. "Okay, nice to know I can hold my own with something. He's smarter, nicer, and for sure, he's made way more progress as a ghost than I have. Capitan Canuck can turn himself solid enough to ring a doorbell. You know what happened when I tried to go solid yesterday? I made a bunch of sparks and almost set fire to the toaster."

We'll talk about your pyrotechnics, later. I turned back to the nurse. "I heard he was a favourite with some of the nurses."

"And easy to—" Serge added.

I shot Serge a death glare and he put his hands up in surrender.

"He was always willing to help with anything. Some of these pre-med kids, they turn their nose up if you ask them to do 'nurse' stuff, but not Kent. He used to help the janitor with the garbage sometimes."

"But the nurses—"

She chuckled. "Yeah, he was like the little brother we always wanted."

"Wait." Serge slammed to a stop. "What?"

"What?" I asked. "I thought he was dating one…"

"Kent? Dating? No. That kid was way too busy with school to worry about girls."

"Maybe he was super discreet," Serge said to me. "Kept everything on the down low."

Maybe. I turned my focus back to the nurse. "I'm sure I'd heard he was seeing a nurse."

She shook her head. "He really wasn't that kind of kid. Trust me. I know a nurse or two that tried, but he was all about the schoolwork and getting into university." The nurse leaned in dropped her voice. "He wasn't supposed to do anything but the bare minimum because he wasn't trained to do anything really worthwhile. Technically, he was there to help with paperwork, hold some babies, read to the older folks. But he was such a nice kid and worked so hard, even the guys in research used to let him help out in the labs." She straightened. "A couple of the men told me he had a real talent for it."

"Did that ever make for bad feelings with the other kids? The other ones that worked here and were also trying to get into med school."

"Nah, not really. There are some people that come along who are so far above and ahead of everyone else, you just can't even feel jealous. Like Gretzky or Hawking."

Great. Once again, Kent the Saint had no one who had anything bad or negative to say, which meant I was still motiveless when it came to his death, and he was still stuck in this plane of existence. Way to go, Maggie. Way to really help the dead.

"Go ahead and wait in here." The nurse swiped her key card and let me into the doctor's lounge.

I stepped inside, expecting leather chairs, potted plants, and a high-end coffee maker. Instead, there was a ratty-looking couch, some plastic chairs scattered around a couple of scarred, pressboard tables, and a regular coffee maker. "Thanks so much."

"No problem, honey." She sighed. "So sad. I hope the cops figure out what happened to Kent."

"Do you think there was anything Captain Canuck wasn't good at?" Serge asked when the nurse left.

"Making and keeping friends."

"That's not true. Everyone liked him."

"Yeah, but no one knew him. Didn't you hear what the nurse said about him?"

"Sure but—"

"But it's what everyone says about him. He was smart, he was good, he was kind. No one has any really personal stories about him. No one saying anything like, 'gee one time, Kent helped me carry my groceries to the car' or 'he used to tell terrible jokes.'"

Serge frowned. "So what do you think it means?"

"It means Kent's got a carefully crafted image, and that makes me wonder about him."

"Don't wonder," said Serge. "It's just his childhood reaching forward."

"Huh?"

"Come on, Mags. Mommy and Daddy spend all their money fighting. So much so, they're *still* married 'cause they can't afford to get divorced. And because they've wasted their money on hate, there's nothing in the pot for Kent's school. Which means when other kids were playing video games or hanging out, he's schlepping garbage because it'll help pay his way. His parents cost him a childhood and a future. Plus, Daddy leaves town just to get away from Mom? That's a special kind of dysfunction."

"Not really. You heard what Kent and his dad said. It was better for Kent—"

"To not have his dad around? You don't have your mom. How's that working out for you?"

"It's not the same thing—"

"He was a kid and I don't care how smart he is. At his core, he wonders what was so wrong with him that his dad would rather have left than stayed and fought for him."

That argument hit close to home because it was something that kept me up at night with thoughts of my mom.

"No kid wants to think they're so unimportant their parent would choose the easy route over the hard route."

And I bet that hit close to home for him.

"If I were Kent, I would've done the same thing. Put on a brave, nice face, keep all my worries and insecurities inside, and never let anyone close to me so they wouldn't know the truth."

I didn't say anything.

"What?" he asked. "Why are you looking at me like that?"

"Just thinking about how sensitive you are."

"Is that code for calling me a wuss?"

"No! Not at all. I just—there's so much depth to you."

He wiggled his eyebrows. "Wanna find out how much depth there is?"

"Trust you to ruin a moment. And to think, I was going to say how much I wished things had turned out differently. That we could've been friends in life."

That wiped the humour from his face. "Yeah, me too."

"Thanks for sticking around."

"Thanks for letting me."

We sat and waited for Dr. Pierson, and to prove I appreciated Serge, I let him choose the TV show to watch. The two of us were watching a classic episode of Scooby Doo when Rori's dad came in.

"Hey, Dr. Pierson."

His eyes widened in surprise. "Maggie! This is the last place I expected to see you."

"I told the nurse I was looking for an update on Rori—"

"Nell's over all the time. I'm surprised she doesn't tell—"

"Really, I wanted to talk to you about Kent."

His shoulders dropped and he gave me a patient smile. "Maggie, we've talked about him before and I told you, I didn't really know him."

"Right. Only, I can't find any information on his scholarship."

"Why are you looking into his scholarship?"

"His parents need help with sorting through his affairs."

"And they asked you?"

I nodded.

"Sorry, I'm definitely out of the loop when it comes to school bursaries or scholarships, but if you like, I can put you in touch with a couple of our residents. Those guys would be able to help."

"Right." It was now occurring to me that confronting him about the scholarship and doing it in a closed room with no witnesses was probably in the top five of my stupidest decisions.

And that included the time at the donut factory.

"Only, I couldn't help but notice that if you rearrange the letters of the Le Lorche scholarship, it spells 'Rochelle—"

"You're a smart person," said Dr. Pierson. "Really smart. And I was stupid to use Rochelle's name."

"If he says '…and I would have gotten away with it, too, if it wasn't for you meddling kids,' I'm stopping his heart." Serge moved to stand by the doctor and put his hand in front of the man's chest.

If he starts quoting Scooby Doo, I think we have bigger problems.

Dr. Pierson sank into one of the chairs. "Don't tell my wife. Please don't tell anyone."

"Huh," said Serge. "That wasn't the plan of action I expected from a murderer."

"If you can tell me what happened?"

"Rochelle's mom a good lady and she's a great mom, but…" He sighed. "We aren't…we live different, separate lives. When I met Kent, he had such promise and talent. It didn't seem right that he couldn't become a doctor because his parents didn't know how to spend their money."

"So you thought of setting up a scholarship?"

"Not at all. Those things can get complicated and besides, I saw potential in Kent. He was a good kid and I wanted to do everything I could to help him. I gave him a letter for university, set him up with my buddy in Edmonton so he could have a doctor as support for school and work, and I helped out with the money."

"So…you made up a scholarship? I don't understand."

"My wife would have flipped if I gave or lent money to anyone. She can be…possessive about our finances…" He waved his hands like he could push away his words. "She's a good person, she can just be self-involved sometimes. It wasn't a lot of money for us, but it was our money and I wasn't giving her a say in how it was spent."

"You couldn't tell her what you were doing with your money?"

He nodded. His eyes looked sunken, his face gaunt. "Giving it away or waiting for someone to pay back a loan…my wife would've made my life a living hell if I'd done something like that. We already fight all the time. It just wasn't worth it. Kent and I quietly made arrangements for the money. He'd help me out with research, do his residency here when he graduated…that's it."

"Not that I'm suggesting this happened," I said, eyeing the closed door, "but is it possible that Kent wanted more money from you?"

That made the doctor laugh. "That kid lived like a monk. I tried to give him *more* money but he was worried that Loni would notice."

There was a beat of silence. "I know all you have is my word, but Kent never blackmailed me. I don't think it would ever have occurred to him. He was a good kid, and he would've made a once-in-a-lifetime kind of doctor. I hope whoever's responsible gets caught, and caught soon."

I thought about the damage to the Piersons' property. "Is there anyone you can think of who would have wanted to hurt him? Jealous students? Ex-girlfriend? Someone who found out about your arrangement and wanted to hurt both of you?"

His mouth pulled down. "There are always petty jealousies in any organization. No one would kill him. Not here. It had to be someone from out of town."

"What about your property and the vandalism?"

His laugh was dark. "The line will form out the door. I dabble in the stock market but I'm not a professional. Risking my money is one thing and I've been successful at it. Risking other people's finances is something I'd never do. Not everyone understands that. There are people in this town that think I'm selfish for not helping them invest their money, that all I want is to be rich and for them to be poor. I'm not surprised people are using the unfortunate events of the Popov family and Kent as a cover to vent their anger." He gave me a quick smile. "But other than breaking my windows, I doubt they'll do anything else. I don't expect to end up on the morgue table."

I'd been hoping for something juicier than an unhappy marriage. I suppose Kent and Mrs. Pierson could have gotten into a fight, but she had a shoulder injury. Whoever killed him had tried to drag his body to another location. She didn't have the strength to that. I thanked Dr. Pierson for his time, then left the hospital, feeling no further ahead and like I was failing in every respect.

CHAPTER NINETEEN

The next morning, I got up too late to catch Nancy before she left for work. After a quick shower and some toast, I headed to the station. I caught her up on Dr. Pierson—survived the tongue lashing for confronting him without talking to her, first—and why I didn't think Mrs. Pierson was a suspect. Then I told her who I thought the killer was. Or at least, where I thought he was hiding.

"Run that by me, again." Nancy set down the police file and swivelled the office chair to face me.

"The murderer's in Edmonton."

"Because…"

"Because there's no one here who had a motive. According to Dr. Pierson and Nell's dad, Kent was one round away from being nominated for sainthood at the hospital."

"Didn't we talk about this? If there had been someone new in town—"

"We would have known because an unfamiliar vehicle would have been noticed," I said.

"Right."

"But what if there wasn't a car?"

Her eyebrows went up. "He walked here?"

"No, what if he hid the car—"

"—and trekked in?"

I flopped into the chair across from her desk. "Okay, so it's a little fantastic but what else do we have?"

She clicked on the mouse. "The preliminary report from the coroner."

That had me sitting up straight. "Seriously?"

"Very preliminary. There was evidence of a fight, a suspicious puncture wound, and he died from blunt trauma to the head. And to make sure, the murderer tossed him down the hill."

"But that's stuff we already suspected. There was nothing…exotic in his wounds?"

"Like the puncture wound being indicative of a one-fanged snake bite?"

I ignored the jab. "I was thinking about drugs, but if you want to pin the murder on an escaped anaconda with a grudge against Kent for having once bought a snakeskin belt, I'm all for it."

Her laugh made the sides of her eyes crinkle. "No snake bites."

"Do you think it was premeditated?"

"I don't know. It seems spontaneous but then there's the mysterious needle mark." She pointed to the note on the medical examiner's email. "If someone drugged him, it would have been a lot easier to toss him down the hill."

He was drugged, his mom was drugged. "Let me go with you to Edmonton," I said. "I can do some nosing around on campus, talk to his friends."

"What do you think you're going to find out that the Edmonton Police Service and I can't?"

"Stuff kids don't tell adults and stuff they definitely don't tell adults in authority."

"If they're keeping something from the police, that's obstruction."

"But they may not think of it as obstruction. It just might be embarrassing stuff and they're trying to keep his privacy."

"Ouch, using my words against me. There's no defense for me against that. So." Nancy cocked her head. "How do you plan on getting them to talk?"

"That's really sweet of you," said Courtney, of the long blond hair, blue eyes, headband, pearl necklace, and a sweater set. She'd been one of Kent's classmates and lab partner. "Doing an account of Kent's last few days for his mom and dad."

A few mornings after our talk at the station, Nancy and I drove to Edmonton, where she'd arranged for me to meet some of the kids Kent had been in class with. They'd gathered in front of the registrar's office. I'd scanned the group of ten and honed in on a tall girl.

The rest of them had seemed curious about why they had been called to the registrar's office. She—Courtney—had sat there, all but vibrating in her seat. She was a girl with a story who was hoping someone would ask her to tell it. Which probably meant her information was going to be more fiction than fact, but I'd asked to talk to her first. The more she talked, the more I'd have when I went to the other kids.

As we'd headed to the Student Union Building, she told me he'd tutored her on their infection, immunity and inflammation class, and how much she missed having him around.

"I thought it was weird that he'd drop out because of class pressure when he was always so in control." She shrugged. "But then you have kids taking all kinds of drugs to keep up, and doctors are among the worst when it comes to drug use, so…" She leaned in. "There was an article about it in the *Journal of Addiction Medicine*. There was an interview with like, fifty-five patients and thirty-eight of them were abusing drugs. Which is why I make sure I do yoga and meditation. I'm not giving up ten years of med school to end up in a gutter or in front of a hearing committee."

We walked for a minute and found a quiet corner away from the crowd. I wiped the crumbs of a muffin from the tabletop, flipped open my tablet and placed it on the surface.

Courtney perched on the edge of her seat, shifted her upper body forward. "Did you know Kent well?"

Let her take control. If it made her comfortable enough to spill her secrets, that's all I cared about. "No, not at all. My best friend had a huge crush on him a couple years back and Kent had worked with her dad."

"Her dad's a doctor?"

"Yes."

"That's funny that she didn't come instead of you if she was the one with the crush."

"We decided I'd do it because…" I pushed the tablet aside and did my best impression of a girl trying to be strong in the midst of emotional trauma. "Actually…I'm the one who found his body."

"No!"

I nodded and hoped I looked vulnerable.

"Oh my God!" She grabbed my hand. "Are you okay? Are you having nightmares or trouble concentrating? What about your connections with friends and family?"

From the questions, obviously, Courtney was heading to the psychiatric branch of medicine. "I'm doing...as well as can be expected, I guess." Seeing the dead had given me a certain immunity when it came to bodies—especially since Dad owned a funeral home. Courtney, I suspected, would respond better to a damsel in distress than a casual dead-stuff-happens chick. I tried to look traumatized and strong all at the same time. Odds were, I probably just looked constipated. "You asked why I was here...I guess, seeing Kent just shook me up."

"I understand."

"It made me question life and death, and I just had to know more about him. I went to see his folks and when I saw their pain..." I shrugged and looked away, trying to buy time and come up with something equally plausible and heart-rending. "...I guess it just made me want to forget my own."

Her face softened and she tightened her grip on my fingers.

Bingo.

"So you asked the sheriff if you could come along? Was it hard to be invited into the investigation?"

Rule one of dealing with people with stories to tell, never give them a reason to close their books, and telling Courtney I was living with the sheriff was going to ruin our sisterly connection. "I'm not part of the police investigation but Sheriff Machio, she really seems to understand—"

"Really? She struck me as a ballbuster."

Oh, boy. Courtney didn't know the half of it. "I think it's a gender thing. Being one of the few women in a male-dominated arena."

There was a flash of connection in her eyes. Double bingo. Courtney would soften on Nancy, now. After all, she was a girl aspiring to be a doctor in a field that men still dominated. Heck, given the rate at which women were still under-diagnosed with heart attacks, I wouldn't have been surprised if they were still talking about female hysteria in class.

"Wow," she said. "Okay, I'm understanding her a little better."

Great. Time to take control. "Look, I know you're missing class and I really appreciate you giving up your time—"

"No problem."

"Really, I'm just here to find out about Kent and his last days, and be able to bring something back to his family. Kent had been so busy with school that he hadn't seen his folks in months and—"

"Tell me about it." She rolled her eyes but her smile took the sarcasm from the action. "I thought I was an over-achiever. That guy makes"—Her smile crumpled—"*made* me look like the grasshopper from Aesop's fable."

"Yeah, he was driven."

"School from eight-to-five, labs from six-to-nine, volunteer on the weekends, plus a courier job. When did he find time to study?"

When did he find time to shower or eat? Her timeline for his classes didn't mesh with my memory of his schedule, and I made a note to double-check it when I got back. "I didn't know he had a job."

She glanced over her left shoulder, then the right, then leaned in. "It was one of those off the book things."

"Off the book?"

"They were paying him under the table."

Huh.

"Something about the family being in Canada illegally but having that go-get-'em attitude. It spoke to Kent."

"Really."

"So he'd help run deliveries—"

"What kind of deliveries?"

She shrugged. "I'm not sure. Stuff."

Something was binging in my brain. Telling me this was important. But I didn't know why "stuff" seemed vital to the investigation. Maybe it was the shadowy family. They were in the country illegally. Maybe something had happened. Could Kent have seen something he shouldn't have?

My imagination raced with images of a poor but determined family smuggling themselves in crates and trucks to live the Canadian dream, only to be screwed over by a dark and evil human trafficker. It sort of made sense. I mean, if you hide people for a living, surely you could hide yourself in a small town. And if you were willing to treat humans like chattel, then maybe you were equally willing to get rid of them like trash if they threatened your livelihood. "Did he do it often? Help out the family?"

"I think he worked almost every day. Just a couple of hours because of his schedule." She smiled. "But every little bit helps, doesn't it?"

It sure did. Even if it created more questions than answers. "Do you think there's any way for me to get a hold of them?" I raised my hands. "Not to get them in trouble or anything, but his parents would love to know that in his last days he was still trying to help people."

"No, I don't know way to get a hold of them," she said with a nose wrinkle.

Okay, ask an open-ended question. "Who could help me with that?"

The nose wrinkle became a full-on frown. "No one. Kent was great and nice, but he didn't exactly get close to people."

"Oh, that's too bad." I injected as much disappointment as I could into the sentence, then I let the conversation lapse into silence.

After a minute, the skin on her face smoothed out. She snapped her fingers. "Does the sheriff have Kent's laptop?"

"Uh, I'm not sure."

"If she does, you should see if she'll let you take a look at it. Kent kept everything in the computer. He was very protective—overprotective—of it."

"Wow." Total dead end. There's been nothing on his computer except school notes, pictures, and the usual inane stuff people kept on hard drives. "Okay, thanks."

We chatted a bit more, but there wasn't much to get from her. After the appropriate amount of time, doing some small talk so I didn't look like I was giving her a bum rush, I stood and said, "Thanks so much for your time."

She came around the table and gave me a tight hug.

If Serge had been here, he would've lost his mind on that.

"No problem. If you need any extra help—" She ripped out a piece of paper and jotted down her number. "Text me. Anytime. And if you need someone to talk to, I'm here, okay?"

I gave her another hug. "Thanks. That's really great of you."

We parted at the main entrance of the building and she left to give her statement to Nancy.

"Hey, Maggie."

I turned to see her coming back to me. "Yeah?"

"You said his folks hadn't seen him in a couple of months, right?"

I nodded.

"Is that what they told you?"

I nodded again.

"Maybe I shouldn't say anything, but his dad's lying."

What? "What?"

"I saw him and his dad having a big fight a couple weeks before he died."

"You're sure it was his dad?"

"That's what he said when I asked," she told me.

"Did he say what they'd been fighting about?"

She shook her head.

"Okay, thanks." I watched her leave and when I was sure she was out of range, I phoned Nancy. "Hey," I said when she picked up the phone. "I think I just figured out how a non-resident of Dead Falls could sneak into town, kill Kent, and no one would notice. I can't believe I'm about to say this, but I think Mr. Meagher may have killed his son."

CHAPTER TWENTY

"Okay, thanks, Frank" Nancy tapped the Bluetooth bud nestled in her ear and returned her hand to the steering wheel. "Frank says Doug denies seeing Kent that night. And he's pissed as hell at the suggestion he might have killed his son."

"Do you believe him?"

"It's about what we can prove, not what we believe. Frank will keep him in one of the cells until we can figure that out if he's telling the truth or lying."

On the other side of the passenger window, the fields of farmers' crops, long since harvested of their grain and corn, sped by in a bleak unchanging landscape of dead grass and grey sky. I put my hands to the SUV's heater, warmed my fingers against the cold landscape and my even colder thoughts. "But in most violent crimes, isn't that the case? The victim's been killed by a loved one? Or at least someone they knew?"

She nodded.

"And what Mr. Meagher said, isn't that what every murderer says? 'Gee, it was an accident. Who knew bonking my son on the back of the head with a'—what was the weapon of choice?"

"They're still trying to figure that out."

"—smacking my son on the back of the head with a yet-to-be-named object would crush his skull."

She grimaced. "I can't imagine Doug would do that to Kent."

I couldn't, either. But he was the only one who fit the non-resident-but-sort-of-resident MO for the killer. Plus there was the fight with Kent two weeks before he died.

"There's no evidence to prove he didn't do it." Nancy took a quick breath. "There's also no evidence to prove he *did* do it. It'll take weeks for the final autopsy report to come in and for us to get an idea of what was used to kill Kent. Until we get that information—the specifics on when Kent died and how—Doug will remain a suspect."

The downside of a town as small as Dead Falls was that we didn't have a designated medical examiner. We had to rely on the one from Edmonton, which was fine. But it meant Kent was at the end of a long line of dead bodies, and it would take a while before we really knew anything.

"Mr. Meagher doesn't seem like the type to off his kid, does he?"

"Nope. They had an amicable if superficial relationship."

"I get Mr. Meagher saying he didn't kill his son," I said, "What I don't understand is why he'd deny seeing him that night when Courtney's a witness to the fight."

"Probably because he's scared it'll turn into suspicion of murder."

"And lying about a fight isn't going to land him in the same boat?"

"No one ever said people are logical when being questioned by the police. He's got a lot to worry about. On both the night he's accused of fighting with Kent and the night Kent died, Doug says he was home, alone. There's no one who can back up his story."

"What about his cell phone? Can't the GPS back him up?"

"Not really. He could have left the phone at home."

Good point.

"Did you talk to Serge or Kent about this?" asked Nancy.

I shook my head. "I figure these are the kinds of things you tell people in person."

"I don't envy you."

"I just want to be there for both of them. Although, I'm not sure I'll be anything but extra baggage. There's so much in common with both their stories—"

"When it comes to domestic crime, the stories are always the same. Only the names seem to change." She shifted into the left lane to pass a slower-moving tractor-trailer.

There didn't seem to be much to add or say, so I went quiet and listened to the soft hiss of the heater.

After a few minutes, Nancy asked, "How is everything else?"

"Which everything?"

"Things are good with you and Craig?"

"Great. I occasionally forget to…" I shrugged. "Act like a traditional girlfriend but he doesn't seem to mind."

"Act like a traditional—what does that mean?"

"You know, text him, send cute photos of me."

Nancy laughed. "Kid, he's ten thousand years old. I think he's fine with a non-traditional relationship. Besides, it's good for you to keep some independence." Her eyes cut my way then returned their focus to the road. "I know I'm not your mom, Mags"—She looked my way again—"but I'm happy he's good to you. I'm happy you're happy, and if you ever need to talk about anything, I'm here. Always, okay?"

I blinked fast and looked out the window. When I trusted my voice, I said, "Yeah, thanks. I'm glad you and Dad found each other, too."

She smiled.

"Uh—" I took a breath and plunged ahead before my second thoughts could become the words I spoke. "Has Dad ever mentioned my mom?"

She frowned. "How do you mean?"

"Well, you got involved with a man who has a kid. You guys must have had The Talk. Where's the baby-momma and all that…didn't you?"

Her rich laughter warmed the interior. "I got to say, Mags, I've never thought of you as a 'baby.' You've always been full grown to me." Her smiled flickered as she added. "Especially once I found out about the cursed-blessing of your abilities."

Cursed-blessing. That was well said. "But he never said anything—?"

"It's not something we talk about and even when I'd asked…" she sighed. "I don't know what happened between Hank and your mom, but it's a hurt he's never gotten over. To ask seemed cruel—"

"Yeah, that's why I don't ask. It's just sometimes I wonder—"

"Why she abandoned you?"

All I could manage was a jerky head nod. "Dad's found a way to love me. What was it about me that made her—"

"Stop." She grabbed my hand and squeezed tight. "You stop right there. There was nothing about you. Nothing wrong. Nothing horrible. You were just a baby—"

"A baby she named after a prostitute. Doesn't that seem...I wonder sometimes, if she knew what I was before I was born. If she felt it when I was in the womb and couldn't stand the thought of having a kid like that—"

"You figure she thought she was about to give birth to Satan's baby?"

"Well—"

"Listen, your dad can be grumpy but there's nothing demonic about him." She tilted her head as she considered her words. "Except his cooking. That's just unholy."

I laughed.

She hadn't let go of my hand and I loved her for that, for keeping the connection between us.

"Mary Magdalene wasn't a prostitute. She was a moneyed woman who helped Jesus, and it's only history and men that have been unkind to her."

"Oh, I didn't know."

"Mags, maybe your mom did know what you were. Maybe she sensed the powers you possessed, and that's why she named you after Mary Magdalene." She interlaced her fingers with mine. "Maybe she wanted you to have the name as a reminder, to know that no matter what life had in store, how hard it got for you or how much you were misunderstood, you had the same power to change the world as the woman who first carried your name."

It was a nice thought and a lot more benevolent to both my mother and me than the thoughts I carried about my name and the woman behind my birth. I didn't say anything but I squeezed Nancy's fingers and smiled.

"How about you?" I let go of her hand to reach behind the seat for the plastic bag of chips and chocolate. "How are things in the police enforcement—other than Kent's murder?"

"Thankfully, the vandalism's stopped."

"Any luck on finding out who was responsible for all the destruction?"

She shook her head. "That kind of damage is a crime of opportunity. It'll take time to track down people's whereabouts. Other than that, Frank said they're nowhere on the fire around the mill."

"Weird, right? Why would you burn a park?"

"I'll ask the idiot who did it when I arrest him." She shook her head. "It feels like people are losing their minds over the murders. Serge was bad enough, but Kent...the longer it takes to find his killer, the worse it's going to get. Right now, we're talking property damage and an unoccupied area of a public park. I don't want to think about what an escalation will mean for people's personal safety."

I didn't want to think about it, either. She was right, and the need to find Kent's killer loomed large and dark over me. How could I have done so many years of helping ghosts cross over, then fail when it mattered most?

CHAPTER TWENTY-ONE

A couple hours later, I walked through the front door and headed up the stairs Serge's room. It was empty. The synthesizer music from that '80s cop show Serge loved seeped through the gap of my bedroom door. I went inside and found my soul brother and my boyfriend on the bed with Ebony and Buddha in between them.

Craig smiled and sat up.

Serge turned his gaze from the TV as I came inside. "Hey, how did it go?"

"Lots to talk about. Any word from Kent?"

"He came over for a little after you and Nancy left this morning, then left this afternoon. I haven't seen him since."

"We need to find him," I said. "His dad's been taken in for questioning."

Serge straightened so quickly, he surprised the cat. Ebony leaped from the bed, then glared Serge's way.

"Sorry, little girl." He turned back to me. "Tell me again about Kent's dad."

I gave him the rundown on Courtney's statement.

"They don't seriously think Mr. Meagher killed his son, do they? That guy couldn't even go in Kent's room."

Craig stood. "You guys need to get going. There's no telling how he'll react and if it goes bad, you'll have to contain him."

"No offer to help?" asked Serge.

"I'll do as much as I can," he said. "This doesn't feel right."

"You don't think his dad did it?" I asked.

Craig shook his head. "I may not have access to Kent's life but somewhere out there is a ferrier who does. I'm going to go and see what I can find." He moved to the door then stopped and looked at us over his shoulder. "Kent's a good guy. I don't like the thought of him wandering for eternity, stuck in the in-between. And I really don't like the thought of him going poltergeist because his murder was never solved."

I looked at the clock on groaned. "It's too late for us to go to Kent's. We'll head over first thing tomorrow." Hopefully, we'd find him before misery does.

"I don't like it, either," said Serge as he watched Craig walk away. "A bad guy's predictable. But a good guy—ghost—who goes bad? There's no predicting what he'll do."

"Hi, Mrs. Meagher." I stamped my feet on the mat and shivered in my boots. "Did I come at a bad time?"

"I don't know," she said dully as she stepped back to let me in. "Doug's still at the station, being questioned by the cops. I've been telling Nancy he's a bad guy, and now, he's been arrested and I find myself arguing that he couldn't have done it, that he's *not* a bad guy." Her jaw trembled. She pulled her sweater close to her body and folded her arms across her chest. "I can't believe it. I just can't believe he did this."

Serge gave me a quick nod then headed down the hallway to search for Kent.

"Is there any part of you that thinks—?"

"No! He—he just wouldn't have." She wiped her eyes. "When we were married, I was the one who had to kill the insects in the house. He couldn't do it. Not even when it was a wasp in Kent's nursery. Doug doesn't have the stomach for death."

"There was an eyewitness who saw them fighting."

"Parents and kids fight. That doesn't mean anything."

Serge emerged from the hallway. *He's not here.*

Does that mean he wasn't around so he doesn't know? Or does that mean he was here, found out, and has gone wandering?

My questions got a shrug from Serge. *I don't know, but if it's all the same, I'm going to head out, see if I can find him.*

Okay, I'll stick around and see what I can find out. Nell was still looking into who'd prescribed Mrs. Meagher the medication. But since

I was here and she was drugged…"Mrs. Meagher, how are you really feeling?"

She shrugged.

"I noticed you were on some anti-anxiety meds. Are you keeping up with the dosage? I've heard if you don't, it can cause problems."

"I'm regular," she said.

"The last time we talked, you said they were adjusting your dose. Did you get a chance to talk—"

"Why do you care?" She leaned forward, swayed. "Why are you asking me this?"

"Because Kent's not here to check up on you—" Bad move. She dissolved into tears.

Twenty minutes later, my efforts had gotten me zilch. I kept asking Mrs. Meagher about Kent and his relationship with Mr. Meagher, but got nothing but the same information I had all the times before. And that was only when she could stop crying long enough to answer me.

There was nothing thing left to do but leave, but before I did, I hazarded one final question. "Ma'am, when I was helping Mr. Meagher sort through Kent's stuff, I couldn't help but notice…notice very expensive clothes. Do you know where Kent would have gotten the money for them?"

She shook her head. "Our finances were strained. I know he worked in town. Maybe he saved up."

"Did he ever mention his job in the city?"

"Which job?"

"The one helping the family?"

Mrs. Meagher stared at me. "There wasn't a family. He didn't have time. If he wasn't at school, he was volunteering at the hospital."

That's what I had remembered about his schedule, too. "There were rumours of him and some"— in case Kent hadn't been lying, I went for generalities instead of talking about the nurses —"some girls he'd been romantically involved—"

Maybe it was the strain of Kent's death compounded by Mr. Meagher's arrest that left her defenceless to my words. Her reaction was instantaneous. A sudden widening of her eyes, her head jerking back.

This wasn't surprise. This was full on disbelief.

There was only one reason for her to have that kind of reaction. "He wasn't dating any girl," I said.

"Oh, well," she stammered.

I frowned, taking in the rise of red in her cheeks, her reluctance to make eye contact.

"He was a grown man, and it's not my place to pry—"

"He didn't like girls," I said.

She scrambled to say something.

"He was gay."

Her face crumpled.

Shifting closer at the same time I put my hand over hers, I let her cry.

"We'd always known," she said when she caught her breath. "Kent came out to us in elementary, but he was worried. None of the other kids had ever mentioned having those kinds of feelings. I told him it was just because they were young. That as they got older, he'd see there were other boys and girls like him."

"Only there weren't."

She squeezed my hand. "I told him no one in Dead Falls would care if he was open, if he told folks. But he felt like he was the only one, and he saw on the news the terrible things that happened to other kids when they came out..." She took a shuddering breath. "He didn't want to risk it. As he got older, it depressed him more and more."

"Was that why you'd freak out if he was late coming home? You were worried that he might have hurt himself."

"He felt so alone, Maggie, and his depressions could rage for months. He would get so dark, so fatalistic. I was terrified for him. He refused to get counselling—I even told him we could go to another town for help, but he didn't want to. I thought about moving us somewhere else, but all I can afford is another small town—"

"Which was another reason he wanted out from this town. He wanted to be in a big city where he could be more open."

"Yes. We argued about it. I told him...I told him it would be okay, that he had to trust his neighbours and friends—"

"Was that why you were fighting the night he died?"

She nodded then shook her head. "We fought about everything that night. He was on edge—he usually got that way before he fell into a depression. And I wasn't helpful. I kept nagging and harping on him. I wanted him to talk to me—I *pushed* him to talk…" Her mouth moved to form the words that didn't seem to want to be spoken. "…And he died that night. The last time we spoke, it was in anger and frustration, and I can never take it back. I can't help but wonder what happened that night and think—had he been right all the time? Did my son come out of the closet that night and end up at the bottom of a hill because he decided to open himself up to the wrong person?"

CHAPTER TWENTY-TWO

"Rori's so excited to see you," said Dr. Pierson as he let me and Nell into his house. "Come on in. You girls want some hot chocolate and popcorn? Maybe some brownies?" His voice receded down the hallway.

I hung back as Nell followed him.

She tossed me a look over her shoulder and mouthed, "What's up?"

I caught up to her, then pulled her back so there was more distance between us and Dr. Pierson. "The night Rori went missing," I whispered, "Mrs. Pierson kept going on about how upset Dr. Pierson had been over Serge's murder."

"So?"

"So, now Kent's dead and he's smiling and offering us drinks?"

"You'd rather us die of thirst?"

"Focus, Nell. I can understand the brave face before, when he had to pretend that he wasn't that close to Kent but now we know, so why's he still acting like this?"

"I am focused. On the hot chocolate. They've got this amazing milk steamer and they use real chocolate flakes, not the powder stuff."

"Nell…"

"Don't worry about the inconsistency with Dr. P. He's a doctor and a scientist, and he's like my dad: emotions are buried deep under intellect and arrogance."

"You're probably right. I hate it when you're right," I said.

"You must live a very unhappy life, then, because I'm always right."

I punched her shoulder and followed her into the kitchen. "Hey, Rori!"

She looked up from the picture she was colouring. "Hi."

Wow. I didn't think six-year-olds could get that depressed. What happened to Dr. Pierson's 'she's so excited to see you?' "You okay?"

Her eyes flicked to her dad, then she shrugged and nodded.

"The machine's all set up for the hot chocolate," said Dr. Pierson. "You girls have fun. I'll check in on you in a bit."

"We're fine, Dr. P," said Nell.

He smiled. "I'll see you in fifteen minutes." He tossed a smile in Rori's direction. "Got to make sure my girl's doing okay."

"Wow," Nell said to Rori. "Has it been like that since you got back?"

Rori gave us a miserable nod. "They watch me all the time."

"Gross," said Nell. "Two parents staring down at you."

"All they do is fight and stare," Rori whispered. "It's horrible."

"I'm sorry." I sat down beside her. "That sucks."

"Can I come to your houses?" Rori asked. "I'll be really good."

"Oh, honey." Nell gave her a tight hug. "You're always really good. I asked but your mom and dad said no."

"Can you stay here, then?"

"I asked about that too, but they said they're not ready to have anyone in the house but you guys."

The crayon slipped from Rori's hand. She bent her head and Nell held her as she cried.

"Hey, girls, what's—oh my God! Rori! Honey, what's wrong?" Mrs. Pierson tossed her purse on the kitchen counter and ran over. She glared at me and Nell. "What did you girls do to her?"

"Us? Nothing—"

"I let you come over because she asked, and I was grateful for your helping us that night."

"Helping you?" Nell's tone was incredulous verging on offended. "We didn't help her," Nell said in a tight, hard voice. "We *saved* her."

"That doesn't give you the right to invade my house and make my daughter cry!"

If Nell's eyes went any wider or hotter, they were going to fall out of her head and set the house on fire.

"Mrs. P," she said, "you know I love you and the doc, but you better check yourself before you wreck yourself. Rori isn't crying because of us, she's crying because of you! The two of you are fighting all the time."

"Don't you presume to talk about my marriage—" Her voice rose.

"Why not?" asked Nell. "You're screaming about it all the time. The entire town knows you're pissing away the finances and he's having an—!"

"Nell!" I grabbed her arm. "Rori."

My friend took a sharp breath and her rage vanished at one look at the little girl's stark, white face.

"Not you too," Rori whispered. "Everybody's yelling—" She hiccupped for breath. "Not you too, Nellie."

"Never, baby." Nell crouched in front of her and wiped away Rori's tears. "Never, I'm so sorry. It won't happen again. Promise. Okay?"

Rori nodded and held out her arms.

Nell wrapped her in a hug.

Mrs. Pierson took a deep, cold breath. "I think you girls should go."

"No, Mrs. P, please don't make us leave. I'm sorry for losing my temper—"

"I don't care," she said, her voice icy. "Your behaviour was inexcusable."

I bit my tongue and fought the overwhelming urge to point out her actions hadn't exactly been saintly.

"No, Mommy!"

Mrs. Pierson brought up her hand and dropped it like a guillotine. "Nell, Maggie, thank you but your time is done here. Good night."

Dr. Pierson came into the kitchen. "I heard yelling. Is everything okay?"

"It's fine, Paul." Mrs. Pierson's tone went from ice to deep-freeze iceberg. "As usual, you're a day late and a dollar short."

He gave her a thin-lipped, acerbic smile. "I maybe a day late, darling, but with you, I dare not be a dollar short."

"Perhaps if you'd been supervising our child—our *only* child—you would have ensured these...*charming* examples of teenage citizenship—"

Ouch.

"—didn't reduce Rori to tears."

"My daughter's fine. In fact, there wasn't any yelling or crying until you came home." He bared his teeth at her. "Dear." Dr. Pierson turned to us. "Perhaps you ladies will excuse us while I remind my wife what good manners looks like. I'm sorry for the short visit. Perhaps another time—"

"No," said Mrs. Pierson. "They're done visiting."

"—another time, then." Dr. Pierson waved his hand toward the hallway. "You know where the door is."

Man. Five minutes with these people and my stomach was an acid bath. How was Rori surviving this? I gave her a final, long hug, held strong as her tears wet my shoulder, then gently nudged her back to her mom.

A little while later, after Dad had decided I was okay to go back to school, I survived the day by avoiding anyone who looked like they were going to ask me about finding Kent's body. After school, I headed to the Tin Shack with the gang.

"Kent is haunting the town. That's why there's been so much vandalism." Tammy issued the statement then went back to sipping her pop.

I, meanwhile, tried not to choke on mine. "Sorry?" I set my drink down on the seat that separated me and Nell. We were in the middle row of Tammy's minivan, scarfing Tin Shack junk food and discussing the weirdness of Kent's death, the fire, and the vandalism. At least, that was my priority. Anything I could do to steer them away from Serge and the Ouija board was good for me.

"How do you figure?" asked Craig. He sat beside Serge in the last row.

"It's only logical," said Tammy.

This from the girl who still thought rainbows had a beginning and end. Still, she was right, and that was weirding me out.

"Serge has been trying to contact the living. Now Kent is dead. It makes sense they'd team up."

"If we set up a séance, we can confirm that." Bruce shot me a pointed look from the front passenger seat. "And help both of them cross over."

"I understand what you're saying," I said, "But they weren't friends in life—"

"Things can change a man, especially death and being trapped in between planes," said Bruce. "It's Kent. Trust me."

"I didn't know Kent when he was alive," said Craig, "but from what I've heard, he didn't seem the type to go nuclear. Would he really want to destroy other people's property?"

"Desperate times," said Tammy, "call for desperate measures."

"Hold on. What's that?" Nell leaned forward and eyed Bruce's food. "A hoagie."

"Why have I not heard of this?" She inched forward and sniffed his sandwich.

I elbowed her in the ribs. "Manners."

"With him? You're kidding right?"

"It's one of the new food items," said Bruce. "It's awesome. Pepperoni, Swiss cheese, turkey, roast beef, provolone, Monterrey Jack cheese, salami, bacon, tomato, lettuce—"

"Trade you one of my burgers for half of yours," said Nell.

"There's more stuff in the hoagie like mustard, mayo—"

"Great. Less talk, more trade. By the time you're done listing all the ingredients I'm going to die of hunger."

"No," said Bruce. "I mean, there's a ton of stuff in here. Your burger won't cut it. Add in your poutine and the yam fries—"

"Half the yam fries—"

"You got a deal."

"Are you done?" I asked. "Can we get back to the issue at hand?"

"Preach. The choir's listening." Nell slid back and started arranging her trade.

"The problem is Serge is trying to move on and Kent's stuck here," said Bruce.

Tammy's eyes widened. "Gee, you don't think they'll start fighting, do you?"

"I'd tell them Kent and I have shared a bed," Serge said. "But I think they'll misconstrue it."

Craig hid his laughter behind a cough.

"I still think the deaths are connected," said Bruce. "There's no way those guys being killed around the same time is a coincidence."

"I'll play this game." I swallowed some hot chocolate. "But who'd kill Kent? And how does that connect back to Serge?"

"They were both athletes," Bruce offered.

"Who were two years apart in school." Nell shrugged at Bruce's glare. "What? I'm not judging, I'm playing devil's advocate."

"More like devil's right hand," he muttered. "Okay, what about church. Serge's dad was the preacher. Was Kent connected to him at all? I mean, the pastor had a thing for—"

"Kent wasn't a churchgoer," said Nell.

Bruce scowled and took a savage bite of his hoagie. "Fine. You throw the ideas and I'll knock 'em down."

"I don't have any ideas," she said. "Kent was a good guy. There's no motive to kill him."

"We're sure it's murder," asked Tammy. "He didn't just fall?"

I kept quiet. The official medical report wasn't out yet, and even though I knew Kent died from being bashed on the head and there was a suspicious needle hole in him, I couldn't tell anyone.

"Of course someone murdered him," scoffed Bruce. "It's the same guy who's trying to kill Maggie."

I punched him on the arm. "Manners."

"What? I'm telling you something you don't know?"

"Something I don't need reminding of, thanks."

"Here." Bruce handed me part of his hoagie. "I'm sorry."

Nell snatched it from his hand. "Too salty for Mags. I'll take that bullet."

"We come back to the same problem," said Craig. "He was a good guy and there's no motive to murder him."

"Uh...I was wondering...did any of you guys ever hear about Kent dating?" I asked oh-so-totally-not-casually.

Bruce shook his head. "That guy didn't even do birthday parties as a kid."

"Are you sure? No flirting or...uh...down-low dating?"

Everyone stopped eating and stared at me.

"What's going on, Johnson?" Nell set down her burger.

"Nothing I was just wondering—"

"You never *just* wonder."

"I don't want to break a confidence—" Oh, stupid move. That just made them lean in.

"Maggie." Nell's voice went calm, measured. "We can do this the easy way or we can do this the hard way—"

I'd seen Nell's hard way, once. I never wanted to see it again. "Okay, don't tell anyone but—" I took a breath, hoped Kent and his folks wouldn't hate me for outing him and said, "—he was gay."

None of their postures changed.

"And?" Bruce waved his hand. "And then...?"

"And then, nothing. That's it. He was gay."

"Oh, geez." Bruce sat back, disgusted. "I thought it was going to be something good. Who cares if he's gay?"

"He did," I said. "He stayed in the closet because he was afraid he'd be judged."

"That's so sad." The fry slipped from Tammy's hand back into the paper container. "He didn't have to be afraid to come out."

"Yeah," said Bruce. "That's not a secret worth keeping or killing for. Now, if he'd been a Flames fan—"

"You mean Oilers," said Tammy.

"Flames—"

"Oilers."

I raised my hand. "Can we—"

"Maple Leafs?" suggested Tammy.

Bruce went quiet. "Okay, Maple Leafs."

"Fantastic," I said, not bothering to hide the sarcasm in my voice. "Now that we've accounted for the true motive behind his killing—loving the wrong hockey team—"

"Hey, don't get snippy." Nell popped some poutine. "Vancouver went nuts back in twenty-eleven because of hockey."

"I bet it was some guy from Vancouver that did it," said Bruce. "Those west coast hippie-Canucks."

I checked over my shoulder, looking for some support from Craig or Serge.

"Fries?" Craig held out his container to me.

"That's all you have to say?"

He looked over at Serge, then back to me. "Fries and ketchup?"

"You were one of the guys who bought tickets to the sideshow back in the day, weren't you?" I took some of his fries.

Craig leaned in. "Enjoy this, Mags. As time goes on and your psychic destiny takes more and more of your focus, these are the things you'll look back on and wish you could relive." He sat back. "That's ten millenniums talking, trust me."

"I'll take the hockey theory to Nancy." I said. "In the meantime, any other theories?"

"The only thing I can think of," said Craig, "was that he was in the wrong place at the wrong time."

"Okay, but he was killed in the forest. How is that the wrong place or wrong time—it's not like he was off'd by a bear." Bruce flicked a look at me.

"No." I held up my hand. "Don't say it—"

"Unless it was a Boston Bruin."

We laughed.

"I shouldn't joke," said Bruce. "I bet Kent was there meeting somebody. Maybe he was seeing someone on the DL. But Maggie, you were in the wrong place at the wrong time, and we know it was no bear or NHL'er who tried to take you out."

I helped myself to some of Nell's poutine. "What could possibly have—oh!" I slapped the food back down. "I'm such an idiot! I bet I know why he was killed!"

CHAPTER TWENTY-THREE

A rapid banging started, followed by the unmistakable voice of Nell, demanding to be let in.

"Answer it," said Serge, "before she takes the door off its hinges."

"You really got to put an emergency key somewhere," said Nell when I opened the door. She barged inside and shucked her boots. "It's cold waiting for you to take your time to answer a doorbell."

"You mean the point-zero-five seconds you waited before taking matters into your hands and trying to break down the door."

"I'm just saying, it wouldn't kill you to move faster." She stopped, sniffed the air like Buddha scenting raw burger. "Nancy here? Did she cook?"

"I made scrambled eggs."

"OMG! You can't cook! You're not going to eat it, though, are you? That's salmonella!"

"Calm down. Serge supervised."

"Oh." She tossed her coat on the banister and headed up the stairs. "In that case, can I have some?"

She jogged into the kitchen and grabbed three plates from the cupboard.

"Two," I said. "Serge can't eat."

She blushed. "Right." Her phone beeped and she blushed harder and giggled.

"Thank you for not sharing," I said to Serge.

"How's Kent doing?" Nell set the plates on the table while I brought the toast and eggs. "Did you find him and check on your theory?"

"Not really. Saying he's 'not doing good' sounds like the world's worst understatement," said Serge. "Every time I try to ask him about that night, he closes his eyes and covers his face."

Nell took a piece of toast, bit into it and slowly chewed. "It's not always like this, is it? The way people die and move on. Most times it's...nice, right?"

I shrugged. "No idea. I get the confused dead. Craig's the better one to ask."

She reached over and took my hand. "It's a crap life you lead, lady, but there's a silver lining."

"What's that?"

"I'll never leave your side."

"That seems more like a storm warning than a silver—ouch!"

"Back to Kent." Nell went back to eating her toast and eggs. "Wow. This is actually good."

"Peppers, mushroom, tomatoes, green onions, some parsley, basil—"

"I'm not asking for the recipe," said Nell. "I'm complimenting you on not turning the eggs into a toxic hazard. Now what do we do about Kent? Does Nancy have any information?"

"Not yet," said Serge. "They're sending in a team to check the location of the fire and see if there's anything they can find in the way of drugs but I'm sure that's why they set fire to the land in the first place. To destroy whatever they were growing."

"You really think that's why he was killed?" Nell asked.

"It's the only thing that makes any kind of sense." I pulled a piece of toast to me. "Nancy said the city cops have been calling her about grow-ops on Crown land, Kent jogs all the time and all over the town. Maybe he stumbled on the crop and whoever's responsible for it saw him, killed him, then burned the crops to get rid of evidence. Maybe he was exactly what he thought: a guy in the wrong place at the wrong time." My mouth twisted as I considered my theory. "Maybe I'm wrong."

"It's a good a guess as any," said Serge. "At least until we can get Kent to talk."

"Then? What happens next?" Nell paused, fork midway to her mouth.

I shrugged. "I don't know."

The fork clattered to the plate. "You don't know?"

"I'm not a cop. I figure Nancy will talk to the police about gang activity or whatever groups grow drugs in this area and they'll go from there."

She shot me an exasperated look.

"What? I transition souls for a living. Solving murders is something else—"

"Serge, where are you?" asked Nell.

"By the window."

She flailed her arm in his general direction. "You solved his, didn't you?"

"No. We knew who killed him. We just had to prove it."

"We don't have anything on Kent," said Serge. "And he still doesn't remember much of anything."

Nell glanced at the text. "That's not true."

"Yeah?" I leaned back in my chair. "What do we have?"

"He was killed over Thanksgiving, his body was dumped in the woods, the murder is tied to the laptop—"

"What about the doctor gossip. Stuff gets around a hospital," I said. "Did you hear anything?"

"I checked with my sources—"

"Your dad—"

"And he doesn't know any gossip about Kent."

Serge came to the table, pulled out a chair, and sat down. "Can he even tell you if the gossip was related to work or a patient? Isn't there something about doctor-patient confidentiality?"

"Yes," she said, "but there's also daddy-daughter trust and I don't break that." She gave me a wicked grin. "Except right now."

"Still..." Serge's freckles bunched together with his frown.

"I have my ways." She gave us a smug smile and helped herself to more eggs.

"By which you mean you whine and beg until he's finally gives in."

"If it works for two-year-olds, then it's good enough for me. Besides, this town only has seven doctors. It's more like a club than a profession in Dead Falls. Dad asked around. No one knows anything. Kent was a good guy and everyone liked him."

"Did your dad know anything about Mrs. Meagher and her medication?"

Nell shook her head. "I'm starting to think she's self-medicating."

"That doesn't sound right. She said 'they're adjusting my dosage.'"

"She wouldn't be the first person to speak about herself in the third person plural," said Nell. "Try it with me, 'we are not amused.'"

"That's it." I took her plate. "No more eggs for you."

"We are not amused." She yanked the plate back.

"Funny." I sat down.

"The pill container she uses to hold the Abriule is an old container," said Serge. "The label is from a billion years ago and it was a prescription to treat strep throat."

"I'm going to say it again, she's self-medicating. If a doctor had really prescribed those meds, they would have come in a proper container. But if they're being kept in an old bottle, maybe she's buying them off the internet."

"Kent paid all the bills," I said. "So much so, that Mrs. Meagher didn't even know he was dead because the automatic payments kept going through. Which means she never goes online to check her bank account. Which probably means she doesn't go online to check any bills. Does that sound like someone with enough tech-savvy to go online and order anything?"

"I suppose not," Nell sighed. Her phone beeped. "Hold that thought." She turned her phone so I could see the screen. "We have a problem."

I took the cell, read the text, and rounded on Serge. "What did you do!"

"That wasn't me," he said, after he'd read the text and stepped back from the phone. "Whatever weird stuff happened last night with the Ouija board, Tammy, and Bruce, that's on them."

I read the text again. **He visited. And he's not happy.** "Text Tammy back." I handed Nell the phone. "Ask her what she means."

She did, and we hovered over the phone, waiting for the responding bing. When it came, our heads pressed together as we read. **Too weird to text.**

"They have to come over and use the Ouija board," said Nell.

"You want me dead? I'm already in enough trouble. Can you imagine what Dad will do to me if he finds out I was playing with an Ouija board?"

"You have to do something," said Nell. "They're messing with forces they don't understand. Who knows what they'll call forth."

"Nothing," I said. "They'll call forth nothing because they're not supernatural."

She pointed to the text. "And yet something came through."

Good point. There was only one thing to do. "Okay, but no Ouija boards." I texted Craig, then hit the send button.

"It was so weird." Tammy started talking as soon as she and Bruce came through the front door. "After we hung out last night, Bruce and I thought we'd try to talk to Kent. Let him know that we may have figured out who murdered him. We took out the board"—She kicked off her shoes and tossed her coat to the side —"and started calling on Serge."

"Wait. You're contacting Kent by calling Serge? What am I missing?"

"More like what screws are they missing," muttered Nell.

Tammy wrapped her arms around me and gave me a hug scented with citrus perfume. "Serge has been dead longer. We thought he could work as a go between."

"That's nice," said Serge. "They gave me a job in the afterlife. Gopher."

Nell read his text and snorted. "Ghostpher."

He laughed.

"We started calling him and suddenly, the board started to shake and rattle," said Tammy. She started up the steps.

"But no roll?" asked Serge.

I gave him a questioning glance.

He rolled his eyes. "Come on. Doesn't anyone listen to Elvis anymore?"

Bruce took off his outer gear and shook the snow from his hair with his fingers. He gave me a hug, then sped up the stairs after Tammy.

I closed the front door, gave myself a quick shake to ward off the cold from the outside and followed them to where they stood by Nell and Craig.

"Like really shake and rattle," said Tammy. "I thought he was trying to come out from the board."

Serge looked at me and lifted his hands in surrender. "I swear to God that wasn't me."

"You should have been there," Bruce said to me. "You're such a death magnet—ow!" He rubbed the back of his head and gave Nell a one-eyed glare.

"Manners."

"I just meant she found Serge dead and now she found Kent dead—" He pedalled backward as she came at him, hand raised. "I'll shut up, now."

Tammy gave me another hug. "Are you sure you're okay? That must have been totally horrible. Landing on a decomposing body—"

"I'm not averse to hitting a girl, either," said Nell. "Leave Kent out of this and get back to Serge. What happened?"

Excitement lit Tammy's eyes. "It was crazy. Like being in an earthquake."

"Wow," I murmured. "Sorry I missed it."

"Don't be sorry." She dropped her bag at her feet and knelt down. "Look what I brought." Tammy brought out the Ouija box with the flourish of a magician performing a trick. "We're going to try again."

Oh, boy.

CHAPTER TWENTY-FOUR

"I thought I told you not to bring that," said Nell.

Bruce waved her down. "Face your fear. A guy's life—afterlife is on the line. Two of their lives. The more help they have, the better."

"I'm not comfortable with this," I said, backing as far away as I could.

"Me either," added Craig as he joined me.

Serge stumbled back to where we stood.

Nell wiggled her fingers. "I think my Ouija hand has got some kind of repetitive stress injury."

"Fine. If you guys are scared, just say so and we won't do anything," said Tammy.

"I'm scared," I said.

"Terrified."

"Consider me petrified."

"Cowards," scoffed Bruce. "It's not that bad."

Oh, yeah. A ferrier, a ghost, and a transitioner of the dead, all hovering around a board that called the dead. What could *possibly* go wrong?

In the background, the radio clicked on.

Serge went still.

Craig's gaze slid to where the radio sat on the counter.

They both looked at me as the static crackled to life.

"Maggie...oh Maggie..."

"You'll see, it'll be so cool." Tammy moved to the wood coffee table. She looked over her shoulder. "I think your radio's broken. Can't you hear the hiss?"

No, I was too busying hearing the boom of Dead Falls exploding from all hell breaking loose.

"Mags, I don't feel good," said Serge. His eyes squeezed shut and he shook his head like a dog. "There's a buzzing inside me."

Me too, Boo-Boo.

"I thought this Ouija stuff was just hocus-pocus."

To regular people, maybe. But you and me are as irregular as they get. I wasn't sure if this was us. None of us was playing with the Ouija, but maybe The Voice's presence was activating it.

"How bad can this get?"

Bad. I glanced over at the radio. *If The Voice doesn't shut up, we'll be drowning in souls.*

Or other things.

Craig's voice sounded in my head.

Serge's face went white. "What kind of things?"

Huh. So I hadn't been the only supernatural in the room to hear Craig's voice.

"Things like that ancient evil thing that attacked us last month?" Serge asked. "Or things like the opening of a portal to hell like last time?"

Maybe. Or there might be other stuff. Craig tossed us a calm smile. *It'll be a good time. Not sure if your house will survive, but we'll have fun.*

No, you'll have fun, I corrected him.

At least one of us will have fun. He grinned.

I hope if anything super bad comes through it ends me, 'cause if I put a dent in the walls, Dad'll kill me.

"Maggie, oh Maggie," The Voice wept. "He's coming for you."

Tammy came toward us, box in hand.

We have to be careful. Craig's ferrier form overlaid his human body. *There's no predicting what's going to come through.*

We backed up as Tammy closed the distance.

"Don't be a wuss—" Bruce cut short his words as the box began to shake.

"Wow, it's happening way faster than last time," said Tammy. "This is so cool!"

Said the girl who was about to start a demon apocalypse.

The lid flew off, hit the armrest and bounced to the ground. Tammy held to the box as tightly as she could, but the Ouija board was shaking hard enough to dislocate her shoulder.

"Hey guys, I've been knocking, didn't anyone hear? I'm sorry I've been so AWOL—whoa!" Kent hit the tops of the stairs, took in the scene. He ducked for cover as whatever controlled the box wrenched itself from Tammy's grip and hurled itself toward him. Kent rolled out of the way as the box slammed to a stop a few inches from his skull.

Everyone stared at the box as it rattled into stillness.

"What did I walk into?" asked Kent.

"A séance," said Serge.

"Something tells me this is the last place I should be." Kent stood, swayed. "Anybody else feeling a weird buzz in their body? My stomach feels like someone put a hot water bottle on it."

"You should leave now," I said.

"No, it wasn't so bad—" Tammy screamed as the pointer rocketed from the ground and clipped her as it sped toward the ceiling. The board shot up, opened itself and began to spin.

Nell launched herself toward the board, but it was as if it had sight, and it dodged out of her way. Spinning ever faster and with the help of its psychic controller it created a wind tunnel in the house. Cold as ice, it froze my throat with every breath I took.

My hair pulled free of its braid, lashed my face like a whip.

In the background, The Voice began to weep. Papers, dirt from plants whipped themselves into a funnel that began to pull us ever closer to the tunnel. The board glowed red and the hellish light shot to the ceiling, changed to a thick fog and poured down. The board flipped so we could see its printed side.

Letters shimmied, rearranged themselves into what looked like words but was of no language I knew. The surface of the board softened into something gel-like as the letters melted into a black goo and dripped to the floor. From underneath the surface of the board, a hand began to push through.

"Serge is trying to talk to us!" Bruce yelled to be heard above the wind. "Look at how fast the board's spinning."

"No, he's not," said Serge. "Because he's too busy trying not to throw up."

"I feel weird, too." Kent was on all fours. "We have to get rid of this thing!"

Craig crouched beside me. "First things. Get rid of Bruce and Tammy. They can't see what we're seeing, but that doesn't mean it can't hurt them."

"Tammy! Bruce!" I yelled. "Get out! Now!"

"No way!" Bruce crawled my way. "We're not going to leave you alone to deal with this!"

Oh, for crying out loud. Why do guys always pick the stupidest times to be heroic?

"I'm staying, too."

I could barely hear Tammy over The Voice crying my name.

She and Bruce crept toward me as my brain spun to think of a way to get rid of them, save the ghosts, and not destroy Dad's house. But the psychic energy from the Ouija board wasn't just affecting Serge and Kent. It was doing funky stuff to me, too. It felt like someone was stuffing my ears with wet cotton balls, shoving them into my brain. My tongue felt thick, my limbs heavy.

"Please," I begged Tammy and Bruce. "Get out!"

"We're in this together!"

A figure loomed behind Tammy and Bruce. It bent close, hit them each at the back of their heads. They went down.

"Learned that in self-defense class," I heard Nell say. "I'll drag them somewhere safe. You guys take care of this."

I turned to the Ouija board. The hand was now a hand, wrist, forearm, and elbow, and more of it was coming through. But embedded in the palm of the hand were smaller hands, grasping, their movement and shape made them seem more like tiny mouths searching for something to tear into.

The fog, too, had taken shape. It had segmented itself into the body and legs of a centipede, the tail of a scorpion, and used the Ouija board as its head.

I didn't know where its sight came from, but it seemed focused on Kent and Serge. "Run for the back door!"

They ran for the door as the creature chased after them.

Craig shook his body like a dog shaking water from its fur. His skin fell off him like droplets as his ferrier form took over. Scales, glittering and dark, covered muscle and sinew. Horns grew from his forehead and his serpentine tail slithered to the ground. His eyes a glowing red, he gave me a sharp-toothed grin. "My turn to play," he rumbled and took off after the group.

I let the guys handle the thing from the other side and helped Nell carry Bruce. We tucked him under the kitchen table, then dragged Tammy to join him. As a parting effort to the cause, I pulled off my sweater—Dad's hoodie—and covered their faces.

"I'll stay here." Nell pulled the chairs around them like a fortress. "I'll knock them out again if they start coming to."

I rushed to the battleground. Snow and wind swirled, blinding me at the same time it froze the air in my chest.

Craig and the thing were locked in battle. He stood ten feet tall and almost as wide and had the centipede in hand-to-hand combat. The creature made a sound, like metal scraping against metal and shoved Craig backwards. Its scorpion tail reared back then honed in on Craig's chest.

He grabbed the trunk of the tail, twisted and rolled, and flipped the creature on its back.

It screamed and my ears pricked at what sounded like human speech. It screamed again and I heard...*mine, belong.* When it rounded on Serge and Kent, crawled towards them, I understood.

It was claiming the ghosts.

Serge jerked back, pushed Kent behind him.

The centipede scuttled to them.

I ran into the fray, the blood pounding in my ears, inoculating me against the ice cold and the fear.

"Maggie, no!" Serge raised his hand to me, in a stop motion.

A wall of air came at me, pushed me back and rolled me to the ground. "Serge!" I rocked to my feet, shaking my head against the sting of snow and wind, and focused on my soul brother.

He stood in between Kent and the creature.

Craig and I raced to them.

The centipede used its tongue like a lasso, whipped it out and lashed it around Serge's body.

His eyes rolled back, and froth poured from his mouth.

Maggie—

I tuned into Craig's voice.

Get ready.

I was close enough to see the whites of Serge's eyes. I grabbed for the creature, retched as I realized its consistency wasn't cloud or fog, but mucus. Its flesh was like quicksand, latched itself to my flesh and began to suck me in. The burning of my skin at contact was nothing compared to *what* it was.

"Maggie!" yelled Craig. "On the count of three, grab Serge and shove him back as hard as you can!"

I nodded, the nausea and the visions too overwhelming for me to do anything else. Bracing my feet and weight on the ground, I tried to pull my hands free of the slime, but it held fast.

Kent ran forward, slipped on the snow as he reached out to grab me.

"No!" I dodged out of his way. "You can't touch me!"

"One!" Craig yelled.

"I have to do something!" Kent looked around. Grabbed a stick from the ground and tried to crowbar it in between me and the creature. He jerked back as the thing sucked the wood into itself.

Serge convulsed.

I pulled harder but it only held tighter.

"Maybe that's why I'm here," screamed Kent. "To save you!"

"No!" There was no time to explain to him why he couldn't get near it. "Stay away!"

"Two!" Craig put his hands—claws—together. As he pulled them apart, a ball of yellow-orange light emanated from his palms.

Screaming in frustration and fear, I yanked and tugged.

The thing only sucked harder.

"Three!"

My hands held immobile, I did the only thing I could. I jerked to my feet and used my shoulder like a battering ram to shove Serge back.

Kent grabbed me around the waist, tackled me into Serge.

There was disgusting sucking noise as Serge twisted free of the thing.

The light from Craig's hands slammed into the creature.

At the edge of my consciousness

—a blinding flash of light

—Serge screaming

—Kent howling

—my skin burning

—sudden silence

—unending black

CHAPTER TWENTY-FIVE

It hurt to blink. It hurt more to breath.

"Maggie, take it easy."

Dad, his tone overly calm.

I tried to talk. And instantly regretted that move.

"No, stay still until Craig's done."

Heat, the kind I imagined on tropical islands—warm, moist, and soothing—travelled from my toes to my head and enveloped me in the scent of jasmine and coconuts. It seeped into my body, quieted the searing hurt in my lungs and throat. When the heat evaporated, I opened my eyes and smiled at Craig. "Thanks, Doc."

Dad helped me to sit up.

Kent leaned against the doorjamb.

"Nancy's cleaning up downstairs," said Dad. His tone remained calm, which meant he was super pissed. "And now that I know you'll live, I'm going to go and help her."

"Was it really bad?" I asked.

"We no longer have windows in the living room. Which is great, considering how cold and snowy it is outside. If you can find a way to predict lottery numbers that would go a long way to helping with the heating bill and repair costs."

"I'll do my best."

"In the meantime, I'm telling the neighbours you had a party that got out of hand." Dad gave me a small smile. "You've been such a good kid, anyway, about time we started giving you a bad girl rep."

"A party in the middle of the day. That is pretty bad girl."

"When I'm done helping Nancy, I'm coming back and we're going to have a nice, long, talk. By which I mean I'll talk and you'll listen." He cupped my chin. "Good?"

"Good."

He gave my forehead a kiss. "Nancy talked Nell's dad into giving us some samples of Tylenol Three for your pain." He pointed at the small packet on my table. "Take as directed. I'm sure Craig fixed everything, but it won't hurt to be extra sure." He left the room.

"He was calm," said Craig. "You're in so much trouble, aren't you?"

"The worst. I'm going to be grounded for life." But I'd worry about that later. "Where's Serge and Ne—?"

Kent pointed behind me.

Serge lay in the bed, his complexion sallow, and a thin sheen of sweat on his skin.

Nell sat beside him, holding his hand.

I blinked.

"Craig turned him solid so I could see him," said Nell. "I had to make sure he was okay."

"You look like death warmed over," I told Serge.

He gave me a weak laugh. "The thing, it liked me because of my past life. Craig fixed me. I just feel shaky and weak."

"I don't understand," I said. "The visions I got from the—" I looked over at Craig. "What do we call it?"

He frowned. "Like 'George' or 'Lester?'"

"Are you purposely being a smartass?"

He grinned. "I do what I can to lighten the mood. It's known by many names. Legion, for one, but that describes any band of souls that group together. We call them The Family."

"The Family?" Nell repeated.

"They're souls that were separated from their bodies violently. In some cases, their bodies have never been found. The Family are the souls that haven't been able to move on or find peace. They're the forever missing. No burials. No solutions to who killed them. In their individual forms, they can become poltergeists. But when they group together," said Craig, "they form a legion we call The Family."

"Shouldn't it be trapped in hell?" asked Nell.

"They've never crossed over, they've never been claimed." I thought back about what it was like to touch and connect with their energy.

"They're like a wind, blowing in the limbo between this world and the next—" I caught myself and stopped talking.

"—blowing and looking for other people who have died they way they did. But we know who killed Serge and why. And we found Kent's body, so he's not a forever missing." Nell's grip on Serge's hand tightened. "So why did it try to claim both of you?"

"It wasn't trying for Serge, it was trying for me," said Kent, "but Serge saved me. If he hadn't pushed me out of the way…I would've been lost, too." He shook his head. "I'm so sorry. I think I called it to your house, Maggie. I've been so screwed up over my death and my mom on those stupid pills—"

"You can take one of those off your list," said Nell. "My dad talked to her and they decided to take her off them. So no accidental overdose. No hospitalizations to fear for your mom."

"When did that happen?" asked Kent.

"Yesterday," she said. "I would've told you but you haven't been around."

"But I'm still around, now." His shoulder bowed. "If she was reason I was lingering, I should be gone, then. But I'm not. I'm not here to save anyone, am I? I'm here because I can't let go of my death."

I nodded.

"Then it *was* me who called The Family. They must have been tracking me or something because—"

"This isn't all on you," I told him. "That was an Ouija board and three supernatural beings in one place at one time when it was activated, and you walked into it. The Family was always coming." That wasn't exactly true, but I didn't want to pile on him. "It just lucked out because you were here."

"Still." Kent looked ready to throw up. "If that thing had touched me, I would've been sucked in." He stood, wobbled on his feet. "I feel nauseous. Can ghosts puke?"

"The bathroom's over there." I pointed at the door.

He gave a sickly nod and walked over on shaky feet.

"You're not going to tell him?" asked Serge.

I shook my head.

"Good. He's dealing with enough crap."

Nell held up her phone. "You guys lost me. What's really going on?"

"I didn't lie," I said. "Supernaturals like me and Craig should never be around Ouija boards, but The Family came because of Kent, it honed on his energy." I paused, debated how much to tell Nell about their rage and hatred, about their lust for revenge. "Serge knew who killed him, but Kent has no idea who's responsible for his death. He's an overachiever and now he's overachieving at being angry."

"Okay," Nell said, "I get it. You can't tell the guy who lived his life according to *do no harm* that he almost killed people because he couldn't deal with his emotions."

"The Family isn't just about finding killers," said Craig. "They're vigilantes. It's why they can't transition, why they get angrier and more dangerous with every soul they ingest."

"That doesn't explain Casper," said Nell. "Look at him. If Kent was their dinner, then Serge was an appetizer. We got justice for you... what are you not telling us?"

Serge didn't speak immediately. Then he said, "I'm not as over my death as I thought." He struggled to sit up but Nell pushed him back down. "Sometimes, I still think of it...think of all the things I'll never get to do and I get mad. My life was taken from me, so was my life's destiny. I was supposed to become a really good guy. Instead, I died a jerk." He took a deep breath. "I know I'm lucky. I have a resolution of sorts and I get a do-over because of my link with you, Mags, but sometimes...sometimes, I wish for revenge."

"It's normal," said Craig. "And it'll pass, if you let it."

I pulled the sleeve of my shirt over my hand and used it as a rag to wipe the sweat from Serge's brow. "I'm sorry, Boo-Boo."

"I thought...I thought this afterlife would be a new chance, a way to start over and erase my past and those feelings, but Craig said—"

"The actions we take in life follow us in death, and follow us into the next lifetime."

"I made some pretty crap decisions in life," said Serge.

"You will always have to guard against giving into the darkness."

Craig put his hand on the ghost's shoulder. "But then again, we *all* have to guard against the darkness."

"Thanks for saying *all*," said Serge. "But we know I'll have to be more watchful than anyone else." His gaze flicked to the bathroom door. "The Family didn't even try for Captain Canuk once they latched on to me. I guess I haven't become as good as guy as I thought."

"Yes you have. And the only reason he's okay is because you saved him," I said. Wait a second. We were two people down on the saving score. "How are Tammy and Bruce?"

"As far as they know, the board flew through the air and knocked them out," said Craig. "I moved them so they didn't wake up under the table but on the couch."

"I told them you bonked your head and were sleeping," said Nell. "And then I got them out and told them to stay quiet."

"Which they will," said Craig, "but what happened didn't turn them off. They want to do it again."

"They're super excited about the whole thing," Nell said. "We're one creaking door away from them pitching us to some network as the next reality series: Dead Falls, come for the small town atmosphere, stay for the poltergeists."

Great, just great. They weren't going to back off. Another thing for me to worry about. Actually two things. One: their safety. Two: them finding out about my secret.

Craig stood. "You're both okay and I need to go. I think I caught all of the energy of The Family and sent it back to limbo, but I need check and make sure it's all back there. Even if one soul escaped my net, it remains a danger. It can call its brothers and sisters back to it, or find new co-hosts."

I thought of the vandalism and graffiti going around town. "How dangerous is it if it's here? Are we going to see petty crimes become something more?"

"It's weak because it's alone, and as long as it doesn't find a host, we'll be fine."

"What kind of hosts does it like?" asked Nell. "Blond, cute girls with a lot of sass or—?"

"You'll be fine. But Serge, you and Kent need to be careful until I find it. The soul won't be strong enough to do anything but whisper in your ear. But if you start having thoughts that don't seem natural, let me know."

"Define natural," said Serge. "I still think about revenge and what I lost."

"There'll be an...*element* to it. It won't just be *I wish I were still alive*. There'll be a push for you to do something more than think about it. You'll feel the urge to go out and do something, to get the bad guy. Since we got your bad guy, that should be your first clue. If it latches in, you'll feel it in your stomach, like worms crawling around."

Serge raised his hand. "Okay, just asking. It's my first stab at potentially being demonically possessed. I want to make sure I know the symptoms."

"Trust me," said Craig as he stood and headed for the door. "You'll know. We'll all know."

I pulled him into the hallway. "You said Nell would be fine," I kept my voice low. "But you didn't say anything about the rest of the living."

"Normally, The Family isn't a threat to the living. They target lost and angry souls, but the more spirits in their collective, the more powerful they can be. And if they ingest a strong soul, that also makes them more powerful. Get enough strength together and they can whisper to the living and latch into them that way..."

"Point taken."

"Nell really will be okay," said Craig. "If I was one of the legion, I'd be too afraid to mess with her."

I laughed, kissed him, and went back to the room.

Kent came out of the bathroom, shoulders hunched, his hand on his stomach.

I wanted to talk to him about the fire and the drugs, but he looked like it was taking all his strength to stay upright.

"You look like crap," said Serge. "You okay?"

"That thing...I feel like I've got the stomach flu."

"Me too," said Serge.

"Yeah," I nodded. "It's the run-off of all the stuff that just happened. It'll pass." I stood and went to him. "Nothing else?"

"Nausea, heavy limbs, lightheaded. Why? Should I be feeling other stuff?"

"No." I took in his pale face, held his clammy hands in mine. "Craig gave us the rundown on what it'll look like if The Family comes for you. I want to make sure you're okay—"

"What are the symptoms?" he asked.

"Voices in your head. Feeling like there's something crawling in your body."

My words managed to make him look even sicker. "God, please," he said. "Help me figure out how to cross over. Please don't let that happen to me."

"We won't," I said.

"You want to lie down or something?" asked Serge. "You really do look like crap."

"I want to go home. Can someone give me a ride? I need to check in with my folks," said Kent. "I want to really be with my parents. Maybe they'll feel—" His eyes filled with tears. "Isn't this stupid?" He swiped them away. "I lived my whole life with the goal of being an adult, not needing my mom. And now, I feel sick and scared and I wish—" He choked back a sob. "I wish she was here to hug me and tell me everything was going to be okay."

"Everything will be okay," Nell said. "I need to head out, anyway. I'll drop you home."

Kent nodded. "I'll wait by the front door." He shuffled out.

"We need to transition Kent," said Serge, once Kent was gone. "The longer he's on this side—"

"The more likely he is to become one of those wandering souls," I finished.

Nell sighed and squeezed Serge's hand. "I hate to think of Kent suffering in death."

It was more than that. In life, Kent had been driven. Motivated. Organized. If he went poltergeist or hooked up with The Family, I didn't even want to think about the damage he could do to both the living and the dead. I gave Nell a hug goodbye, then sat with Serge and tried to figure out how to solve Kent's murder and get him to move on before The Family claimed his soul.

CHAPTER TWENTY-SIX

I spent the next day at home and Nell played hooky and hung out with me. Around three o'clock, she got up from the kitchen table. "Come on, we're going to be late."

"Late for what?" I asked.

"Do you not read your texts? Or listen to Harriet or—"

"The fact I'm asking, 'late for what,' should be your answer."

Nell rolled her eyes. "There's a town meeting about the vandalism and the murders."

"Wait. *Now?*"

She nodded.

I stood and turned to Serge. "You coming?"

"Definitely," said Serge.

I texted Dad and Nancy to let them know where I was going—and that Nell the Enforcer was with me. Then we headed out to the meeting.

"Whoa, this place is packed." Nell's gaze swept the gym.

Town hall hadn't been large enough to contain the crowd, so the meeting was moved to the school. The bleachers were full, so people lined the walls or sat in chairs by the podium.

My cell binged. Technically, Dad's cell. He'd leant me his until the weekend, when we'd go and buy a second-hand one for me. With the way I shorted them out, he'd said there was no point in buying me anything new.

I took it out and read the text. "Dad says he and Nancy are on the north side of the bleachers, which means they're…" I opened my compass app.

"Stop before you hurt yourself, Johnson," said Nell. "They're over there. Is Craig coming?"

"No." I pushed through the crowd. "He's still looking for The Family."

We found them and Nancy hugged me then pulled away. "I wanted to bring popcorn. Your dad wouldn't let me."

"You know she'll throw it," said Dad. "And when law enforcement goes rogue, what hope is there for the rest of us?"

"This is the kind of stuff that creates relationship baggage," said Nancy. "You're restricting me as an individual."

"Ignore her." Dad gave me a hug. "She's been grumpy all day because of the city police."

"Still?" I asked.

She snorted and shook her head. "Getting a straight answer from those people—"

"Let's go for a walk." Dad took her hand. "Outside, in case your head explodes. Maggie, text Nancy when the meeting starts."

"Don't," said Nancy. "Council made a last minute decision to have me head the meeting, which is politician speak for *let's get the sheriff to take all the heat.*"

Dad pulled her away. "Let's get you some air..."

I tracked them as they left and in the mass of humanity, I spotted Dr. Pierson, alone. "Do you think Rori's here?"

"No dice," said Nell. "Last I heard, Mrs. P was packing them up to leave town."

"Seriously?"

"A couple nights ago, I tried again to see Rori. I phoned but the whole thing was a hot mess. Mrs. P said I broke her trust. And that she and Rori need to concentrate on healing the family. Which is just crap. She's just mad because Rori would rather be with me." Her eyes misted. "It got worse from there. Mrs. P and the doc started screaming at each other. He was yelling that I should be able to come over, she was yelling about him being an absent father and husband." She took a long breath. "The worst was hearing Rori crying in the background, begging them to stop fighting...I may have said some things that I don't regret saying, but do regret the way I said it."

"Oh boy. I can imagine."

"Mrs. P got off the phone pretty quick." She winced. "She slammed the phone down on me."

"What are you going to do? Can your folks help?"

She snorted. "The adults are smart enough to stay away from a couple on the brink of a bitter divorce."

"But you on the other hand—"

"Am planning to stop by and see Rori tomorrow. Wanna come?"

"Wouldn't miss it."

The gym went suddenly quiet. I followed the direction of everyone's gaze and saw Principal Larry striding into the gym and toward the podium.

Nell groaned. "They're having him open the meeting? He's never going to give up that mic."

"I guess because the school's hosting the meeting. Anyway, that works out great for Nancy." I tuned out as he did the usual spiel of acknowledging the staff, students, and the townspeople.

Nell crowd-watched, then grabbed my hand pulled. "Isn't that Mr. and Mrs. Meagher?"

I followed the direction of her gaze. "Yeah, those are the Meaghers."

"Last month," Principal Larry said as the crowd collectively leaned forward. "We suffered a tragedy. Actually, we suffered many tragedies. But this school has now seen the loss of not just one but two of its students. Sergei Popov and Kent Meagher."

Ignoring the principal, going on my tiptoes, I scanned the area around the Meaghers for Kent. "But I don't see Kent..."

"Hey, guys."

"Hey, I was just looking for you." I swung around to face Kent. "Holy crap!" I pedalled back. Then forward. "Nell, quick. Stand here." I pointed to the spot directly behind the ghost.

"—Today, however, we focus on the graffiti and damage to public property"—The principal stumbled over his words —"and, of course, the tragic deaths of our young men."

Serge, his attention on the principal and not the drama unfolding to his left, snorted. "Yeah, cause he really cares about my murder."

"Serge." I tugged the sleeve of his sweater. "Look alive."

Serge turned to see what was going on. "Damn! Kent, what the hell happened to you?"

The ghost turned his focus from me to Serge, then back again. "What are you talking about?"

I dropped my voice so only my friends could hear me. "Something's wrong with your skin."

"It is?" He reached up, touched his face, and I tried to keep my food down. His flesh had gone opaque, not enough to reveal bone and muscle, but enough to make his blue veins stand out against his skin like a 3D rendering of a topographical map.

He pulled at his skin and it came off in one, long, thin, transparent layer. "Is that supposed to happen?" Pieces of it hung off his jaw and forehead.

I shook my head.

"What's going on?" asked Nell. "I can see the conversation but not the action."

"You don't want to know," said Serge. "I better text Craig and get his opinion on this."

In the background, Principal Larry droned on.

My senses told me the crowd had lost interest. There was the shuffling of feet, the crinkle of candy wrappers opening, people looking around, glancing at their watches.

"How are you feeling? Does it hurt?" I asked Kent.

He shrugged. "I've been sleeping all day. When I got home, I was so bagged, I just crashed out in bed. I only woke up because Mom and Dad were fighting. I got up to get out of the house for a bit. When I realized they were coming here, I figured I'd come along."

Nell elbowed me. "What does he look like?"

"An albino snake shedding its skin."

"Has he eaten?" she asked. "Developed any taste for human flesh?"

"I'm not going ghost-zombie." Kent stepped away from her. "I can't even feel hunger."

Craig materialized beside me, looked at Kent, and swore.

"Yeah, so I'm hearing," said Kent. "But I don't feel bad—"

"That's bad," said the ferrier. "You've been infected. Didn't you feel it in your stomach? You should've called us—"

"I thought it was the flu—"

"I have to get you out of here—"

"Wait. Infected? With what?" Kent's face went even whiter. "Oh, God. The Family," he said. "It's in me."

"Which is why we have to get you out of here," said Craig. "There are too many people and too many of us with psychic energy to be in one spot—"

"How did it infect me without me knowing?" asked Kent. "Without you guys knowing?"

Craig, Serge and I made eye contact. We all knew the why and how, but now wasn't the time to talk about it.

"Let's get you somewhere safe," said Craig, "we'll talk about this later."

The mic screeched and put Principal Larry on pause. Another screech.

Crap. Too late.

Static hissed through the speakers, The Voice began to weep.

CHAPTER TWENTY-SEVEN

The lights flickered. Light. Dark. Light. Dark. Light. Around me, people murmured. No fear. Just confusion. A few of them pulled out their phones and started recording.

Through the strobe lighting, I tracked Craig, Serge, and Kent. Craig went into ferrier form, wrapped his wings around Craig and Serge, and disappeared. I pulled out my cell and texted Nancy and Dad an SOS.

Principal Larry waved his hands. "If we could all stay—"

The gym plunged into darkness and confusion gave way to fear.

"If we could all stay calm!" he yelled.

No one was listening. Least of all me. I sent the message, tucked the phone in my back pocket. Did a quick eye-contact vibe-thing with Nell, hoped she'd feel it in the pitch black. Going by my memory of where everyone had been before the lights went off, I grabbed her hand and moved us toward the exit.

Light from camera phones lit up the dark interior, bobbed and weaved like fireflies.

"People—"

The lights snapped back on.

"PLEASE!" The last part of the principal's command, caught by the now-powered mic, boomed in the gym and made the speakers screech.

There was awkward laughter, shuffling as folks found their seats.

"Now." Principal Larry adjusted his tie, craned his neck as he straightened his collar. "As I was saying—"

The lights brightened, dimmed. Throbbed.

"What are the odds this is a short-circuit?" Nell asked.

"What are the odds of you swearing an oath for a life of celibacy?"

"That bad, huh?"

"If we could all focus—"

Nell snorted at the principal's instructions, then turned back to watching the humming lights. "Is this Kent or Serge, or the two—"

"It's The Family. There must have been a leftover soul and it latched onto Kent."

"What about the worm—"

"He thought it was the flu. The rest of The Family honed in on them."

"So get Kent out of here."

"That's been done," I said, "Serge too, as a precaution."

"Then why the freaky light show?"

I kept pushing through the crowd, moving for the exit. "Craig said time and space aren't the same on the other side. Maybe there's a delay in communication and The Family still thinks Kent's here."

"Great," she muttered. "You'd think with that many souls, they'd have a better honing device."

"The Voice is here, too."

"Doubly great."

The principal stepped back from the mic, powered it down, and shut off the speaker.

A second later, the microphone surged to life with a squeal and static poured through the speaker.

Maggie, oh, Maggie.

The crowd went silent. They couldn't hear The Voice, but they could see the light show. There was no sound, save the pulsating hum of the lights as they brightened and dimmed, no sound except the shallow, frightened breaths of those around me, no sound but the beating of my heart.

"Find Dad and Nancy," I told Nell. "Get the crowd out."

"*Maggie, oh, Maggie.*"

"Get them out, now."

The lights flared, bright and brighter still, and Nell moved into action. So did the rest of my family.

"People," Nancy's voice boomed with authority and confidence. She strode to the front of the gym. "This section—" She swept her hand from the middle of the gym to the left. "Exit through the doors on your right. The rest of you, exit through the left doors. People in the front row, move out. Now!"

He's coming, Maggie. He's coming for you.

The crowd may have ignored the principal, but no one questioned Nancy. As though they had practised the exit drill before, people turned to their respective sides, waited for those in front of them to leave the bleachers.

"Maggie. He's coming for you—"

"Faster, people!" Nancy glanced up at the lights.

I didn't know what the wattage of the bulbs was, but the gym was five times brighter than normal and the luminosity was increasing. As was the heat. I wiped the sweat from my eyes, thankful as Dad directed one group through one exit, Nell the other, and Nancy supervised.

"Maggie, oh, Maggie. He's coming, Maggie. He's coming for you—"

I fought off the panic, pushed forward to the doors.

"Let's go! Let's go! Let's go!" Nancy spun her hand like a windmill. "Pretend your PVRs are broken!"

The Voice screamed.

The lights exploded and the gym plunged into darkness.

There was a moment of shocked silence, punctuated by sudden screaming. Mothers and fathers cried out their children's names. In the distance, I heard a faint buzzing. The static pull of my hair on my arms and the back of my neck told me what was coming.

The legion came through the ceiling in a red cloud. It wasn't just its shape that was different this time, though I found the cloud way creepier than the centipede. There was something about it...the specks of gold highlighted by its internal lightning that said this was a bad development, that somehow The Family had evolved and morphed into something that could affect the living. But whether that was knowledge from a previous life or instinct, I didn't know. And right now, I had other things to focus on than its evolution. The legion's evil energy lit up the gym in a crimson glow. Moving one way then the other, it tried to hone on Serge and Kent.

When it couldn't find them, it spread out, thin and rectangular and rained itself on the remaining people in the gym.

Oh, crap.

They coughed, blinked as the specks of the souls was absorbed into their bodies and turned their flesh luminescent.

I moved in the direction of the fire exit and used the demonic light cast by the infected to see if anyone I cared about was still around. Nancy was still here, directing people to stay calm and exit in an orderly fashion. Dad and Nell were at separate entrances, making sure everyone got out safely.

Craig, Kent, and Serge were gone and that meant any of the specks of the legion hitchhiking in people's bodies wouldn't be able to find them. Which meant I could turn my attention back to the fog. Getting it to pool together into one mass.

And deal with it.

Only, I hadn't a clue how to handle it.

Think. Think. Think.

I had a cell phone. Somehow, I didn't think I'd be able to scare the fog with my overage charge or monthly fees.

Think, Maggie, think! Your boyfriend and best friend are off, protecting a soul from evil from hell and you're standing around like a moron.

I glanced at the panicked crowd.

The frenzied crowd.

Bodies pushed against bodies as they turned from fighting for the exit to fighting with each other. The Family's infection made them more violent and angry.

The Vancouver riots were going to be nothing compared to the injuries and assaults if these people didn't get into open space, soon.

C'mon, c'mon. I didn't want to be one of those stupid girls who needed to be rescued all the time. But I couldn't think of how to save them.

Craig had said once that my destiny was to be a guardian, a watcher of worlds. I wasn't even doing a passable job watching over a crowd. How was I going to solve this?

Evil versus good.

Craig had cleansed me with heat.

Setting fire to the gym was probably out of the question.
Plus it wasn't just heat, it had been good heat. Clean energy.
And that told me exactly how to save them.

CHAPTER TWENTY-EIGHT

I called Serge to me.

"I thought you didn't want me near this," he said when he appeared.

"I know, it's risky but the fog is infecting the living. I think we have a way to save the people."

"Okay. What do you want?"

"Give me a hug."

Serge's jaw went slack. "You're kidding."

"No. Hug me."

"Isn't this the wrong time for a comforting—?"

"Serge! When you and I hugged that time, we gave off energy, remember?"

"Okay." He dragged out the word like he was wondering if I'd suffered some kind of head injury.

"The Family is using their collective energy to become more than they are and to evolve into something that can influence the crowd."

"I noticed."

"So why can't we do the same? You and I put off energy once when we hugged and it was powerful enough for Dad to see—"

"Oh, yeah! Okay, come on. Hold me tight." He stepped close to me, pulled me into his arms, and hugged me hard.

Which felt nice but I could still hear the crowd wailing and pounding on each other.

"This doesn't seem to be working," he said into my hair.

"No, it doesn't."

"Should I hug harder?" He suited action to words.

And I was in line to break my ribs. "I can't breathe."

"Oops, sorry." He loosened his grip and stepped back. "What are we doing wrong?"

"I don't know. It was the morning after you exploded—"

"Please don't tell me I have to explode again—"

"No—"

"Thank God."

"But..." I closed my eyes, thought hard and fast. "The morning after, we had a talk. That's when I forgave you for all the horrible stuff you'd done and you forgave yourself—"

"Yeah."

"We glowed. *That's* why there was an energy between us. Because of the emotion behind the action," I said.

"Oh. Oh! Okay, so if I remember how I felt that day and then, when we hug, it should work?"

"Something like that."

He stepped close.

I wrapped my arms around his waist and pulled in close. Inhaled the freshly fallen rain scent of him. "I'd spent so much time being mad at you. Then all of a sudden, I saw what your life must have really been like, and I felt so bad. So bad for you that you'd lived it. So bad for me that I hadn't been smart enough to see what was really going on—"

"That wasn't on you, Mags, that was on me. I should've been strong enough to get help. Should've reported what was going on. I thought for sure my death meant an eternity in hell, then all of a sudden to get that second chance, and to have it start with your forgiveness—"

He was crying and so was I.

"You're everything to me, Mags."

"You too, Serge."

We held each other tight and I felt the heat, the light. It started where our heartbeats connected and spread out. Still holding him, but opening my eyes, I watched as the white light rose like a beacon, expanded and washed over the crowd. It passed through them, outlined their forms in a golden yellow, then faded to dark.

Nell picked me up at the parking lot. I climbed into an interior warmed by both the vent and the cup of Tin Shack coffee-hot chocolate sitting in the cup holder reserved for me.

"Should we really be doing this?" I asked. "I just defeated an ancient evil less than an hour ago."

"Calm down. You didn't defeat an ancient evil. You delayed a bunch of loser ghosts."

"Thanks. So nice to have you to put my life in perspective."

"Sorry," she sighed and took my hand. "I can't stand silently by with Rori, anymore."

I laughed. "Nell, you weren't standing silently by before. And if you're going to get vocal now, then I'm super afraid for the Piersons."

"You should be. They should be, too. How stupid are adults?" Nell scowled at the steering wheel as she pulled out of the lot.

"Is that a trick question?" I belted in and freed the cup from its holder. "Because if you're asking it seriously, we may be here awhile."

"Huh. Ain't that the truth. Mom and Dad say to stay out of it, but there's a kid involved. How do you not step in?" She put the car in gear and eased onto the slippery road.

"I don't think they're worried about you stepping in, as much as they're worried about *what* you're stepping into."

"It's a kid, Maggie. That should be the beginning, middle, and end of the story."

"I don't disagree—but are you sure *you're* the one that needs to do something?"

"I have to. No one else is listening."

I frowned. "That doesn't sound right. Your folks—"

She laughed. "They're good people, Mags, but I'm not tight with them the way you are with your dad." She gave me a quick glance then turned back to the road. "You guys have a special relationship. He looks at you like you're an equal"—She shrugged—"for the most part, at least. My parents look at me like they're stunned I no longer need diapers. I've tried to talk to them but I'm getting a lot of pats on the head and 'there, there, dear.'"

I took the hard set of her mouth and jaw. "—But there has to be a better way than storming in and…what exactly are we doing?"

"Going to the Piersons."

"Yeah, I know. But what's your grand plan after we get there."

"Channel The Family and bring some Old Testament justice on their—"

"That's not funny." I glanced around, as though the legion could be called by us speaking its name. "Don't even joke about it."

She took her foot off the accelerator and sighed. "I don't know what I want to do, other that get Rori away from them. Even for one night."

"Maybe Nancy can step in and—"

"I talked to her but she said if she stepped in and pulled Rori out—even for a night—it could have detrimental consequences because Rori would be flagged in the system. Plus, she's not in a dangerous situation. There's no reason for them to take her out of her home."

"You were asking Nancy to step in as town sheriff?"

"I thought some law and order might serve to smarten them up. And if that failed, Nancy could give them that look she gets when people are wearing on her patience—you've seen that look—"

"I have nightmares about that look."

"—exactly. But she said no."

"Maybe to stepping in as a cop, but we both know Nancy, no way is she letting Rori suffer through in silence." I squeezed Nell's shoulder. "And I know your mom and dad. They'll do something."

"But when?" she cried. "When are they going to step in for this kid?" She pulled the car to the shoulder and put it in park. Her hand gripped the top of the wheel and she bowed her head over the steering column as though she was about to offer up a prayer. "I see what's going on, I hear them fighting and Rori crying, and I lie awake at night, thinking about how much pain he must be in, how scared and terrified he must be, and all I can think of is, 'I've got to do something. I've got to help before it's too late.'"

I let silence speak for a little while. Then I unbuckled my belt, scooted as close to her as I could, given the console, and rubbed her back. "You said 'he.' This isn't just about Rori, is it?"

Crying, her forehead on the wheel, she shook her head. "I think about Serge all the time." Her words were muffled but audible. "All the abuse and beatings, and I feel so *bad,* so horrible." She lifted her head and looked at me, the tears formed a wet layer on her cheeks. "He's such a good guy, Maggie. He's such a *nice* guy. And he's been so sweet to you and protective." The tears overtook her and she struggled to get the words out. "I was horrible to him in life. Rude and mean and cutting. And when I think of all the times I was so proud of myself for taking him out at the knees, all the joy I got when his face flushed with embarrassment or shame—"

A light glowed from the back and Serge appeared in the middle seat. "Hey, Mags, were you calling, 'cause—"

Don't text anything.

His eyes locked on Nell. *What's going—? Why's she crying?*

I'm sorry. I was connecting with what she said and it must have acted like a beacon and brought you here.

His eyebrows pulled together. *What's she talking—*

"Every time I think about Rori crying, I see him, and I feel like such a bad person," Nell said.

"You're not." I rubbed in between her shoulder blades. "You're not."

Serge scooted forward, his face etched in worry.

"There's so much guilt I carry," she continued. "And no matter what I do, I feel like I can't get rid of it."

"You shouldn't feel guilty—"

"Of course I should! We all should! He was talking to us every day about what was going on at home—"

Is this about Kent? asked Serge. *Did she find out something bad?*

"—and none of us was listening because we couldn't understand his language."

"Nell—"

"It was violent and brutal." She reached out, grabbed my hand in an awkward, painful grip. "But what else could it have been? What other language did Serge know except one that was violent and brutal?"

From the corner of my eye, I saw Serge's face go slack with surprise.

She's crying over me? Crying for me?

"It was a hard life he led," I told her, "and I feel the guilt—we all feel the guilt. But life isn't about making the right decisions. It's about being right with the decisions you make. Did the town step wrong with Serge? Yes. Did Serge step wrong with the town? Double yes."

"I know." She took a shuddering breath. "Intellectually, I know all of that but my heart…it just *hurts*."

Serge reached through the middle space, put his hand on her shoulder. "Mine too. And it hurts every day—"

Nell went still. "Is he here?"

I nodded. "You feel him?"

"Yeah." She wiped her eyes with the back of her hand. "Where are you, Casper?"

Her phone beeped and she turned toward the back of the car. "I don't think I ever told you I was sorry." The tears came again. "But I am and I wish I could've done it differently—"

"Me too."

"—that I could have a do-over."

He laughed softly. "You do. We both do. Right now."

Nell read the text and her face crumpled. "But I want a do-over from the beginning. So I could be a good friend and step in for you and—"

"That time is done," he said. "It's not good for either of us to hold on to the mistakes of the past."

"Easy to say."

"I know," he said. "And harder to do. But I'm in a really good place now and I'm happier in death than I ever was in real life."

"Come on, Nell," I said. "Let's switch places and I'll drive. You and Serge can talk, okay?"

She jerked her head in a nod and climbed out of the car.

I took her place, seat-belted in, and as she opened the passenger door, I said, "We'll do a drive by of the Pierson house. Make sure everything's okay. Maybe Rori will be outside or by the window and you can talk to her."

Nell gave me a watery smile. "Thanks, Maggie. You're my best friend."

"I know, and if that isn't a sure sign you need therapy, I don't know what it."

She laughed, then went quiet as her cell binged with a text.

Serge went quiet on my end and texted his words privately to Nell.

I left the two of them alone, though I caught the gist of the conversation when one of them would laugh softly or make a small sound of sympathy or connection. A couple of blocks away from the Pierson home, I frowned, slowed the car, and did a quick check of the skyline.

The night was cold and the wind speed was stiff but it didn't explain how fast the clouds seemed to roll overhead. And it was dark enough that I shouldn't be able to *see* any clouds. I gave a quick thought to asking Serge to comment, then dismissed it. He and Nell needed to talk.

I kept driving but as I closed the distance to the house, I had to stop. It was like someone in the Great Upstairs had turned their fan on high. The clouds raced across the dark sky, their undersides occasionally lit up as though contained lightning flashed within them. I stopped the car and watched as the sky went from black to dark violet.

After a second, Nell looked up. She tracked my gaze and peered out the windshield. "What's going on?"

"You don't see the sky?"

"Whoa," said Serge. "I do." He wriggled forward so the three of us were in a line. "That can't be good, can it?"

"I don't see anything," said Nell.

I described what was going on.

Hurriedly, she shoved her phone in her pocket. "Mags, it's Rori. It has to be. We need to get there, now!"

"I know—I just—give me a second because I don't know what we're walking into."

"Last time it was a portal to hell," said Serge.

Nell jerked out her phone and read the text. "This little girl is living in hell. C'mon."

"I'm going." I put the car into gear. "Text Craig. Just in case something's here."

Serge stared out the window. "Do you think it's The Family?"

I shook my head. "We're about to find out." I pressed on the accelerator and hoped whatever was going on at that house, we weren't too late to stop it.

CHAPTER TWENTY-NINE

I pulled to a stop in front of the house, climbed out, and took it in.

Whatever "it" was.

The clouds over the Pierson home continued to streak across the dark kaleidoscope sky. But they would suddenly freeze, the sky would reset to the beginning, and the weirdness would start again.

Serge slowly climbed out of the car. "What the—?" He glanced at the sky that bordered the neighbours. "Everything's fine with them. That's so…bizarre."

That was one word for it. The house was a black silhouette, with occasional bright, white light that beamed from the windows, then disappeared.

"It's like there's a lighthouse inside their house," said Serge. "This is what my house looked like when everything went down."

And that meant, big, bad things were on the inside.

"Okay," said Nell. "Lighthouses talk to ships. What is the house talking to?"

Nothing I wanted to meet.

The air crackled, then crackled again. Static electricity hummed along my skin. "Nell, get inside the car."

"What about you?"

"I'm getting in, too! Hurry up!" I wrenched open the door, dove inside, and slammed it shut.

Nell and Serge did the same.

I turned over the key, again, and again, on the third time, I realized I couldn't hear the engine start because it was already running. Not bothering with my seat belt, I tossed the car in reverse and slammed on the accelerator.

The crackling grew louder as did the rising throb of thunder.

Just as I spun the wheel to turn the car around, there was a loud *crash*, an ear-splitting *crack* of thunder. Then a giant fork of lightning split the sky and exploded on the rooftop. Chunks of tile and stucco flew into the air as the house burst into flame.

"Maggie! Maggie!"

I jerked back, blinked, then did a combination freak-out and jerky chicken dance. "What the—! Where—" I panicked as hands reached out for me, fought against them, then stopped when I realized they belonged to Nell.

"Geez, girl. Where did you go?"

I squeezed my eyes shut, then opened them and looked around. We were still in Nell's car. Only, I was in the passenger seat. "What just happened?"

"You told me to change spots with you, then you totally zoned out," she said.

"I—we didn't change spots?"

"No."

"I didn't drive to the Pierson home?"

"What part of 'no' are you not getting?"

I turned to Serge. "What about you? Did you see anything?"

"You drooling a little," he said. "But nothing to put on YouTube."

Okay, don't freak out. Just think. I rested my hand against my forehead. No fever. Okay, so no delusions based on illness. "I thought I'd changed spots with you, Nell. We drove to the Piersons and there was this weird sky and lightning. Then everything exploded and the house caught on fire."

Nell spun in her seat, jerked on her seat belt. She put the car in gear and rocketed onto the road. "What else did you see?"

"Nothing, just what I said. A weird sky, thunder, lightning, and a house on fire."

The scenery turned into a grey, blurry shadow as we sped through the night, racing for the Piersons. A few, tense moments later, we pulled up to the house.

The dark, quiet house.

"It's fine," she said, scanning the area. "Nothing's on fire." She turned to me. "Was it a vision or a premonition?"

"I hope neither. I have enough to deal with when it comes to the dead. I don't need to add prognosticating to my list of trials, too." I undid my seat belt and got out of the car. "This is too weird. I've got to take a look."

Serge and Nell came with me and we headed up the steps to the front door.

"That's wrong," Nell said. "They always have their porch light on."

"And their door locked, too, I bet." I pointed to the front entrance and the crack of space in between it and the jamb.

"I don't like this, Mags."

"Me neither. Call Nancy. Tell her what's going on. And tell her we're going inside to make sure everyone's okay." I stopped. "No, don't tell her the last part. Just tell her to come right away."

Nell started texting.

"Actually." I closed my fingers over hers. "Don't. Let's see what happens when we go inside."

"I think dead happens when we go inside."

"If we call them in, they'll tell us to stay outside."

"I'm already dead," said Serge, "and I think that staying outside is a good idea."

"Yeah, but I have to transition Kent. He and Dr. Pierson have history. This could all be related. Let's just look and then we'll bring in the grown-ups."

Serge sighed and nodded.

"Fine," said Nell. "But if I die with a hatchet to the head, you and I will have a long, long talk about my eternal disfigurement."

"Just a sec." I stepped back. "Serge, get Craig."

A couple seconds later, the ferrier appeared. "Kent's okay," he said. "I cleared the spirit from him and sent it back. He's home, freaked out, but okay."

"One problem solved." I gave him the two-second rundown on our next one.

He nodded. "Okay, got it. Did you call Nancy?"

"That's on our list of things to do after we check out the Piersons' house," said Nell.

Craig shot me a disapproving look. "You should really get in the professionals."

"That's what I did. I called you, the professional supernatural. We should move on this."

"Nell, text Nancy. Let me go first." Craig stepped in front, gently pushed open the door, and moved inside.

I followed, then Nell, and Serge. The interior of the house was cool, quiet, and dark.

"Should I turn on a light?" whispered Nell. "They never do in cop shows."

"That's because they're creating drama," I said. "Turn on the light. We need to see if the house has been tossed."

There was a click, a flash, then the interior lit up under the chandeliers and lamps. The house looked perfect.

"This doesn't make me feel better," said Serge.

"Me either. If there had been a mess, you could say it was robbers, get out and wait. But with the house being so tidy and the door left open..."

"You start thinking domestic violence," finished Craig.

I scanned the floors and ceilings. "I don't see any fog and everything looks fine."

"Maybe they went out and forgot to lock up?" suggested Serge.

"Unlikely," answered Nell. "They like their stuff too much."

Quickly, quietly, and not touching anything, we did a check of the upstairs, main floor, and basement. I rifled through Dr. Pierson's computer—just to see if there was some reason to explain their disappearance. A sudden trip to Mexico they'd forgotten about, a spontaneous drive to the outskirts to check out some meteor shower that NASA had emailed him about. But the only emails in his inboxes and archives were friends, work, and shipping notices from factories.

Nothing was out of place. Mrs. Pierson's purse was on the kitchen counter, the doctor's bag in the living room. There was no sign of the family.

"There's only one place left," said Craig. "The garage."

I took a breath and followed him to where Nell directed. The four of us looked at each other, then Nell nodded, and gripped my hand.

Craig opened the door, turned on the lights...

There was a brief second of relief when I didn't see three bodies in one of the cars. No murder-suicide by carbon monoxide poisoning. But the relief was short-lived.

"One of the cars is missing," said Nell.

I ran back to the kitchen, searched through Mrs. Pierson's purse and the doctor's bag. "Both their wallets are here," I said as the group joined me. The family was missing and wherever they'd gone, the adults hadn't taken any cash or credit cards. There seemed to be only one explanation, one that ended with three coffins and a dead six-year-old.

"I'm trying really hard to think of reasons not to ground you for the rest of your life."

I gulped at Dad's words, then gulped again at the death glare he was shooting my way. "In my defense—"

His eyebrow went up and I shut up.

"I don't care how super your supernatural boyfriend is or how kick-butt Nell can be or even that Serge can do weird magic voo-doo with people's hearts." Dad leaned forward, rested his hands on the kitchen table. "If you ever, *ever* walk into a house that may have a murderer or burglar, you will never see the sun again. You get me?"

I put my hands up in a surrender gesture. "Not that I'm arguing or playing chicken with how serious you are about grounding me, but this isn't the first time I've had to walk into a murderer's den..."

The skin around his lips whitened.

"...and it probably won't be the last." I rolled the dice and took a step toward him. "Maybe I should've waited for Nancy but we were worried about Rori and—"

"This is dangerous stuff. It's my job to protect you, Maggie. Even from yourself. Especially from yourself."

"You protect me with everything else." I took another step. "Trust me that I know how to deal with this."

"Maggie—"

Another step, then the hard truth of my life that we rarely acknowledged. "There's nothing you can do," I said. "When it comes to the otherworldly weirdness, there's no way for you to protect me."

He didn't say anything, only looked away.

I stepped back and went to my room.

"What's the damage?" Serge asked as I came into the bedroom.

"I think I crushed my dad's soul a little."

He frowned. "Shouldn't it be the other way around?"

"You'd think, but my reminding him he can't protect me from this part of my life trumped his threats for grounding."

"Yeah, I guess it would." Serge sat up and muted the TV. "So, what's our next move?"

"Stay out of Dad's way with this."

"But keep connected about it with Nancy?"

"That's about it." I looked at my watch. "It's been an hour, think they have any information on what happened to the family?"

"I'm sure they've solved both cases and are at the Tin Shack celebrating with some poutine and hot chocolate."

"Sarcasm isn't becoming on a ghost."

"Impatience isn't becoming on a guardian."

"I know," I sighed. "But something just feels off about everything, y'know?"

"I know. I thought we would've solved Kent's murder by now. But we're no further along than before. He's dead. He's been dead for weeks." Serge ticked the facts off on his fingers. "He died in Dead Falls. And there we have all the facts we know for sure. Did he know his attacker? Who knows—probably, because someone came in to his dorm and moved all his stuff."

"Which kind of nixes the idea of a gang offing him."

"But we have no motive and no suspects."

"Except his dad," said Serge, "and I just can't see it."

"Me neither." I stood. "Come on, let's go for a drive."

"Think it'll help?"

"It can't hurt and besides, now I want poutine and hot chocolate."

I grabbed my gear—coat, wallet, boots—and headed downstairs. Dad wasn't around, so I dropped a note on the kitchen table, and put lots of hearts on it.

Serge and I headed out.

"Should we call Nell?" he asked. "See if she wants to come with?"

"Give it a shot but I bet she's probably grounded."

He did, but after a couple of minutes, when the phone stayed quiet, we figured she'd been separated from her cell. We drove in silence. The streetlights washed over the car as the steady hum of the tires sounded in the background.

"Do you feel bad for him?" Serge asked.

"Who him?"

"Kent."

My eyebrows pulled together. "Bad that he died so young?"

"Bad in general," said Serge. He pulled the harness of the seat belt away from his chest then let it fall gently back into position.

"I think you always feel bad for the lingering dead—at least, I do. The elderly or those at peace with dying, they just move on. There are no regrets. But those who linger. There's so much sadness and anger and confusion. It's a terrible way to exist."

"Well, I feel doubly bad for Kent," said Serge. "Look at what a waste he's been—"

"Ouch."

"This guy's life was tragic," said Serge. "Completely tragic."

"Double ouch. He was studying to be a doctor and save lives."

"No, he was wasting away. He ignored everything—friends, having a life, doing stupid things like vegging in front of the TV all day—all of it, so he could become a doctor. And for what? He's dead and he'll never be a doctor."

I waited.

"He's gone and no one really mourns for him, except his mom and dad. Folks feel bad and say it's a shame, but no one really cares."

"Okay...?"

"If I could go back in time, I'd have been a nicer person," said Serge. "I think life's about when you die, people actually miss you."

I had no idea where he was going with the conversation, but it seemed like a circuitous route. Figuring he needed more time to get his thoughts out, I hung a left and decided to circle the town, drive the highway for a bit, then come back to the Tin Shack. Hot chocolate and poutine could wait.

"I was an asshole to everyone—and granted, I had good reasons, I guess—but Kent, what's his excuse? He had parents who loved him, people who liked him well enough. But he never extended himself to anyone because he was too busy trying to make a name for himself. All I'm saying is that his textbooks won't mourn him. He must realize that. And it must suck to know you were so unbalanced, such a workaholic that you've left behind nothing for people to say about you, except, 'he was driven.'"

"Okay, but that's not his fault—"

"Yeah, but having no friends. That's his fault."

I cut a quick glance at him, then turned back to the empty road. "Are you talking about him or yourself?"

"I may be dead but I've made friends. You, Craig, Nell, your dad, Nancy, Ebony and Buddha. Can you say you know more about Kent now than you did when he was alive?"

"Not really, but he's not exactly in a talkative mood—"

"Exactly my point. He's as incapable of making friends now as he was in life." Serge's hands peddled the air. "It's just—" He sighed. "I don't know. I guess I'm not making sense. It just seems to be such a waste to have been so...obsessed with your future that you forgot about your present."

Something in his words made the hair on the back of my neck stand up. I took my foot off the accelerator.

"What?"

"He was obsessed with his future, wasn't he? Determined to get out of town, make a name for himself." I pulled the car onto the shoulder.

Now it was Serge's turn to give me the look like I was taking the switchback trail through logic and reasoning. "Okay."

"How far would he go for his future?"

"Can you give me another hint?"

"The money," I said. "We need to figure out where he was getting the money."

"He was getting it from Dr. Pierson."

"The thousand bucks a month from Dr. Pierson would barely have paid for his tuition and books. We need to corner Kent and make him talk."

Serge watched me for a minute. "I'm still lost. Explain the connection."

"Kent's totally responsible with money, right? Pays his mom's bills on time...and however he makes his money, he has enough to buy expensive clothes. Clothes, that when we asked him, he said was because of the women he was dating."

"Which was a lie," said Serge, "because he was gay. Is gay."

"Right. So where did the clothes come from?"

Serge's eyebrows pulled together. "A sugar daddy?" His frown deepened. "You don't think he and Dr. Pierson were—"

"Maybe, but I doubt it. Plus, we've still got this mysterious family Kent was working for in Edmonton. *Making deliveries.*"

"I hear the emphasis in your voice, but if they exist and he wasn't working as an escort, then what was he doing?"

"Think about it. What other illegal profession has deliveries?"

There was a beat of silence, then, "Drugs! I should've guessed..."

"We know Kent's getting money from Dr. Pierson and all of it is being hidden from his wife. But the big question—"

"Where was Dr. Pierson getting the money?" finished Serge. "And the answer is drugs, not the stock market."

"Right. He's not investing his money," I said. "There was nothing in his emails about trades or investment. There's no mail coming in. There no evidence to support him playing the stock market. But he's got tons of cash coming in, enough to pay for his family and Kent..."

"Hold on, hold on," said Serge. "Let me think. Dr. Pierson must have been dealing for a while, right? All those trips his wife mentioned. Business is good, then along come Kent, wonder-science kid."

"Dr. Pierson must have seen a chance to increase his profit by making a better drug."

"What was Kent hiding in his bedroom. ADHD research, right? But ADHD drugs are great stimulants. They're perfect for the overachiever who needs extra energy."

"And Kent's in med school, surrounded by overachievers."

"So Dr. Pierson was using him as a mule," said Serge. "No, wait, more than a mule. The research."

"That field that burned. I wonder if that's where they'd set up the lab. It was private and out of the way…"

"Makes sense. Dr. Pierson supplies the building and the raw materials. Kent plays mad scientist and sells the drugs. Then they split the money."

"It's a great scheme," I said. "Till it all goes wrong."

"But what went wrong?"

"Nancy said the city police had been calling her. Something about kids OD'ing."

"Kent's all about saving the world," said Serge. "He's selling the drugs, telling himself it helps students to do better at school. Then someone dies and he has to face reality that he's nothing more than a dealer."

"He wants to close the lab, but Dr. Pierson's lifestyle's been built on dealing. There's a fight and Kent's killed," I said. "More than a fight. Kent had a needle mark on him. Dr. Pierson wasn't going to let him walk. He couldn't. And now the good doctor's gone missing just at the moment we could've have confronted him with this," I said. I put the car back in drive, checked the road, then pulled out into traffic. "I still don't understand how that entire family could just disappear into the night. They couldn't have left town—not without their wallets."

"Unless they're running with cash. If your theory's right, then he'd have money."

I snorted. "If I'm right." I swung off the highway and back into town. There were too many questions, too many mysteries…too much of everything, except answers.

CHAPTER THIRTY

spent the next half-hour driving aimlessly. We were heading for the outskirts of town, on Garden Drive to loop back for the Tin Shack, when my headlights illuminated a figure in the distance. I slowed the car, squinted. "Who is that?"

"Someone drunk."

I went into the other lane—no need to hit the stranger if they wove onto the wrong side of the white line—then slowed to see who I was passing. "Dr. Pierson!" I slammed on the brakes.

If he heard me, he didn't acknowledge it. He kept weaving down the shoulder of the road. Streaks of dirt smeared his jacket and there were rips in his clothing.

I pulled ahead, then blocked his path with my car and kept the headlights on him. Getting out of the car, I called, "Dr. Pierson?"

He slowed, more because of the light than me.

"Text Nancy," I said to Serge. "Dr. Pierson."

"Be extra careful." Serge stepped out of the car. "His body—it's like a reverse negative."

I walked towards him. "Sir? Are you okay?"

He turned his unfocused gaze to me. Blinked then blinked again. "Maggie?"

"Yes, sir. Is everything okay?"

He looked down at his dirt-caked hands.

So did I. "Sir." I stopped walking. Took a step back, then another. "Sir, where's your family? Where are Mrs. Pierson and Rori?"

He began to cry.

Oh, man.

"Sir? Your family?"

He shook his head.

Serge, get ready to zap him.

"Already there." He took a position behind the doctor.

"Dr. Pierson. Where is your family?"

"I don't know," he sobbed. "I don't know. It's all gone. They're all gone."

"Did you—" Okay, wait. Don't ask him if he's killed his family. Ask something else. "What do you mean?"

He lurched toward me. "Rori—" He grabbed and held me by the shoulders. The smell of fire came off him. "She's gone."

"What do you mean?"

"Missing! She took off, again! Loni's driving around and I started walking, looking for anywhere she may be."

"And you ended up here? Rori couldn't have walked this far."

He wiped the snot and tears from his face. "I don't know how far she's gone—"

The smell of copper and sweat came off his pores and I noticed a dull stain of red on his forearms. He knew exactly where his wife and child had gone and chances were, they were at least three feet under the ground.

"Help me—help me find them. I can't lose Rori. And Loni—" His face went ashen. "She has to stay with me."

I tried to tug myself free but he only tightened his grip. "Why don't we call the police?" Big mistake. He tightened his hold on me hard enough to cut off blood circulation.

"Again? And have her taken away by child services? I have to find her."

"Dr. Pierson, you're hurting me!"

"Should I do something? I can grab his heart," said Serge, moving toward him.

Only if you can use the electricity like a Taser. If not, then don't do anything. Maybe Mrs. Pierson and Rori are still alive. We have to play along until the cavalry comes. "Dr. Pierson. Which direction did your wife go? Maybe we should go in the opposite direction to look for Rori."

But he wasn't Dr. Pierson anymore. He was a wild, primal thing, and what he would do if threatened was anyone's guess.

He shook me. "Help me! You have to help me find her!" His breath was rank with fear.

"Okay! Okay!" I saw headlights in the distance. Nancy or one of her deputies.

"Who is that?" He twisted me around, held me tight as his narrowed gaze stared into the horizon.

The driver behind the wheel lit up the police lights and removed any doubt.

"Was this you?" He flung his forearm around my neck.

Dr. Pierson was too big for me to flip but I knew what to do. As his arm came around my neck, I gripped him on either side of his elbow, ducked my chin and tucked it into the small pocket of space I'd created. That gave me enough breathing room, not much, but enough.

I lifted my foot and brought it down hard on the top of his foot. He howled in pain, let go, and I started running for the car.

Behind me, Dr. Pierson grunted then gave chase.

"I'm sorry, Mags," said Serge.

There was another howl, sharp and thin, then the thump of Dr. Pierson as he went down.

I turned, looked.

He was curled into a ball, screaming and holding his knee.

"I figure electricity is electricity," panted Serge. "If it could stop his heart, surely it could work on a less lethal body part."

If it hadn't been for witnesses, I would've given him a high-five. "Good work," I said as the patrol car pulled onto the shoulder.

Frank stepped out of the vehicle and I stepped away.

"He says he didn't kill them," Nancy said an hour later, as she handed me a cup of tea and pushed the plate of store cookies my way.

"Jails seem full of people who say they didn't kill anyone. Him, Doug Meagher." I wrapped my hands around the warm mug and blew a cloud of steam toward the cabinet.

"I can't speak for Dr. Pierson, but Doug was telling the truth."

"What about Dr. Pierson's story about Mrs. Pierson going to look for Rori? Can you track her car's GPS?"

"It's not as simple as that. If she had committed a violent crime, sure. But as a missing person, no, the police just can't ask dealerships and GPS services to pull up private information on their subscribers."

"Too bad," I sighed. "That would have made it a lot easier."

"It's Dead Falls, so all's not lost. I've put the word out. If someone sees her car, they'll phone in."

"Dr. Pierson said something weird earlier, just before Frank pulled up."

"Just one weird thing?" Nancy asked, a wry smile on her lips.

"About his wife. He said they had to stay together, that she couldn't leave him."

"That's not unusual for men like Pierson."

"But to say it like that—"

"The idea that someone is your possession is what lets them justify anything they do in order to keep that possession."

"But did Dr. Pierson ever strike you as that kind of guy? The one who always had to know where his wife was at all times?"

"No," she sighed. "They did everything to stay away from each other."

"Exactly. And..." I scooted closer to her chair. "I may have done some digging around before calling you to their house today."

She dipped her chin.

I scooted back. Took another look at her face. Scooted back some more. "Now, in my defense—"

"Talk fast and justify later, kid."

"I went through his emails. He doesn't have any mail from his brokerage company."

Whatever she was expecting me to say, it wasn't that, because the thunderous look rolled from her face and confusion took its place.

"Dad has mutual funds and those guys are always sending snail mail and email. I know Dr. Pierson is supposed to be doing all the stock stuff himself, but don't you think it's weird that there's no research or materials in his house?"

"You know the worst thing about you?" said Nancy. "You have a terrible way of mitigating the punishment you deserve by being so perceptive."

"Does that mean there's a chocolate cake in my future?"

"Your distant future and don't push it, kid."

"If he literally can't divorce her because of the money, then maybe that's why he's so freaked out. Not because he killed her but because if she gets Rori and files for divorce, the lawyers will start looking into his finances…"

"I hear you."

Since she was listening, I gave her a quick rundown on our theory about Kent, Dr. Pierson, and the drugs.

She stared off into the distance. "He travels a lot. Says it's for work but who knows who he's working for…" A focused light came into her eyes. "I'm going to get Frank to start tracking the last six months of Pierson's activities. See if there's anything we can connect." She pulled out her cell and started texting. "We can start with his vehicle, call up the history of the last few places he went. I'm going to have them recheck the pictures on Kent's computer. How much you want to bet they were steganography?"

She finished her text, sent it off with a whoosh, then set down the phone. "Thanks for the help, kid. I'll put in a good word for you with your dad."

"Put in a few. Try to include the words, please, don't, ground, and her."

She chuckled and waved me to the door.

I headed to the exit, then turned back. "Hey, when will the lab tests come in?"

"What lab tests."

"For Dr. Pierson's hands."

Her face went blank. "His hands?"

"The blood on his hands."

She cut a quick glance to the other deputy in the office—who was now watching me with keen interest—then stood and came to me. "Wow, kid, you sure you're not in shock?" When she got closer, Nancy put her hand around my shoulders and spun me to the exit. "There was no blood on his hands," she said in a low voice. "Whatever you saw was otherworldly." She squeezed my shoulder. "And if what you saw was right, you better go and let Nell know that she's not going to be babysitting Rori, anymore."

"Large double-double, please," I told the cashier on the other side of the Tim Hortons drive-through.

"You think a coffee going's to help her?" asked Serge from the passenger seat.

"Nothing's going to help Nell," I said, "but at least it will give her something warm to hold on to." I'd debated not telling her right away, to give her a good night of sleep—a final night of rest—before I told her about my suspicions regarding Dr. Pierson and his family. But Nell would've killed me for doing that. Spare no pain. Tell the truth.

I pulled the car ahead, paid the cashier and took the drink.

"We should give her a head's up."

"And what should we text?" I pulled out of the drive-through lane and headed onto the main road. "Hey Nell, got some news about Rori. Be there in ten? She'll see through it right away."

"I know," he sighed, "but this is going to hit her hard. I wish I could be there."

I reached over and took his hand. "You're doing the right thing. The whole point of us being a team is so we can divide and conquer. I'll tell Nell and—"

"—and I'll search for Rori and her mom." His gaze flicked toward the sky. "Did you text Craig?"

I nodded. "But he hasn't texted back."

"I haven't seen any ferriers flying overhead, which means no one came to get Rori and Mrs. Pierson, and now, they're the confused dead."

"If they're together—"

"It won't be so bad," I said, "but if they've been separated..."

"At least I had you." Serge ran his hands over his face. "I don't want to think about Rori, alone and confused."

Me either. "Dr. Pierson smelled of smoke. If he buried them, I bet it was around where the fire was."

"That seems risky. What if someone came by?"

"No one was going to come by. The fire came, went...the arson guys already took their samples...Dr. Pierson was smart. The ground's been disrupted and raked over. Who's going to notice anything if he adds two graves?"

"Hey!" Serge tapped me on the leg then pointed to the right. "Is that Craig or another ferrier?"

I twisted my head to follow the direction of Serge's finger. "That's Craig and he's heading to the fire site." I did a quick safety check for cars, then stepped on the accelerator.

A few minutes later, I pulled into the entranceway of the path. I put the car in park and climbed out, zipping my coat up as I went. "Can you see him?"

Serge shook his head.

We started down the trail, my feet leaving tracks in the shallow skiff of snow. There was a muffled thump of wings behind me, then, "Hey guys. What's going on?"

I pivoted to face Craig. "Whoa. What happened to you?"

He touched the bruise on his cheek. "I had a call in to retrieve an escaped soul from *Duat*—it's the place of judgment for the ancient Egyptians. One guy decided he didn't want to risk being eaten by Ammit, the devourer of souls. Based on the fight he put up with me, his heart is definitely heavier than a feather."

"Ancient Egyptians. Time really doesn't make sense on the other side, does it?"

"Time is a human concept," he said.

"You'd think you guys would have better security," said Serge.

"Not every soul wants to be claimed, and believe me, as you get higher in this existence, whatever skills you learn, the bad guys are equally educating themselves—"

"Does anyone feel weird?" Serge held up his hands and showed us his trembling fingers. "Because I feel—" He closed his eyes and swayed. "I feel something in my stomach." His eyes snapped open. "There's a buzzing and someone's whispering in my ear."

"The Family?" I swung to Craig. "I thought you got rid of all the souls."

"I did but they can still come back if there's one member on—"

Oh, crap. "Kent. He was infected."

Serge shook his head as if trying to clear the voice from his mind. "I thought you swept him clean."

"I did. I checked his energy levels—"

"But he can manipulate energy," I said. "He'd been working on it—"

"So he did the equivalent of hiding his pill under his tongue," said Craig. "He faked the energy I was looking for and hid his infection from me. No wonder I can't sense The Family. He must still be masking them."

Serge swore. "What did you say about the bad guys always learning and The Family being as smart as the souls they hold?"

"Great," I said, "We're tracking down a horde of angry ghosts with a genius IQ. This won't go horribly wrong."

CHAPTER THIRTY-ONE

Snow began to fall from the sky as Craig said, "We need a game plan. One that takes Kent into account."

"What do we know?" asked Serge. "Other than he's crazy smart and powerful."

"We know he joined them," I said. "On a deep level, he's sympathetic to what they do." I thought about what Craig had said in the beginning, about why Kent had slept for so long after his death. "He lost everything, including his identity. That's why he was vulnerable to their influence."

"Nothing like taking on the guy with nothing to lose," muttered Serge. "And we still have to find Mrs. Pierson and Rori's bodies."

"What about the Piersons?" Craig asked. "What did I miss?"

I told him about Dr. Pierson and ended with, "I think he might have buried his family here."

"When did all this happen?"

"Within the last couple of hours."

"Then he didn't do it. At least, he didn't kill his wife."

"How do you know? Did you see him?"

"No," said Craig. "I saw her. About fifteen minutes ago. She was looping make out hill in her SUV."

I took a breath of the icy night air. "So he was telling the truth about what happened tonight…and if both Dr. and Mrs. Pierson are looking in such remote areas, Rori must really be lost."

"God." Serge's voice was tight. "That kid's been outside for hours. In the snow. I'm texting Nancy, right now."

"This is so much worse than last time. Did you sense any ferriers?" I directed my question to Craig.

"Nothing," he said. "There's still time for her. I'm just not sure how much."

Serge swore. "We have to split up. Mags, leave me here and I'll walk the park's perimeter, then head back into town through the trails."

"You deal with them," said Craig, "I'll find Kent and The Family."

"Shouldn't Kent be my responsibility?" I asked. "He's my charge to transition over to the other side."

"Kent is your responsibility," he said. "I won't be able to do anything to help him. But you're not strong enough to tackle The Family, not without help. If you find them instead of the Piersons, call me. Don't do anything by yourself."

"Okay, deal. When you saw Mrs. Pierson at the hill, was she heading up or down it?" I asked Craig.

"Down, to Millers Ave."

"Okay, I'm going to loop past their home again—just in case." As I spoke, I texted Nell about Rori. "Then I'll head on McKenzie Way and check the north side of town."

Nell texted back, said she'd get everyone on it. Serge, Craig, and I broke up and headed out. I climbed in my car, headed south on Garden Drive and wished I could teleport to the Piersons' home.

The chances of Rori being anywhere near the house were slim, but I figured it had worked before, maybe it would work again. I slammed the accelerator to the floor and hoped I wasn't too late to save a life.

The closer I got to the house, the more it seemed I was looking at its reflection through a watery lens. Edges and lines of the structure seemed to ripple, the walls bent concave and then bloated out. The slow motion of the ripples combined with an eerie silence that made the scene far creepier than if I'd seen ghouls or demons rising from a fiery pit.

I parked the car, stepped out into a night devoid of cold or wind. The air wasn't still. It was immobile. There was no sound, no scent. Just...nothingness. I headed to the backyard, to Rori's playhouse. As I turned the corner, my gaze lit on the tree and I slowed to a stop. And blinked. Then blinked again.

The tree was in full summer bloom, thick with leaves that softly flowed with an invisible wind. But the tree was also covered in a blanket of snow. It encircled the base and rested on the branches. The playhouse itself had no snow but seemed to be in the full spotlight of a warm and orange-yellow sun.

These were the times I wished my mother had been around. Or that Dad had also possessed the dubious abilities we called my gift. I didn't know what the image meant. Was I looking at the psychic manifestation of Rori's love for her tree house? Or was it some kind of otherworldly message on where to find the little girl?

I moved closer to the tree and as I closed my distance, I noticed a figure standing in the shadows. "Kent?"

"Hi, Maggie."

He was calm. If Hollywood hadn't lied to me, then his peaceful demeanour could only be the precursor to big, bad things. "Hey." I gulped some air. "You okay?"

"Never better."

I pulled out my cell to text Craig.

"Don't bother," he said. "It's amazing what you can do when you're working with hundreds of other minds. Your cell won't work." He looked at me from the corner of his eyes. "Neither will trying to call Serge. We've created a dampening field."

Not that I didn't believe him, but just in case, I tried to call Serge and Craig to me. My mind felt fuzzy and heavy, like my brain was full of cotton balls.

"I told you, but it was good you tried. Speaks to your initiative."

Great. The possessed ghost was giving me an A for effort.

"Uh…" I crept closer. "Kent, remember how you were feeling sick earlier? Your skin was doing that weird snake thing?"

"A necessary process of the mixing of the souls."

So he knew he was playing host to the legion. "I think it's having a negative effect on you. How are you feeling?"

"You already asked me that."

"That was before I knew that you knew you were possessed."

He laughed. "I'm not possessed, Maggie. I'm body sharing. Soul networking. You'd think having hundreds of spirits in my body would be claustrophobic, but I've never felt more free, more myself."

"That's because they're influencing you."

"No one influences me."

I went for a hard punch. "That wasn't true in life. You've suddenly changed in death?"

He stiffened but still refused to look at me.

"Kent, you know these guys aren't good for you. You need to separate from them."

His back was to me as he stared up at the tree. "It's something else to see, isn't it?" Kent stepped closer to the tree. "Beautiful, isn't it?"

"The tree?"

He shifted, planting his feet shoulder-width apart, lifted his gaze to the treetop. "I always wondered what it would be like. To have a house like this."

"You wanted a play—"

"To have a life like this."

Oh.

"Never to worry about money. When the school planned extra activities like a day in Edmonton at the water park, to never wonder if my mom and dad could come up with the money to pay for it. What must it be like to walk down a mall and wonder *what* you'll buy, not *if you can* buy something?"

"I don't know," I said, trying to psychically call the guys and failing, again. I stared at the leaves of the tree. They rippled, but no puff of wind whispered on my skin. "Money's never really flowed in my house, either." I stretched my hand out into the shaft of sunlight. There was no warmth to it, no substance. I touched the snow. It was the same. Empty of feeling and sensation.

"It's not fair." His back was still to me. "I'll never know this life, not even vicariously. I'll never have kids to buy stuff for and play with. Never know what it'll be like to have a family or pay a mortgage." A hush settled between us. "I'll never know what it'll be like to have a spouse. To be married...Still, it was a beautiful dream I dreamed, wasn't it?"

I put his words together with what I was seeing. The summer images, the soft wind, the lush vegetation, those must be Kent's manifestation of his fantasies. Rori's reality was evidenced in the snow, the barren quiet. And the fact I saw both was probably because of my connection to both of them.

"Life is never like the fantasy," I said. "Reality always has it corrections."

"I'll never know. That doesn't seem fair, does it?"

"Nothing is fair, Kent."

He faced me.

I'd expected him to look grotesque. Maggots and peeling flesh. But he was beautiful. Hyper beautiful. Golden hair, crystal blue eyes. His skin seemed to glow. That got my danger radar pinging. He was being possessed by a legion of angry ghosts. No way should he be looking like he'd just walked off a photo shoot.

He cocked his head, gave me a condescending smile. "But things always work out for people like you, don't they?"

I bit back the response that sprang to my mouth, reminded myself that Kent was being influenced by an army of idiots, Rori was missing, and now wasn't the time to play a game of who'd had the crappier life. "Nothing is ever perfect. Look at Rori."

"She has everything."

"Is that what the tree tells you?"

"She's too young to understand the blessings of her life."

"Her parents fight all the time, they don't let her have any friends."

"So did mine and look how I turned out. The town wunderkind." He sounded amused. "She would've been fine."

"*Would've* been?"

He smiled.

"Kent, what did you do with her?"

"I did nothing. *We* freed her and she will be the justice for the father." He bent, took a handful of snow from the tree. "Had she grown, she would've understood the blessings of her life. Rich father. Rich mother. The snow would have faded from the tree."

"Her life wasn't blessed." I had a theory about Kent's appearance, the tree, and The Family, and decided to roll the dice on seeing if I was right. "But yours was." I said and hoped I'd survive what I was about to do. "You have a mother who did her best—"

"Don't talk about my mother." His voice changed, became a chorus rather than a single speaker.

"Why not?" I stepped close to the tree. "She has to live with your murder. Has to live with all the things she'll never see you do. Graduate med school. Date."

"That's not my fault."

"No." I took another step to the trunk. "But when she's up late at night and crying over all she's lost, and you're consoling her, whose hand will be on her shoulder? Yours or the legion's?"

"I know what you're driving at," he said, his voice back to normal, "but it's only because you don't understand them or the partnership between us."

"Partnership?" I laughed. "That's a nice word. Is that what they told you? Because you and The Family aren't anything alike. They hurt people, feed on wounded souls." I looked him from over my shoulder. "That's a nice, homey image. You, visiting your mom after you and the gang have unleashed violence on some unsuspecting person—"

"Don't say that!" The chorus was back. "We will find justice for victims!"

I shook my head. "No you won't." I addressed Kent. "You don't belong with them. They're lying to you."

"They're going to help me," he said.

"Like Dr. Pierson helped you?"

His face slackened.

"We know he's involved in your death and your life. That he wasn't a partner or a friend to you. Just like The Family isn't a partner of friend—"

"Don't say that!" His demigod appearance sputtered out. For a second, I saw The Family wriggling under his skin. They were small, thick, worm-like apparitions that scuttled along his cheekbones and jaw, wriggled over his forehead.

A psychic energy wave blasted from him, hit me like a solid thing, and slammed me into the tree. I did a mental check for broken bones before I rolled onto my hands and knees. "Is that the way they're going to help you? Like this? Hurting the people that care about you?"

"You don't care about me," he said bitterly. "If you really cared, you'd have figured out what happened to me sooner."

"I could've figured out a lot of things if you hadn't lied. You never had a girlfriend."

"I didn't lie." The golden god image was back. He held out his hand.

I ignored it, tried to call Serge and Craig, failed, and got to my feet.

"I just didn't think it was relevant."

"Like your after-school job with Dr. Pierson?"

The skin on his face tightened. "I didn't tell you about that because I thought you wouldn't help me if you knew what I'd done."

"It's not my place to judge you," I said. "It's my place to help you. Although, right now, I'm judging you." I made a show of limping to the tree and rested against the thick trunk. "Nancy has Dr. Pierson. It's just a matter of time before—"

"Before what? He blames me? Says it was my idea to make and sell drugs? That it was my fault those kids died? I'm the one who has all the formulas hidden on my computer, not him." His voice shook as he continued, "I was trying to help. He said I was helping. The drugs weren't party crap, they—"

"—they were ADHD drugs, tweaked so kids could stay up longer, study harder. That was your intention, wasn't it?"

He nodded. "It's so hard, med school. All the homework, the pressure. I thought I was prepared, that I could handle it."

"You were handling it."

"Not as well as I should've. The drugs helped. I told Dr. Pierson what I was doing. He convinced me to make more. Said we couldn't wait for funding and government permission, that kids like me needed help with school and work. I thought if I could help others…"

"Then a couple of them died."

"They shouldn't have," he said. "Not if they'd taken the meds like I told them."

"They were under pressure and struggling. They were always going to abuse the drugs."

"I wanted out but he wouldn't let me. That night, that's all I wanted, to stop." His face went to a shadow. "He killed me. Murdered me.

And you think he's suddenly going to confess? No. It's up to me to stop him."

"They're lying to you," I said. "The Family. Think it through, Kent. Be logical—"

"I am."

"You're not. Dr. Pierson had a high-end lifestyle before you were even born. There's no way he wasn't already selling drugs. You were just his first employee. If you stop and think, you'll see I'm right. And you'll see the cops have it handled. They're going to find the money trail and the drugs. I saw shipping notices in his house. If nothing else, they'll be able to track the supplies he ordered. Dr. Pierson may be smart," I said, "but Nancy's tenacious. And she always gets her criminal." I gave him a minute to digest what I said, then went for the kill shot. "I can't believe you're letting them manipulate you like this...for a smart guy, you're being awfully stupid."

The air crackled and popped. "I'm not stupid!" His voice morphed into the chorus. "We're not stupid!"

Bingo. Plan A, done.

He faced me and raised his hands.

Plan B, don't die.

CHAPTER THIRTY-TWO

An energy wave exploded from his hands and rocketed my way. I dived to the ground, let the fireball hit the tree. Sparks of ember ignited the bark as the trunk crackled and exploded into flame.

Kent howled in pain.

I ducked, rolled from the fire, and I called Serge to me.

Craig appeared, too.

"What's—whoa!" Serge took in the scene and turned his disbelieving gaze my way.

The wood cracked. Chunks of tree and branch flew into the air in jagged pieces and slung firebombs.

I jerked, reared up, slapped at my shoulders and back as my coat caught on fire.

Serge grabbed and hauled me down, and kicked snow at the flames. "What the hell's going on?"

I pointed at Kent, who looked like he was having some kind of seizure. His back arched then bowed, his arms jerked and his legs spasmed. Craig went to his ferrier form and circled him.

"Don't hurt him! Don't take him!" I rushed to Craig.

"They're dangerous," he said. "I have to take them back."

"But Kent is melded to them—he'll re-die at his lowest point."

"Maggie—"

"Please, Craig, he's my charge." I pointed to Serge. "He's our charge. Let us try to separate them."

"No, with this power and intelligence, and their ability to affect the living—"

"Let me try," I begged. "Please. I'm supposed to be a guardian and I know how to do it. I know how to save him."

"And a gatekeeper. You have to protect both worlds. We can't let this thing loose—"

"One try, just one."

His head cocked to the side. "They're telling me to give you the chance." His voice growled with frustration. "One chance, Maggie, then I take it down."

"They have him convinced he's some kind of psychic saviour. That's why he's helping them. He's always to be somebody." I struggled to my feet. "When I saw him, he was uber-gorgeous. Too good-looking to be housing evil spirits in his body." I motioned behind me. "And the tree. They've done something to it—made it part of his delusion. He's connected to it—I figured setting it on fire would hurt them. They created some kind of dampening field, that's why I couldn't call you to me. But it takes energy and resources. I figured if I could get them mad enough at me, at each other, I could break their focus, weaken the field. The madder they get, the weaker they get, the easier it'll be to separate Kent."

Craig came our way, ducking as the wind swept burning twigs in our direction. "Time's ticking. Do something or let me take them."

An explosion rocked the ground as the house caught on fire.

"Maggie. Serge."

We turned as Kent came our way.

He gave Craig a dismissive glance. "I don't think we need to call in the supernatural help, do we?"

"You will," he said to The Family, "but they don't." Turning to me, he continued, "One chance, that's it." He stepped back.

Flames and wind heated the air.

"There's one of him, two of us," said Serge. "I say we beat the crap out of him until they separate, then let Craig have some playtime."

I was up for that plan, too.

"See?" said Kent, his voice going to chorus. "It's good to work as a team." His body shivered, shook.

Then there were two of him.

Four of him.

"If this was a movie," said Serge, "right now, I'd make some smart comment about him needing more than four clones to takes us on."

"But this isn't a movie," I said, "And we're totally outnumbered. He knows where Rori is—I'm sure of it. Use his mom to take him out."

"His mom?"

"It was the only thing that seemed capable of separating their bond."

Serge smiled grimly. "I'm assuming we're not talking about a bunch of yo momma jokes."

"No, I mean anything that plays into his not being a good son." I went to the left, picked out the two Kents I'd deal with. "Ready?"

He nodded and we ran to confront the legion.

If this were a movie, this was where there'd be battle music—some kind of intense orchestral music with drums and violins. Maybe hard rock or even metal.

But it wasn't, and there was only the silence punctuated by my breathing as I ran to confront the legion.

My Kents stood, confident, and waited.

And I realized had I been *really* smart, I would never have run to them. I would have waited and let them come to me. After all, I was mortal. They weren't. Of the two of us, I needed to conserve my energy.

I put on the brakes and lurched to a stop four feet from them.

They smiled. "Second thoughts."

"I met you halfway," I panted. "Time for you to do your share."

"I can wait for you if you're tired."

This was officially turning into the worst battle scene ever.

I peeked at Serge who was doing a passable and enviable job of battling his Kents.

"What are we going to do?" I asked. "Battle it out with paper, rock, scissors?"

The Kents smiled. "Best out of three?"

They were playing me, but why? It took me a second to figure it out. "You can't fight me, can you?"

"I can do a lot of things," said Kent One.

"But not fight. There's too much for you to keep track of. Serge, the real Kent, the tree, Craig, your clones. I start throwing fists and something'll give."

He shrugged. "Try me."

It was a bluff and I called it. I closed the distance between us.

"Think carefully," said Kent Two. "We have the training of hundreds of souls. Karate. Judo. Boxing. It's the advantage of being a collective. Do you really want to grapple with us?"

I raised my hand as if to slap Kent Two.

He grabbed it.

I raised my other hand.

Kent One grabbed it.

As fast as I could, I brought my knees up, one at a time, and got them both in the crotch.

They let go, doubled over.

"I have the collective training of being a girl and knowing what happens to boy parts when you kick them."

The Kents grunted their rage.

I back-pedalled and as Kent One lifted his head, I closed my fist and swung hard.

Flesh connected with flesh and I heard the crunch of bone breaking, but I didn't know if it was his face or my hand that suffered the injury. Adrenaline thrummed through my body, dulling my pain, and I readied myself to hit him again.

Kent Two jumped, grabbed me around the waist and hauled me sideways. He imprisoned my arms with one of his. "Our turn," he said in my ear, his tone gleeful.

Kent One came at me.

I used Kent Two as a combination wall-springboard, jumped up, pushed all my weight into him and drove both feet into Kent One's chest.

We all went down.

I looked skyward, saw flashes of orange and red. A drive of my elbow into Kent Two's ribs freed me from his grasp. I rolled out of their way and stumbled to my feet.

Their faces flickered and the glowing light snuffed out. The worms were visible now.

"If that's how you want to play." They shivered and shook, but instead of splitting, they joined into one Kent.

Too fast for me to do anything, he grabbed me by the throat and slammed me to the ground. Kent pinned my arms to the snow and put his full weight on my chest.

"Suffocation is a funny thing," he said as he released his fingers from my neck. "It looks so violent on TV but it doesn't have to be." He smiled. "At least for me. It's simple, really. I'm heavier than you and my weight is slowly crushing your chest. You're not strong enough to breathe, to get in the necessary amount of oxygen. You're going to suffocate to death," he grinned, "and I'm going to sit and watch."

CHAPTER THIRTY-THREE

"Your mom will be so proud," I said. "Another death courtesy of her golden child."

The worms pulsed under his skin, stretched out his flesh.

"My mother will never know."

"Of course she will. If my dad doesn't tell her, Nancy will."

"I'll kill them right after I'm done with you."

"Craig will tell her."

He loomed over me, put his face close to mine. "She won't believe him."

"She will," I wheezed the words. "He knows things about you, things no one else does. Things about her that he couldn't know unless you told us. All those nights you visited her and came back to talk about it. All the searching we did for your killer. All the crying you did. He's going to tell her everything. And she'll know you slaughtered me, Nancy, and my dad. Then what?"

He grabbed my throat.

"She has no friends, no family. She'll be all alone in her grief. There'll be no one she can talk to about you. No one will want to listen to her mourning over a drug dealer."

His fingers tightened.

"What do you think she'll do with those meds, when she's all alone and hurting?"

"I'll watch over her, make sure she doesn't hurt herself."

"Think she'll want your guardianship? Think she'll even visit your grave? Her murdering son?"

"Stop it!" He shifted his weight, raised his hand to punch me.

It was all I needed. I rolled with his movement, spun out from under him. Scrambling, I planted my hands and feet in the snow, crawled away and clawed for air.

I didn't know where he was, didn't know what he was doing until I felt his foot make rib-cracking contact with my torso. He kicked me so hard I thought I was going to vomit.

"I tried to do right." He stood over me, grunted the words. "When Dr. Pierson came to the city with the shipment, I tried to end it, but he wouldn't let me."

"That was the fight Courtney saw. You told her you were fighting with your dad."

"He was like a father to me." Kent's voice went to the legion's chorus. "I trusted him with everything. He knew my life, my passwords. He murdered me then humiliated with the email to the registrar. He betrayed me. It's time to even the score."

"And you're going to make him pay with Rori?"

"He left a mother without her son. I'm leaving a father without a daughter. Fair is fair."

"But what about Rori? Think of her!"

"Sacrifices must be made for justice to win."

"And adding child-killer to your roster. Your mother will be so proud."

Grabbing me by the back of my head, clutching a fistful of my hair, he hissed, "At least I have a mother. You have nothing. Some whore your father knocked up who bailed the moment she pushed you out."

He brought his hand back to drive my head into the ground. I reached back and clawed his skin.

He grunted, let go.

I spun around, kicked out his legs as I rolled to my butt.

Kent went down, landed on his stomach, and I crawled on top of him. Hooked my legs around his waist as he struggled to get up, locked my arm around his throat, and squeezed.

"You *had* a mother." My voice didn't sound like mine, anymore. "She loved you, cared for you. And what did you do? You got yourself killed." I tightened my grip. "And turned her into a drug addict. Isn't that ironic? The boy savior destroys his mother's life"

He tried to claw himself free, but I had rage—and fear for Rori—on my side. "We both know it's not a coincidence that she went on the pills after the Thanksgiving weekend. What happened? When she found you that night, it was around the area you grew the drugs. Did Dr. Pierson see her? Did you tell him? Did you sic the man who murdered you on your mother, too?"

He gasped for air. When that didn't work, he threw himself back, slammed me to the ground. Tomorrow—if I lived through tonight—that was going to hurt. But tonight I was too focused on separating Kent to notice the pain.

"Did you tell him about your mom being in the park? Good old Doc Pierson. I bet she opened her door when he knocked. Her son's favourite role model. Of course she answered the door. Of course she listened and believed every word when he lied and told her you'd taken him into your confidence. That you were worried about her anxieties. I bet he's been the one feeding her those meds. Lovely little samples, just like the Tylenols Nell's dad gave me. No prescription to fill out, no records to keep. Just quietly dosing her until she's too stoned to worry about her missing son. You want to kill me? You're just going to murder your mother."

Kent went still. His hands fell to the sides and he started crying. His body wriggled, his skin bloated, and I heard the sound of flesh ripping.

I shoved him up, crawled out from under him.

His eyes rolled back in his head, froth poured from his mouth, as The Family ruptured his stomach and poured out of his body in a mass of worms.

The souls crawled away from the husk of Kent's body. I backed out of their way, preparing for another round, but they seemed more focused on regrouping with the others than dealing with me. When they'd gone, I crept to the skin.

"Kent?" I spun in a slow circle, checking out the worms to see if I recognized any. But the worms all looked the same, sickly pink, sparse hair covering, sightless, with gaping mouths. They slid along the snow.

Serge was dealing with one Kent and the worms headed to it, which meant the legion was trying to conserve energy. Good. We were gaining ground.

My team had their sections under control. Time for me to step up and find Kent. Which meant checking the skin tent. Pushing down the rising nausea, I moved toward it. The flesh had taken on the consistency of a deflated balloon. Wrinkled, stretched out.

"Kent, are you in there?" I got down on all fours, picked up a section of the flap in my thumb and forefinger, and lifted. And gagged. The smell coming out of the flesh bag was a combination farm fertilizer, boys' locker room, garbage, and decomposition. I dropped the flap and scuttled backwards.

The skin wriggled. A small bump, the size of a rodent, moved up from Kent's stomach to his head.

I got on my knees, ready to either deal with Kent or another one of the legion.

The rodent-thing pushed from under the skin and as it emerged, it turned into a full-sized Kent. He crawled on his hands and knees. "Maggie?"

"Yeah."

"I feel like crap."

"You should. You've been a Class-A jerkface."

"It's not my fault." He coughed, gagged, and vomited up a thick, green mass.

"You lied to me and now a little girl's missing."

"That wasn't me, I didn't want—"

"God, Kent, stop! Just stop! It's not your fault you decided to make and sell drugs, it's not your fault The Family inhabited you, it's not your fault they took Rori!" I jabbed my finger at the burning skeleton of the tree, now burning with a psychic fire of purple-black flames, tinged with white. "That's your fault. The only way you could have known about the snow on the bark is if you had a connection to her." I took a breath, trying to calm the rising hysteria. "You talk about betrayal, but what have you done to that little girl? You saved her life. Her dad called it a medical miracle but it wasn't. It was you. She hurt herself, you fixed it."

"I could see the brain injury," he said. "I could see how to fix it."

"How can you save her life only to take it from her? How could you violate her trust?"

"I didn't—"

"You did! You're nothing but a liar! The only way—the *only* way for you to have fixed her injury was through energy. You knew you were dead. You've *always* known you were dead. You lied to me the first moment we met, and you've been lying the whole time. No wonder The Family loves you! What did you do? You lied about going home or doing loops around the town, and you went to visit Rori. Practised your ability to manipulate energy. Rori couldn't hear Serge or see him clearly after her accident. But the only way you would know how she really felt about her family, the only way you'd see the snow on the tree was if you'd spent time with her."

"I just wanted to see her, to see if I'd done a good job. She woke up and when I realized she could see me…"

"You befriended her. But this—" I swept my hand at the destruction burning all around us. "This is how you repay her love for you?"

"I didn't mean to. I didn't even know The Family was inside me—"

"Liar—!"

"No!"

"Your skin was peeling, you were shedding. That could only happen if you had combined. You had to agree to the joining, which meant you believed whatever they were telling you…Is that why you left the house that night? Told us you had the flu, but really you wanted privacy for you and your new friends?"

"They offered me a place to belong! Told me I could get justice from Pierson."

"It's a lie, Kent! Rub your brain cells together—it's not justice to kill a child. That's revenge. Do what's right. Separate from them so Craig can come in."

He started to cry. "I can't. I can't."

"You have to! I can't help Rori until you do!"

He kept crying.

"Is this what you want? This is the legacy you leave your mother? Kent the Child Killer? Kent the Murderer of Little Girls?"

"No! No!"

I tried not to get angry. Reminded myself he'd been vulnerable and The Family had manipulated him. Reminded myself I had a part to play in this drama. I'd believed him, taken his words at face value and that made me responsible, too. "As long as The Family is in this plane, they can come after anyone they like—including Rori. Especially Rori. As long as you're linked with them, they can use your knowledge. They're linked to you and that means on a psychic level, they're linked to your mom. You don't think she won't dream of this, that on some level, she won't know?"

"Don't you understand! I *can't* separate! Once you join The Family, you can't get out."

The fires raged, throwing heat and flame, but I went ice-cold. "They have you?"

He sobbed, nodded.

"You can never transition and I can't help Rori. Not unless Craig destroys you."

"I didn't know—" Behind him, a wave of worms rose up. Swallowed him.

"We are family," said the legion. "We don't leave our own."

"I think *he's* trying leave *you*," I said, rising to my feet. A quick look in Serge's direction confirmed what I knew. They'd gone back to one form.

Serge struggled to his feet, wiped the blood from his face and ran to help.

Behind him, Craig followed.

"We are family. We don't leave our own." They melted into each other, formed a transparent glob with Kent at the centre, struggling for air and escape.

I grabbed a branch burning with the psychic fire and plunged it into the creature.

It screeched and shrieked as I shoved it deeper and twisted a ragged opening big enough to pull Kent out.

He coughed and spat the sticky phlegm of the legion. "As long as I'm here, Craig can't come through. I melded The Family's energy with mine, and I made sure it's not reversible. If Craig hurts them, he hurts me."

"It's time, Maggie," said Craig. "You had your chance—"

"Just a second!" Serge had died at his lowest point but had found redemption. If Kent died like this, there would be no redemption, there would be no chance for him to save himself. "Are you saying there's no way to separate you?" I glanced over to the legion and Serge who held them at bay with the psychic fire.

He started to shake his head, then stopped. "There is one way."

"What is it?"

"I have to die first." He crawled over to the fire, took a torch, and held it out. "End me, you end their connection to me."

"But you die—re-die—at your lowest point. That—"

"It's too late for me," he said, "but not for Rori. I can't let her die. Not for my mom, either. Not for who I thought I could be."

I wasn't sure I could do it—I was supposed to cross him over. But there was a kid's life on the line. I reached for the stick.

"How did it all go wrong?" The torch in his hand trembled but he didn't let it go. "Save Rori. You'll find her in the glades, on the northeast side of the forest. Tell her I'm sorry. Tell my mom I tried to be good—" He took the torch, ran it into his stomach, and set himself on fire.

Once Kent had killed himself, The Family couldn't stand against Craig. A blur of fire and screams, them breaking into their individual souls and scaling him like demonic Lilliputians, him heating his skin, turning his scales to knives and slicing them into jagged, bloody pieces, then tossing a net over them, trapping them, and disappearing.

Serge, and I sped to the open field where Kent said we'd find Rori. He texted Nancy and Nell.

I spent the entire drive hoping Rori would be okay and trying get the memory of Kent, on fire and screaming in agony, out of my head.

I parked the car and we took off running. Serge saw her first. She sat in the glow of a supernatural light, a circle of emerald grass under her, her red coat the only other colour amidst the background of hazy sky and snow. Her hand rested on the back of a large grey wolf.

"Hey Rori," I said, my breath puffing into white clouds. "I see you found a friend."

She turned. "Hey Maggie." Her breath fogged the air. "Isn't she nice? Mom and Dad won't let me have a dog. I'm calling her Sabrina."

The wolf watched me, panted quietly.

"She's beautiful." Serge sat beside the little girl and rubbed Sabrina's head. "Has she been keeping you company?"

Rori nodded. "She knew I was cold and alone. She came and kept me company. I feel warm 'cause she's here. She said the wolves always come to the lost. They protect us from anything that might try to hurt us. She's a good girl, isn't she?"

"The best."

"I love her."

I feel the same way about my dog." Sitting down, I scratched Sabrina under the chin. "They're loyal and protective."

"Uh-huh." Rori moved closer to the wolf. "I'm going to love her forever."

Sabrina's muzzle parted in a smile.

"I'm glad she's here to keep you company. Your mom and dad are really worried about you," I said. "You need to come home with us."

Rori shook her head. "I like it here. It's quiet."

"It's cold here," said Serge.

"Out there it is. But it's warm here with Sabrina. If I go home, I can't stay with her."

"Maybe she'll come visit," said Serge.

"You know that's not true." Rori hugged the wolf close. "I won't get to see her if I go home. I like her. I want to take care of her. She wants to take care of me, too."

"Rori—"

She shook her head. "It's quiet here."

I watched the wolf. The cold was seeping into my clothes, leaving my jeans wet, and time was running out.

"It'll get quiet at home."

The little girl shook her head, again. "It'll be a bad quiet. I feel it."

"Rori, you're a smart kid," said Serge, "but you're still just a kid. And I don't mean that in a bad way—"

"I know—"

"—you need your mom and dad." Serge raised her hands in a pleading motion. "You need to go home."

"They don't need me."

"Of course they do," I said. "Their lives won't be the same without you."

"They fight all the time. They don't see me." Rori hugged the wolf. "Not like Sabrina. She sees me."

The wolf rose, circled Rori, then lay down.

"See?" asked Rori. "She wants me to stay with her."

"Are you sure about this?" I asked. "You're still here—"

"I was waiting." Rori stopped talking as Nell ran our way. "I knew you'd call her. I didn't want to go without saying goodbye."

Nell screamed Rori's name, again and again. She slid toward us, collapsed into the snow, grabbed the little girl's body and held it tight. "I can't feel her pulse! No! Rori!"

"It's too late, anyway." Rori watched Nell holding her body.

Serge transcribed her words for Nell.

Nell dropped her phone but kept clinging to Rori's body. "Please don't. Give me another chance to help you—"

Rori got to her feet. "You know that." She lifted her face as the steady beat of wings came our way.

A ferrier—Rori's ferrier—touched down. In her supernatural form, she looked like Craig, except bigger and darker.

Rori smiled up at her. "I'm ready."

The little girl wrapped her arms around Nell's neck.

"She's not supernatural," I said to the ferrier. "She can't tell what Rori's doing."

The ferrier put her hand on Rori's shoulder. White light surrounded her spirit and turned her visible to Nell.

When Nell realized the spirit of Rori was hugging her, she let the little girl's corpse slip gently to the ground. Sobbing, she threw her arms around Rori's spirit. "Please, Rori. I love you—"

"I love you too, Nellie."

"I can make it better."

Rori pulled away. "No you can't. Where I'm going is all better. It's going to be quiet and sunny. There's peace there, Nelly."

"I know but —"

Rori turned to me. "Tell her, Maggie. Tell her all the things you see when you're on this side."

"But I won't see you, ever again," said Nell.

Rori hugged her. "But you'll feel me all the time because I'll think of you all the time."

Nell cried and tightened her hold.

Rori gently pried herself free, took the ferrier's hand, and called Sabrina to her.

A rectangular portal opened. The love and peace of the other side surrounded us in a halo. A bright light enveloped the group and they disappeared from this plane.

I stood off to the side, holding Nell, and watching as Nancy led Mr. Pierson—his hands handcuffed—and Mrs. Pierson to the location of Rori's body. Mrs. Pierson fell to her knees beside her daughter, cradled her, and keened her name.

The yearning, the loss, and the heartache in her voice made my hair stand on end, gave me so many goosebumps my skin hurt.

Mrs. Pierson's voice stabbed my heart and in the rising octave of her mourning, I had a flash of memory, a shocked moment of understanding, and I knew it was something I could never tell Dad. The Voice was my mother.

CHAPTER THIRTY-FOUR

Craig drove us home in Nell's car and the four of us sat in the silent interior.

"It sucks," Nell spoke. "No matter how much I try to live in the love Rori's now living in, my heart's been blown apart."

"I'd say give it time," said Craig, "but even now, I have cases I can't let go of."

"I don't know that I'll be able to let go of this, either," I said. "I was supposed to transition Kent and not only did I fail, but a little girl died because of me."

"That's not on you, that's on Kent." Serge spoke up from the backseat. "But I didn't help—I was supposed to be your partner in helping him cross over."

"No one failed," said Craig. "Ghosts have autonomy, the same way the living do. Decisions were made and this was the outcome. Ultimately, Kent decided his fate. So did Rori. If you love her—" he made eye contact with Nell via the rearview mirror. "You have to respect the decision she made."

"But she was just a kid!"

"A smart kid who saw both sides and made her choice," he said. "And we all have to live with it."

The car went quiet, again. Streetlights cast their shadow on the interior in an alternating pattern of light and dark. After a few minutes, I told them about The Voice and my theory.

"Are you sure?" Nell asked.

I nodded. "I didn't realize it until I heard Mrs. Pierson wailing for Rori. She sounded exactly like The Voice when it's calling out to me."

"I think you need to call back because she's done some seriously psycho stuff with you."

"It's her fear and the different dimensions getting tangled," said Craig. "Unless you have the power to communicate through the dimensions, trying to get a message from that side to this one is like a PC talking to Apple without the right software. Everything gets garbled. She's calling out to you because she's trying to warn you. She's scared and by the time it manifests on this end—"

"It's more violent than she intends," I finished. "But how is that possible? Is she stuck somewhere or lost or is she some other kind of supernatural thing..."

Craig shrugged. "I don't know. I don't get to access that kind of information."

"Are you going to tell your dad?" asked Serge.

I shook my head.

"God, Maggie," said Nell. "Seriously? You and your dad don't keep secrets."

"He carries a weight with her. When she left us, I think he hoped she left to find happiness. I can't tell him she's dead. You know my dad. He'll start wondering how she died, and what if she died in a bad way? He'll blame himself. It's better for him to think she's alive and happy."

"Are you sure you can keep this from him?" asked Nell.

"It's for his own good," I said. "I can keep this secret. But I have to find out more," I said. "I need to know what happened to my mother."

"I'll do everything I can to help," promised Craig. "Though it might take a while."

"What about Kent?" asked Nell. "Or Rori? Can you find out about them?"

"Time on this end and time on that end aren't the same. I'll ask, but it could take a long time before we find out anything."

"What do you think they'll do to Kent?" I asked.

"When he deals with his life," said Craig, "it won't just be the decisions he made in this one. It'll be the decisions he made in his past lives, if there was any growth in this incarnation, why he made the decisions he did."

"But he kidnapped a kid," I said.

"But he sacrificed himself to save her," said Craig, "and that will count for something. He made some terrible mistakes in his life, and he'll be held responsible for them. But he'll also be held responsible for the steps he took to try and fix those mistakes."

"In the meantime," said Nell, "he's gone, Rori's gone, and two families are decimated. Dead Falls is living up to its name a little too well."

"What about you? How are you feeling?" I asked.

She shook her head, the tears fell. "I don't understand why she had to die. I did everything I could, I did everything right—I even did the wrong thing to help her—"

"The lesson that sucks the most about living," said Craig, "is sometimes you do your best, you give it everything, but everything falls apart and terrible things happen." He looked over at me.

I nodded and squeezed his hand.

Serge turned to Craig. "How do you handle this? Don't you get tired?"

"Sometimes, but I remind myself there's hope and where's there's hope, there's joy. And that's the thing I hold on to. Amidst all the terrible things, there's good."

"What's the good in this?" challenged Nell. "Dr. Pierson's life is over, Kent's dead. His parents hate each other even more. Mrs. Pierson's probably going to find the end of her life at the bottom of a bottle. Rori will never know what it's like to grow up." Her voice cracked. "Where, Craig? Where is the good?"

"Here," he said. He reached back, and she put her hand in his. "With us."

It was all we had, but tonight, it was going to have to do. We continued down the quiet road.